Man or Monkey

Rosalyn Marie Francis

DEDICATION

To my children, for driving me crazy so I wrote this book.

ACKNOWLEDGMENTS

Thank you to B. Heather Mantler, my publisher at Lit-N-Laughter.

CHAPTER 1

Dr. Brandy Hollander holds a file full of scientific evidence in her hands; she shivers and contemplates tossing it in the garbage bin.

"What's wrong Doc?" Scott, her new lab assistant, asks bringing her out of her revere. "You look like someone canceled Christmas, your birthday, Valentine's Day and banned chocolate all at the same time."

"The creature has gone into some kind of hibernation and is not reproducing." She grimaces before trying to smile. Anything to smooth out the frowns lines that were becoming deep furrows in her forehead beneath her bangs. "I need time to make sure our observations are accurate before I release information to the media."

"But the news conference has already been scheduled. Dr. Manley is pressing for national coverage." The tall young man with broad shoulders leans against the wall beside the door.

"I will have to find something I can tell them." After dropping the file on her desk, she presses her fingertips to her forehead to straighten the skin then combs back the curly dark brown hair back with her fingers. "I suppose this is why he called me back in from the field. Having to deal with Manley and turning fifty in the same week should be outlawed."

"Speaking of your birthday, I was wondering if I could buy you a drink to celebrate seeing as it's a big one." Scott asks. "I know the rumor is that you don't drink but the big five-o, it's a reason to celebrate."

"Celebrate being unemployed and over the hill? I don't think so." She drops the file folder on her desk. A grimace mars a face which still attracts its share of male attention.

"No one's going to fire you, Doc, you got tenure." Scott teases with a smile.

"I've got three hours to come up with something big enough to justify a press conference." She sags into her chair and glances at the phone. "Or get Manley to cancel it."

"Publish or perish." Scott heads toward the door. "I will leave you alone to deal with the dean."

Taking a deep breath, Brandy picks up the phone. "Rosemary, may I speak to Dr. Manley?"

"Yes, he can phone me back."

"Before the press conference if he would be so kind."

She opens the file and reads it again. She closes her eyes and presses her fingers to her eyelids then opens them again. "This should not be released." She whispers. The fierce concentration that had enabled her to rack up two doctoral degrees before the age of thirty betrays her and Dr. Manley is standing over her before she even hears the door.

"What is the problem, Dr. Hollander?" The dean asks

while leaning over the desk and Brandy jumps three inches. She presses a hand above her ample bosom pulling the material tight to her upper chest and causing her lab coat to show the mature but still attractive curves beneath.

"Sorry, Dr. Manley I did not hear you come in." She manages to say before she restores her regular breathing.

"You called Rosemary." A definite twinkle enters his eye at catching the dignified Dr. Hollander off guard.

"Yes. I cannot release these observations. They are ludicrous and don't prove anything." Brandy shutters. "We will be the laughingstock of the scientific community."

A thin hand reaches for the results. He turns the papers to get a better view then leafs through the file. "You have conclusive proof of the theory of evolution. A definite blow struck for pure, unsullied scientific research. In the face of all the publicity the Intelligent Design proponents are receiving, I say announce it." The dean slaps the file and his hand on the desk. "If you don't, I will."

Brandy watches him stride away after catching her breath after this last assault on her nerves. She rises to pace the small room. The large clock hanging over the door ticks off the seconds leaving her closer to the deadline without a providing a compelling reason for canceling.

She ticks off her options using her fingers. "I can burn the results and lose my job. I can run away and lose my job. Or I can stay and point out this is a one-off and is therefore not scientifically significant. Or I can become Manley's poster girl for evolution." She sighs. "Or I can say I just do the research and leave the conclusions from my work to more qualified people."

She straightens up. "Fifteen more years and you can retire." She mutters then goes back to her files and practices what she intends to say to the press.

Two hours later, Brandy Hollander steps to the podium set up inside the auditorium, especially, set up to give the press access to the speaker.

"Ladies, gentlemen, and members of the press;" She reaches over and taps a computer key. "I would like to introduce you to the world's youngest species. It's a small creature found in the sub-Sahara. My team and I watched as the parent split then one of the offspring broke down to form him. He is the only example in the world of one species turning into another species that has ever been recorded." The screen shows the formation of a one-celled animal from his more complex parent.

"We believe this change is permanent in so much as there is enough lost DNA that he cannot return to what he previously was. The adaptation may be required for survival as the desertification is becoming extremely advanced in this area and this allows him to cope with the more arid conditions. I have had samples taken from numerous places surrounding where we found him and we have found no other creatures like him. We are, of course, continuing to look."

"Dr. Hollander, would you say this is a modern day example of evolution?" The first question is yelled out and she does not see who yelled it as she is looking at the screen.

"That depends on how you define evolution. If it necessarily requires an increase in the degree of the complexity of the nature of a creature, then no, we cannot call it classical evolution." Brandy answers honestly. "What is noteworthy in this case is that the breakdown of the DNA did not destroy the creature's ability to reproduce itself or, at least, we believe it still is capable. We have it under observation but it has yet to reproduce."

"So the new creature is really just a mutation?" A second voice asks.

"The creature is a new creature. Mutations happen all the time in nature, but nowhere in the scientific literature has a creature that lost this much DNA and remained a viable species." Brandy insists. "This is not the equivalent of the difference between a Doberman and a terrier. This is the difference between a Doberman and a lizard. This organism and its parent do not share any scientific categorization. A human and most apes share between ninety-eight to ninety-nine percent of similar DNA, these creatures share seventy."

"What does this prove?" Someone else asks.

"In scientific theory, one occurrence of something usually has little merit, we like things to be repeatable but discoveries like this are a bit different. What it proves will be a subject for debate. All I am here to do is announce the discovery. Then I will go back to the desert looking for more such creatures in areas of climate change to see if I can spot a pattern or find a similar change."

A young man steps forward. "Dr. Hollander, did you know your divorce from Norman Kettering is not legal?"

Brandy blinks before she steps back as much as the podium allows. "Excuse me."

"Did you know you are still legally married to Norman Kettering?" He pushes the question.

"I think that is an extremely sick joke." Brandy reaches her hand out to touch the lectern. "My association with Mr. Kettering ended twenty-five years ago. I will take no more questions." She turns and walks toward the door of the auditorium.

Manley stops her. "You have to finish."

"You finish. My notes are there. I have to leave before I throw up." Brandy steps around him and heads for the exit.

Brandy stops her rental car at a laundry mat to wash the clothing she has yet to remove from her trunk after her plane touched down early that morning.

After doing a rough sorting, she fills three washers and plugs in coins. Once they are operating, she goes and sits in a nearby chair. Memories ambush her.

The pain; the shame; the fear; they all rush back to her as her eyes pop open. She shivers and searches for anything to divert her attention. She notices an abandoned paper on the seat next to her and opens it to a random page. It takes a minute for her mind to accept the information on the page. Rev. Norman Kettering will speak on Intelligent Design at the Mount Vernon Presbyterian Church at seven thirty on the twenty-third. Brandy pauses, "That's a week from today."

She throws the paper back down on the chair. "That little performance today was to get publicity. It isn't really true." She takes a deep breath and releases it. For a second she laughs until she feels tears on her cheeks. "He used me again." The thought echoes through the empty room. She pushes aside her thoughts and stands too agitated to sit still.

Brandy goes to check on her washing. "I never was anything to him but a pay cheque and someone he could use." She finds a cart to take her clothing to the dryers. She still has to wait another five minutes. As the seconds tick past, emotion ferments within her. She is blazing mad when she pulls the clothes from the washer and slams them into the dryer. She is nearly frozen with fear by the time they are dry and she's folding them.

"What should I do?" The question hangs in the air. Her cell phone rings. She opens it.

"Dr. Brandy Hollander."

"This is Dr. Manley. I've canceled your flight back. I've got media dates for you to do radio, television and other public appearances over the next week."

Brandy pauses, "You what?"

"Be, at the local television station at eight tomorrow morning, you'll be doing a live interview on the morning news." The line cuts out.

Brandy finishes her laundry repacks it and takes it out to her car. Returning to her hotel, Brandy goes straight to her room. The phone is blinking.

Brandy hits the button for the message. "Dr. Brandy Hollander. I am Jared Kettering. We met at the press conference today. I have proof that you are still married to my father. If you want to see the evidence, meet me in the lounge of your hotel at ten tonight. If you don't show up, I will turn it over to the media."

Brandy glances at her watch. Nine thirty. She picks up the receiver. "Yes, I would like Directory Information please." She hesitates while her call is going through. "I would like a local number for Norman Kettering." "There is no phone book in my hotel room or I would look it up myself." "I consider it urgent." She hangs onto the receiver with both hands. "Unlisted." "No, there's nothing else you can do." Brandy drops the receiver into the cradle.

She paces the room for ten minutes deciding what to do before she goes downstairs to the lounge. She takes a table near the door and orders mineral water. She sits concentrating on her watch when the same young man steps forward. She stares at him for a minute to see signs of her ex-husband. From the chocolate brown eyes to the chiseled cheekbones and perfectly proportioned nose, Jared looks just like her memory of his father.

"Dr. Hollander."

Brandy glances down at her glass. "Why are you doing this?"

He pulls up a chair and sits down, "Lots of reasons." He takes a paper from his pocket and slides it in front of her.

Brandy glances down at the paper. "This proves nothing."

"It's your final divorce decree. It's not signed." He frowns. "Neither of you signed it."

"Judge Herman Gregory Golden decreed it to be valid without my signature."

"Yes, but does that make it legal without my father's consent? What does my grandfather have to do with this?"

"He pushed the divorce through so you could be born legitimate. I was out of the country doing research and so he did what he thought necessary to see that the law allowed his daughter to marry Norman."

"That would put him in a blatant conflict of interest."

Brandy sighs. "Take it up with him." Brandy rises to her feet.

"My father never married Chastity Golden." The young man rises with her.

"Yes, but he slept with her while he was legally married to me. Adultery still can lose a preacher his pulpit. Your father and your grandfather have more to lose than I do."

"The validity of your research..."

"How does being a duped wife twenty-five years ago

have anything to do with my research?"

"You came back to make your announcement when you found out about my father's new lecture series! To discredit him!"

"How? I returned to the country this morning after an absence of twenty-five years. Had Manley said one word about your father and his lecture series, I would have refused to return." Brandy shakes her head. "The only one discrediting your father is you, by stirring up a scandal."

Jared's face turns three shades of red before he turns and strides off.

CHAPTER 2

Brandy checks her makeup in the rear view mirror of her car before she steps out into the street in front of the television station. She locks her car and crosses the sidewalk to the door. Taking a deep breath, she opens the door and steps inside.

Dr. Manley jumps out of a waiting area chair at the sight of her. "Where have you been?"

"You said eight o'clock." Brandy glances at the receptionist. "My watch says two minutes to eight." The woman behind the desk glances down and grins.

"We have to get you ready." Dr. Manley reaches for Brandy's arm. His fingers dig into her skin. "Couldn't you have worn something fashionable?" He drags her through some doors and into a dressing room.

Brandy digs in the heels of her comfortable shoes and brushes off her business suit. "I am a research scientist. I will remain dignified." She frowns at the skimpy clothing on the racks.

"You don't understand what's at stake. Flaunting a

little bit of skin--"

"I don't care what's at stake. I hold two doctorates in science. I will not dress like a prostitute."

A man steps through the door. "You are on in five." He directs his comment towards Dr. Manley

Brandy grips Dr. Manley's wrist between her thumb and forefinger before she squeezes hard. His hand pops open. She follows the man from the room.

"I am Dr. Brandy Hollander. Just how is this going to be set up?"

"You just have to smile and be pretty. Dr. Manley has agreed to do all the talking."

Brandy stops and stares at the man for a moment. "Tell Dr. Manley that I am returning to the university and he will find me having words with the university president." She turns and walks out.

"Dr. Hollander, what can I do for you?" The university president, Dr. Jamison Forester leans back in his large, well-padded chair. His fingers lace together and rest upon the mound of his stomach.

"You can tell Dr. Manley to cease and desist!"

"And just what is Dr. Manley doing?" The chair comes forward and he leans on the edge of the desk.

"He is insisting that I publish unfinished work. He canceled my plane tickets back to where I have serious fieldwork happening. He scheduled me for a television spot and when I get there, I find out that I am not the one being interviewed. He asked me to appear in clothing more suitable to a bimbo than a university professor. He was so insistent he grabbed my arm and dragged me into a dressing room leaving me with bruises."

"Do you wish to lay an official complaint?"

"I wish him to stop. I am willing to follow whatever

procedures you think are appropriate. Unfortunately, his position as dean will leave me with little choice but to make the complaint official if this treatment continues past this meeting. I have two doctorates, I refuse to sit there and *look pretty* while he puts words in my mouth."

"I understand your chagrin, Dr. Hollander. I will speak to Dean Manley." The man pauses. "You were married to Rev. Kettering. I've been trying to get him to teach an ethics class. You will put in a good word."

"I hardly think it would be to your advantage if I did. I have not spoken to Norman Kettering in twenty-five years."

"I was hoping to get a group of faculty to go to his first lecture. Show him that we have open minds towards his subject. You could come along."

"That depends on when my airline ticket is reinstated."

"A week one way or the other is not going to change the fate of your research."

"I have a dozen experiments on the go and fifteen students to oversee. To be dragged away from my work to engage in Dr. Manley's media circus is ridiculous." Brandy frowns.

"Your students are doing the field work. One week home is twenty-five years is not going to destroy your research."

Brandy has to restrain her tongue.

"Then you will come with us on the twenty-third?"

"Only as long as you keep Dean Manley from using me and my research to fuel his ridiculous media vendetta against the boogie man of intelligent debate."

"I will direct Dr. Manley to leave you out of his media blitz."

Brandy goes to her office and marks off today's date

then counts. "Six days, six days and I can breathe easy again."

The phone rings. "Dr. Brandy Hollander."

"Doc, it's Scott. There's a Ms. Chastity Golden here. She says I must allow her in to see you."

"Actually, you don't have to let her in to see me."

"You want me to send her away?"

"As far as you can kick her," Brandy answers, "use steel toes."

"I'll do my best." Scott answers.

"Thank you." Brandy hangs up the telephone. It rings again.

"Dr. Brandy Hollander."

"This is Herman Golden."

"Judge Golden. Just what are you calling about?"

"That's somewhat formal considering-"

"Your daughter destroyed my marriage twenty-five years ago."

"My grandson came to visit me. He had questions about your final decree. What exactly did you tell him?"

"Nothing more than is in the official record."

"It won't do you any good to open up this issue."

"I have no intention of staying in town long enough to deal with complicated legal issues." Brandy answers. "I'm here because my job requires it."

The judge chuckles, "Norman's got them on the run with his new lecture series."

"I have no idea what Norman Kettering is doing nor do I care."

Brandy's attention is distracted by Scott's voice. "You can't go in there."

The door bangs open to reveal Scott attempting to stop a pencil-thin, professionally groomed woman in a business suit. "I'm sorry, Dr. Hollander."

"Call security," Brandy tells Scott, who leaves.

Brandy places the receiver on the desk rather than the cradle. "What do you want Miss Golden?"

"You aren't busy, he lied. Nor are you important."

"What do you want?" Brandy sighs.

"I told you to leave town and never come back."

"My job brings me here. Sorry, job, a place where you work and they pay you. Something women need if they don't have rich daddies who protect them from such mundane things as rent and grocery bills."

"Gutter swipe."

"No, I am a fully tenured professor with two doctorates and over twenty years of experience teaching field work to undergraduate and graduate students. This is my office."

"Not once I get through talking to Doctor Forester. He'll do whatever I ask."

"Go talk to Doctor Forester. Maybe he has a tape recorder so your father can play the last messages you left on my answering machine."

"You whore."

"I wasn't the one sleeping with a married man. Mrs. Forester might like to hear that piece of history if you are getting too friendly with her husband. I am sure Rev. Kettering would be interested in doing a marriage counseling session for yet another of your victims."

"Rev. Kettering? Since when did you start to call him something other than meal ticket?"

"I believe I was the one who held the job while you were the only thing he held."

"I will have my father throw you in jail."

Brandy reaches for the receiver and holds it out. "What a coincidence. Judge Golden is on the phone. You can ask him for the favor right now."

"You filthy liar, he's not on the phone. I should strangle you with my bare hands. All, Norman saw was those big tits. I had to rescue him from himself." Chastity steps close enough to lean over the desk.

The deep voice comes through quite clearly over the receiver. "Chastity get out of there before security shows up! How do you expect me to keep you out of trouble when you act this way?"

The woman pales. "I'm leaving but only because I want to torture you so you die slowly."

Scott and a security guard come through the door in time to hear the threat. "Now Ms. Golden it is time for you to leave." The guard takes the woman by the arm.

"She threatened me." Chastity bursts into tears.

"Should I stay Dr. Hollander just in case she comes back?"

"No, I need those results reviewed by fresh eyes. I have to finish my phone call."

Scott leaves closing the door behind him.

"Hello." Brandy puts the phone back to her ear.

"Who was the second man?" The judge asks.

"My lab assistant."

"You said you have tapes?"

"Tapes of your daughter threatening my life. I will send them to the justice department along with the relevant papers from my divorce unless you and your daughter quit harassing me."

"You don't want Kettering back?"

"I want everyone to forget that I was ever stupid enough to believe his lies."

"He refused to marry her."

"The fact you have a grandson is more than enough evidence." Brandy picks up a pen and twirls it between her fingers. "I believe the Biblical sentence would have been stoning for both of them."

"Luckily we live in more enlightened times."

"Enlightened, or immoral?" Brandy sets the pen down, "On the other hand in cases where judges expedite cases where they have a conflict of interest, the law still has some teeth."

"I've retired."

"Hardly surprising, I take it the voters got enough of your brand of injustice. Unfortunately, for you, the law is still the law."

"Kettering won't like it if you reopen this divorce."

"Really and you've discussed it; probably right after he married your daughter." Brandy answers.

"I've never figured that one out."

"You sent him unsigned divorce papers, and then expected him to commit bigamy. Norman Kettering is not stupid and he knows that I am not. Why would he set himself up for blackmail by you and your ditsy daughter?"

"That divorce is legal!"

"Explain how to your grandson. He's the one that raised the issue." Brandy drops the receiver back into its cradle.

She has just opened up the file when Dr. Manley enters her office.

"Forester has told me that you are not to be put on display so I will do the publicity leading up to the lecture."

Brandy glances up at him then back at the file. "So why are you here?"

"I need your files." He reaches for the ones in front of her.

"These ones have just arrived and I have not yet analyzed the data. I will instruct Scott to supply you with the files on my discovery once they had been analyzed."

"I need the latest information."

"Fine, once I am done here, I'll break out that piece of information. I'll send it to Rosemary via e-mail by the end of the day."

"You are not taking this seriously. If people begin to see intelligent design as legitimate science, then their *experiments* will start drawing resources away from real scientists. It's hard enough to get grants now. Then what would you know you've spent years in the field while I've been tracking down funding?"

Brandy wants to roll her eyes but self-preservation keeps her lips sealed. "The sooner you leave, the sooner I get this done, and the sooner you get your information."

"Just make sure that I get it." He stomps out of the room.

Brandy works until Scott sticks his head in the door. "Doc?"

She glances up. "What?"

"I'm taking off now unless you really need me."

She turns and glances at the clock. "Go. I've got a few things I need to finish up. I will see you in the morning."

"See you tomorrow."

Brandy is another hour before she sends off her daily e-mails. Then she separates data into two file folders and locks one set into the bottom drawer of her desk. The other she drops into the to-be-filed basket.

She gathers a few things then leaves the office locking it as she goes. As she walks down the hall of the science building someone calls. "Dr. Hollander?"

She turns and sees a security guard. "Yes."

"If you wait up Dr. Hollander, I'll walk you to your car."

She frowns but waits for him to catch up. "Is walking

people to their car common practice these days?"

"If you're nervous, you can ring security anytime, but a woman uttered threats against you to another guard today after you had her removed from your office. He did report the episode so it is on the record. If she causes you any further trouble, we will call in the police. We were keeping an eye on your office in case she came back."

Brandy walks in silent to her car. The security guard checks the back and the trunk before he bids her goodnight. She takes a deep breath before starting the car.

Listening to the radio on the way, Brandy hears an advertisement for the lecture. She shakes her head and turns off the broadcast. She finds a parking spot on the street behind a Cadillac.

She enters the hotel lobby. A young woman jumps up at the sight of her.

"Can I speak to you, Dr. Hollander?"

"Right now all I want is to change clothes and find something to eat." Brandy frowns.

"I'll buy you supper."

The newspaper of the man sitting in a chair at the other end of the couch rattles.

"Why?"

"I need some advice. I thought you might be in the best position to tell me what I need to know." The woman glances around as if she's nervous.

"On what subject?"

"The Kettering men and Chastity Golden."

"I'm certainly no expert on the Kettering men." Brandy frowns as the man, at the end of the couch, rattles his paper again.

"It's just I'm dating Jared, and he won't even introduce me to his mother."

"Be grateful." Brandy sighs.

"Jared says he wants to marry me. His grandmother's will states he needs Chastity's permission to marry."

"That piece of advice doesn't require buying supper." Brandy answers. "Run for the hills and don't look back."

"You don't think I can change her mind?"

Brandy sighs and looks at the young woman. "Even if he's willing to leave her circle of influence and the money behind, Chastity Golden and Anna Kettering will make your miserable."

"Dr. Hollander?" A young man approaches from the registration desk.

"Yes."

"I regret to inform you that someone ransacked your room. The police have come and gone. They asked that you go down to the police station to make a statement."

The young woman's face pales.

Brandy pauses. "Are any of my belongings salvageable?"

The man shrugs. "The police ask you not to go to your room as they have forensic experts on the way."

"How do I get to this police station?"

"If you will come to the front desk I will find you a map." He leads her toward the desk.

"What should I do? I've got his car." Leia grabs her arm.

"Return the car. Then go home and consider whether Jared Kettering is worth the pain those women will cause you." Brandy answers.

Brandy stops at a fast food place to take out a meal before driving to the station. She sits in the car and eats then goes to the front desk.

"Excuse me but I was told to come down and make a statement."

"Name?"

"Brandy Hollander, my room at the Georgetown Hotel was ransacked."

"Yes. We've been expecting you. I'll just put call the detective in charge of the case."

Brandy steps back away from the desk to sit in one of a row of plastic chairs lined up against the wall. She is no sooner seated than a tall man of about thirty-five arrives behind a short wall at the gate. "Dr. Hollander."

Standing on her feet, Brandy steps forward, "I'm Dr. Hollander."

He opens the gate. "Come this way please."

Brandy follows him down a hall then around a corner and finally to a cubicle. It holds one desk and chair that backs onto another desk and chair. "Dr. Hollander, I'm Detective Kevin Lang and this is my partner Detective Jon Turner."

The second detective, a man of similar age and height but much thinner, snags a chair from another cubicle and offers it to Brandy as a place to sit. "Do you have any idea who might have something against you, Dr. Hollander?"

"There are a few people who are not happy with me at the moment. I lodged an unofficial protest against my boss this morning with the president of the university."

"University?"

"I am a professor at Lakeview University. Dr. Manley is dean of the biology department. I teach field research skills, environmental ecology, and genetics. My specialty at the moment is climate change and desertification. Dr. Manley is attempting to force me into releasing information on a discovery that he says will prove the theory of evolution."

"Will it?"

"I don't know, and until I have more time to complete

my observations I refuse to state an opinion on the subject. I objected to his tactics to the president of the university."

"Anyone else?"

"Retired Judge Herman Golden and his daughter, Chastity."

"And why would a retired judge want to ransack your rooms?" The detectives trade off on asking their questions.

"To find telephone answering machine tapes from twenty-five years ago, Chastity Golden claimed to be having an affair with my ex-husband. She threatened my life if I did not leave town and stay gone."

"Where are the tapes?"

"In a storage locker with everything else from the apartment I was living in at the time." Brandy pulls keys from her purse. A card is attached to the keys. "I haven't had time to clean it out but I was going to do so before I left."

"When exactly did you leave town?"

"Late September, twenty-five years ago."

"Where did you go?"

"I went to a research station in Chad in the sub-Sahara that the university runs in partnership with international organizations."

"Have you seen either Herman or Chastity Golden since you returned?"

"Herman Golden phoned me this afternoon. Security at the university removed Chastity Golden from my office today and a security guard showed up to walk me to my car after work. He told me that they had filed the incident and that the next time, there would be a police report."

"The judge knew she was there?"

"I was talking on the phone with him when she arrived. He knows these tapes exist."

"Anyone else?"

"My ex-husband's son showed up to see me last night. He wanted to inform me that my divorce from his father might not be legal. A woman claiming to be the son's girlfriend showed up at the hotel tonight. She asked for advice on how to handle the Kettering men."

"And what did you tell her?"

"To go home and think about whether she considered him worth the trouble." Brandy sighs.

"Can I ask the name of your ex-husband?"

"Rev. Norman Kettering of the Mount Vernon Presbyterian Church." Brandy answers.

"Have you had any contact with your ex-husband since you came to town?"

"No."

"Do you intend to have any contact with him?"

"I have agreed to attend a public lecture given by Rev. Kettering in his church on the twenty-third of this month as a member of a group of faculty from the university. I wouldn't have agreed to go except the president of the university asked me and tied getting a ticket back to the research station to my attendance."

"You've been in the sub-Sahara for all of those twenty-five years?"

"No. I shuttle between four research stations; one in Africa, one on the Arctic Circle in Finland, one in the Alps and one in Australia. I have done so for the last twenty-five years although Chad has been the base for most of my experiments." Brandy answers. "Now I would like to ask you one question."

"What's that?"

"What is the state of my belongings?"

Detective Lang glances at his partner and winces. "Your clothes were shredded. I think you're going to have to replace everything."

CHAPTER 3

Brandy walks up and down the aisle in a ladies wear store the next morning. The hotel had found her another room but she feels sticky in yesterday's clothing even after a shower. Unfortunately, the clothes on the racks were sized too small.

A saleswoman approaches. "Can I help you?"

"Only if you have something in my size," Brandy frowns at the label.

The woman looks her up and down. "What have you tried on?"

"Nothing, who in the world is a size zero?"

"You have not been shopping lately."

"Only internationally at irregular intervals." Brandy frowns.

"The sizings have changed in the last few years. Choose something and try in on in at least two sizes."

Brandy picks a dark blue suit in the two largest sizes and follows the saleswoman to the dressing rooms. To her surprise, she has to send back for the next smaller size. "I've never been a ten."

"Some manufactures are making their clothing sizes larger." The saleswoman tells her. "Did you need more than one outfit?"

"I need a whole new wardrobe. From underwear to jackets and I need to look professional."

Brandy gets to work about noon. Scott whistles when he sees her in the hall outside her office. "I don't know if going shopping is a good reason to be late."

"Did the reports come in?" Brandy asks.

"On your desk, you had a visitor but he couldn't stay."

"Who?"

"Rev. Norman Kettering. He came and stayed for a while. He left a note." Scott hands her a folded piece of paper.

"Anyone else?"

"Dr. Manley called demanding your report earlier in the day, something about a two o'clock interview."

Brandy sighs and unlocks her office door. She goes to the desk and glances at the note. *Meet me for dinner. The Melon Ball on Jackson. 7:00 pm.* Brandy tosses the demand aside to glance through the pile of file folders on her desk. She is deep in her analysis of the latest information when the phone rings.

She picks it up. "Dr. Brandy Hollander."

"Dr. Forester here."

"What can I do for you, Dr. Forester?"

"Meet Kettering for dinner."

"Why?"

"He dropped by my office this morning. He said you were avoiding him."

"I was not avoiding him." Brandy frowns. "I ran a necessary personal errand before coming to work. I will need to work this evening to make up the time."

"Getting Rev. Kettering back into academic circles is of utmost importance. I want you to persuade him to teach a class. I will count it towards making up the time."

"I cannot promise to persuade him of anything."

"Blackmail him then."

"I don't have any blackmail material." Brandy answers.

"I think you do. The gossips have been having a field day."

"If everyone knows the story then why would he bother to teach a class to stop me from talking about it?"

"Do whatever it takes."

"You do understand that he is, at least, three times as ruthless as I am. I am never going to win."

"That's a poor attitude, Dr. Hollander, what you need to think is I'm going to nail his hide to the wall for what he's done to me."

"First I would need to want his hide and quite frankly I don't."

"I will send you a copy of a book called The First Wives Club. My wife insisted I read it. Very educational about what happens to men who cheat."

"Some other time, Dr. Manley wants his report on our one-celled little friend before two, and I am behind schedule."

"Has he reproduced yet?"

Brandy flips through the file. "No."

"Keep working on it." The phone goes dead and she sets it down.

Dr. Manley enters her office at one thirty. "What do you mean sending me this?"

"I relayed to you what information was sent to me. The creature has not split."

"What have you been doing to hurry it along?"

"The field station hosts an international cast of graduate students and they all are taking great interest in the little fellow. It would cause a scandal if anyone were to *hurry it along.*"

"I need more than this, and I need it soon."

"I cannot rush observational research." Brandy rises to her feet. "You placed yourself in this position so don't expect me to be able to bail you out of it."

"But it is your research!"

"Then you should have waited until I was ready to report out on it."

Dr. Manley pauses. "Now you buy some newer clothes!"

"Not by choice." Brandy sits down.

The dean frowns. "What do you mean?"

"Someone ransacked my hotel room and shredded my things."

"Someone from the university?"

"I don't know. The police are looking into the incident. Hopefully, they will turn up something."

He pales. "What did you tell them?"

"I answered their questions as fully as possible." Brandy answers. "Now if you will excuse me I have more information to analyze."

He frowns at her before he walks out.

Scott sticks his head in the door. "I'm gone for the night."

"See you tomorrow." Brandy waves him away. Splitting the files, she tucks the confidential information away in a locked bottom drawer.

The phone rings. "Dr. Brandy Hollander," Brandy says.

She listens to a lengthy explanation as she sits back in her chair. "Okay, I will have to send a replacement. You can keep sending the data for me to analyze. I will send the information off to the appropriate people until I train someone to take over." She puts down the receiver. She closes her eyes for a second then picks up the phone again.

"Yes, this is Dr. Hollander. Could you set up an emergency meeting between Dr. Forester, Dr. Manley and myself?" "As quickly as possible, please." "Thank you, I will be there."

Brandy leans forward to rest her arms on the desk and puts her head down.

"Somehow the local Muslim cleric has learned via the publicity the discovery received in the press that I am a divorced woman. The cleric has deemed me unsuitable to head a facility where young men and women are taught. Therefore, I cannot return as the chief of the research station in Chad."

"Preposterous!" Dr. Forester comes to his feet.

"Unfortunately if I do go back the place is likely to be firebombed as the result." Brandy answers. "We've got fifteen students from around the world and three dozen paying experiments taking place. I don't want to jeopardize everything I've built."

Dr. Manley frowns. "We have to keep that station running. We have crucial research happening there."

"Are you volunteering to go Dr. Manley?" Dr. Forester asks.

Dr. Manley frowns. "We have others who are better qualified."

"They will continue to send me the data for a week. After that, I need to give them a new boss. Who on your staff is willing to relocate to the sub-Sahara desert on a week's notice?"

Dr. Manley frowns. "You are the only single member of my faculty."

"Then you are going to have to find someone who is willing. I have seven days to get that person up to speed on all the experiments and confidential reports that need to go to organizations funding the research and it's going to take every minute of that and more."

"What organizations?" Dr. Forester asks.

"There are about a dozen different organizations that are interested in global climate change who have approached me in the over the last twenty years. They have offered to fully fund experiments including the buying of expensive equipment to have our four research stations send them data under confidential agreements. I have contracts for forty million dollars' worth of research over the next fifteen years. If we can't put someone qualified into my position at the Chad station in the next seven days, those contracts are at risk."

"Dr. Manley, you will go." Dr. Forester tells him. "You can fly in and out until we find someone else to take the job but for right now it is yours."

"Who is going to take my duties here at the university?"

"I think someone who manages multi-million dollar contracts can handle your job at least until we find a specialist in global warming to take Dr. Hollander's position."

"I suppose then we need to start briefing me on the experiments." Dr. Manley answers.

"Anytime you are ready to start." Brandy answers.

"Just let me tell Rosemary to hold my calls until further notice."

"I think I have to call it a day." Dr. Manley yawns. "You have graduate students who know this stuff?"

"They know their parts but I'm the only one with the whole picture." Brandy pauses. "The confidentiality agreements require that level of clearance."

"I'll be back at seven o'clock tomorrow morning if my wife doesn't kill me when I tell her that I am going to Chad." Dr. Manley leaves Brandy. Brandy clears up the files and locks them in the drawer.

She picks up the phone and calls the hotel. "Yes, this is Dr. Hollander. Are you still willing to rent me a room?" "Thank you. I'll be about an hour."

Next she phones security to request an escort to her car. She stops by a fast food restaurant and eats before returning to the hotel.

The next morning she is at the university before seven with more information and more files waiting when Dr. Manley arrives.

"My wife says I can travel to and live in the sub-Sahara, so long as I don't expect her to join me."

"Once you're in place I will put out feelers for someone to take the position on a permanent basis." Brandy answers.

"You know someone who is qualified?"

Brandy nods. "I keep up with people in my field. I could begin the process while you read unless you want me here to answer questions."

"I'll save the questions while you start the process." He picks up a file.

Brandy goes to the phone. She starts calling people all over the world. She comes back two hours later. "I have a qualified person who may be willing to take over at the end of his doctoral process."

"Who? Where?"

"A Swedish student who was with me last summer but had to go home to finish his thesis, he's defending it in late May. He's right up-to-date on the subject matter but he'll need to be brought up to speed on the contractual obligations."

"Sounds good," Dr. Manley stares at the pile of files. "I asked Rosemary to bring you up-to-date on what you will need to do here in my absence. Most of it is administrative, although I do teach one class of third and fourth-year students. I have all the lecture materials including the tests on file in my office. The only other big thing is Rev. Kettering's lectures. You must refute his stance, we cannot afford to lose research money to people touting intelligent design."

"I doubt the reverend will be applying for grant money anytime soon." Brandy frowns. "He's not a scientist."

"No but others are just waiting for public opinion to swing far enough to make the whole idea legitimate in the mind of the money people."

"People fund what they believe in. If they believe in creationism, then they will fund those experiments. Nothing will change their minds."

"Yes but we do not want to make it easy for science funding to lose out to philosophers. You are too far away from the university to know the heat we are taking."

Brandy shakes her head.

"How would you like it if you lose funding because a large foundation changed its criteria to only accept Intelligent Design scientists?" Dr. Manley stands to his feet.

"Sit down." Brandy points to a chair. "One of our contracts is with a group called Stewards of Earth. They are an organization of Christians who believe God appointed men as stewards of creation. Their experiments are designed to reveal parameters for environmental best practices."

Dr. Manley sits with a thud. "Why would you accept the contract?"

"Their experiments fit into the same criteria as the other experiments that the research stations carry out. I don't have to believe their philosophy to design and carry out the work, which is one reason they choose me to do them. No one could accuse me of slanting the results to suit their philosophy."

"Any others?"

"Christian organizations, yes, one of the biggest experiments at the Chad station is funded by a Christian international aid agency. They want to know the best and fastest ways to reclaim land back from the desert and make it arable again."

"Who else has you under contract?"

"A few environmental organizations, three governments agencies, an alpine guiding organization, and--" She stops and hands him a file. "Copies of the contracts are in this file."

He opens the file and starts flipping through it. "That is this?"

Brandy moves to read over his shoulder, "A standard contract for the graduate students."

He points to a clause, "Anti-malaria drugs?"

"Yes, you need to start them as soon as possible. Malaria is a killer in the sub-Sahara. The drugs are a prophylactic measure against the disease."

"Where do I get them?"

"The drug store," Brandy answers, "talk to a pharmacist."

CHAPTER 4

Ten o'clock that night, Brandy enters the hotel lobby. She passes the desk to have the clerk wave her down. "A young man is waiting for you in the lounge."

"Any idea who he is?"

"Jared Kettering."

Brandy sighs and goes to the lounge. She sees him sitting at a table and approaches. "What's it about this time?"

"Leia."

"Leia?" Brandy frowns.

"My girlfriend came to see you."

Brandy nods. "Sorry so much has happened in the last two days."

"She never came home after meeting with you." He frowns. "What did you tell her?"

"The last thing I told her and I remember this distinctly was to return your car."

"She didn't- return the car- but that's the least of my worries. I even had her best friend phone her parents and they say they haven't seen Leia."

"Has anyone reported her missing to the police?"

"I've been keeping our relationship under wraps." He sighs. "I know the sorts of things what my mother will do if she got her hands on Leia."

"Sorry, I don't even know which way she left. The front desk person came and told me that someone trashed my room and wanted me to go to the police station to make a statement."

He sighs. "I'll have to go to the police. What if they won't listen?"

"Go to the detectives who are working on the trashing. Tell them she spoke to me just before she went missing. Their names were Lang and Turner at the local station."

"Thanks."

Brandy leaves the lobby and goes up to her room. She has showered and is about to climb into bed then Detective Lang phones.

"Jared Kettering is here."

"He stopped here looking for someone he called Leia." Brandy answers.

"We would like you come down and make another statement."

"I will be there in a few minutes." Brandy reaches for her clothes again.

She enters the station.

"Dr. Hollander, I'll call the detectives."

"Thank you."

Detective Kevin Lang comes out from the back a few minutes later. "Dr. Hollander."

Brandy follows him back to the cubicle. Jared was sitting on their guest chair. Turner finds her another one.

"You want to tell us that happened between you and Leia Gerron."

Brandy nods. "She was waiting for me in the lobby of the hotel. She wanted advice on handling Kettering men. We spoke for a few minutes then the front desk clerk came over to say my room had been ransacked and I needed to give you a statement. He found me a map. I didn't talk to her after that."

"Did Leia hear about your room?"

"She was standing right beside me. She paled when he said it so I think she did." Brandy frowns.

"Does Leia own a car?" The detective asks.

"She borrowed mine." Jared answers.

"Have you found the car?"

"No." Jared shakes his head.

"Did you consider reporting the car missing?"

"Not if I knew it was Leia who had it." Jared shakes his head.

"She said something about your grandmother requiring Chastity Golden's permission to get married and you refusing to introduce her." Brandy frowns.

"The only reason I even hesitated to dump the will and the inheritance was it would leave grandmother's housekeeper without a job. She's not quite ready to retire." Jared frowns. "And I don't care what anyone says I am not marrying the woman my mother picked out for me."

"Your mother chose a woman for you to marry?" Lang asks.

"Marianne Gilford. Everywhere I turn Marianne is there. I got a job at the library and immediately she gets a job at the library. I take an elective at the university and Marianne is in my class. I've told her that I have no intention of touching her never mind marrying her and the next time I go with the varsity team to a tournament she bribed one of the guys into letting her in my room so she can strip down and be waiting in my bed."

"So what did you do?"

"I left and took another room." Jared sighs deeply. "Grandmother threatened to have Mrs. James tossed out on the street with no prospects if I don't marry Marianne."

"Have you laid a formal complaint about her?"

"I don't have enough money to get the law involved."

"The Kettering fortune?" Brandy frowns.

"Grandmother tied up every penny so I don't have enough money to even talk to a lawyer so I couldn't get the will overturned. Between her, the Goldens and the Gilfords, I don't have a chance if I took the matter to court. They can afford to tie everything up for years."

"You could have this Marianne Gilford arrested." Turner leans against the desk.

"All I want is someone to take me seriously and look for Leia."

"The last thing I told Leia was to return Jared's car." Brandy frowns.

"So we look for the car."

"What have you learned about who trashed my room? Maybe she saw someone she recognized."

"We interviewed Ms. Golden. The statute of limitations on uttering threats has passed."

"She repeated them the same day as my room was trashed. A security guard and my assistant heard her."

"The security people did not file a police report."

Brandy frowns. "Now you have a missing young woman in the same position I was in twenty-five years ago, are you going to write her off?"

"We are going to look for Miss Gerron." Turner

answers. "We need reasons to go search people's houses. We can't just walk in because he's Chastity Golden's son."

"No, but maybe he can." Brandy turns to Jared. "You upset your grandfather by going to him with the divorce accusation. Why don't you use that influence to locate Leia?"

"I don't see my mother." Jared frowns.

"Why not?" Lang asks.

"At my sixth birthday, she and my best friend's Dad were caught naked in the swimming pool. His mom grabbed Keith and left. I never saw him again. I refused to see her ever after that if I had a choice."

"You think she meant for them to be seen," Turner asks.

"My mother told me she did it because she didn't think Keith was good enough to be my friend." Jared sighs. "The woman is a menace and I don't mean that is any way that's nice."

"You do apparently see your grandfather." Brandy frowns.

"I phone him, mostly to complain of that my mother's latest stunt." Jared shakes his head. "Not that it does any good. It's like your divorce he pushed it through illegally because my mother wanted it."

Brandy stands. "I have just worked two sixteen hour work days. Unless you have more questions I need to go."

"Where did you go after you left Miss Gerron?" Lang asks.

"Here, I got in my car, stopped to pick up a fast food supper and came here to give my statement."

"Did anyone overhear any part of your conversation with Miss Gerron?"

"A man, sitting on a chair in the lobby, with his face behind the newspaper." Brandy answers. "The paper rattled after my comments so I felt he was listening."

"Did you see his face?" Turner asks.

"No." Brandy shakes her head.

"We'll call if we need more questions answered." Lang starts to walk her out.

Brandy walks out in silence.

Brandy stops by Scott's work area the next morning. "You need something, Dr. Hollander?"

"Yes, I want to know why Ms. Golden got as far as my office when I asked you not to allow her in."

"She acted as if she was leaving. I thought she had gone so I turned around to do some work. Next thing I know, she's gone past me. I caught up with her at your door."

"She didn't come on to you?"

"From the second she arrived. But Doc, she's way too old for me."

Brandy nods. "Okay, has Dr. Manley arrived this morning?"

"He's been in there reading files since before I arrived." Scott tells her. "Rosemary asks that you stop by her station so she can bring you up-to-date on your morning class."

"I'll go over there now." Brandy changes direction and heads for the dean's office. She stops in front of the secretary's desk.

"Dr. Hollander, I've cleared enough space for you to move your files." Rosemary pauses. "I've put the class list on the desk and Dr. Manley's prepared lecture. You do know you that you have an eleven o'clock class this morning?"

"I knew I had a class but not the time." Brandy goes into the office and reads through the lecture. She changes the examples in her head then goes through the class list. She glances at her watch then goes through the rest of the papers on the desk.

"Anything you need explained?"

"No, I think it's self-explanatory. I need to check with Dr. Manley then I'll go directly to class. Just make one note."

"What's that?"

"If Herman or Chastity Golden shows up or phones. I'm tied up until sometime mid-century. If they don't take no for an answer call security and have them escorted out."

Rosemary nods, "Got it."

Brandy takes the lecture notes and leaves.

Dr. Manley has a list of questions that Brandy takes the time to answer. She makes a long distance call and introduces Dr. Manley to the caretaker at the research station. Then she goes to class.

"I am Dr. Brandy Hollander. I will be taking Dr. Manley's place until the end of the semester. You can, as you have in the past, drop assignments off in the dean's office. To give you some background, I hold doctorates in genetics and environmental biology I have taught field research for the last twenty years. I believe in hands-on learning.

Today I want a general discussion on what you have gotten out of this class so I know what you still need to know before the end of the semester."

Brandy stops at dean's office and rewrites the outline for the rest of the semester then goes to her office to answer more of Dr. Manley's questions. The phone rings just as she steps through the door.

"Dr. Brandy Hollander."

"Dr. Hollander, it's Jared Kettering. I need to talk to you."

"About what?" Brandy asks.

"Not on the phone."

"How about we meet in the cafeteria at the university in about thirty minutes?"

"I'll be there." He answers and hangs up.

"What was that about?" Manley asks.

"Just a student wanting a meeting, do you think you have a good grasp of the contracts?"

"The contracts aren't the problem. I deal with them all the time. It's the specialized knowledge to know how to analyze those reports."

"You can send me the reports, so long as no one in Chad is wiser." Brandy answers. "There is a conference in May. Sweden, this time, I think. You can pick up the information there."

"By June, your friend should be in this position." Dr. Manley answers.

"I intend to go if you miss these things you get behind. I may not know the politics but I know the science." Brandy shrugs. "Don't forget to take your malaria medication."

"Get out of here. It's the weekend. I'll leave a list of questions in an e-mail."

"What day are you flying out?"

"Sunday, just don't miss Kettering's lecture."

Brandy just nods.

Jared is waiting in the cafeteria. Brandy buys a bowl of soup then comes to sit down across from him. "Have you found Leia?"

"No, the police aren't giving me much hope. She was

missing forty-eight hours before they were notified."

"They find your car?"

"It was towed for over limit parking from beside the hotel the same night that she went missing." Jared nods. "I got people to go visit my mother. They say she doesn't seem to know Leia exists."

"Do the Goldens own any other properties?"

"The detectives are looking into it. Who else would have been at the hotel?"

"I don't know. The man at the desk wasn't any help?"

"The detectives say no. They promised that they talked to everyone working that night."

"So why did you want to talk to me?"

"You're the last person to see her."

Brandy frowns. "You're a student, but what did Leia do?"

"She was a part-time student and worked at a restaurant not far from campus." Jared frowns.

"Have you gone to her place of work and asked her boss if he's heard from her?"

Jared shakes his head. "I went there once. One of the other waitresses said that she hadn't been in."

"Then let's go talk to them. I know it's a long shot, but maybe she did run." Brandy frowns at her soup and leaves it. She drives to the restaurant and gets out.

"Is the food any good?"

"Passable." Jared shrugs. "Leia's the waitress, not the cook."

Brandy enters the restaurant and takes a table. "Do you know who owns it?"

He shakes his head.

The waitress comes over and takes out her order pad, "Jared, who's the new lady friend?"

"She's" Jared frowns, "my stepmother. You haven't

seen Leia have you?"

"No." The woman shakes her head and lifts her order pad. "What do you want?"

"A burger and fries."

"And your step-mom?"

"What kinds of soup do you have?"

"Beef vegetable and white clam chowder."

"Beef vegetable and a chicken sandwich on multi-grain bread with tomato and lettuce, go light on the mayo."

"Sure thing."

"Who's the manager here?" Brandy asks.

"That would be Mr. Duff."

"Is he here, tonight?"

"Yup."

"Could you get him to come out here and speak to us for a few minutes?"

"I could ask."

"Please do." Brandy manages half a smile.

The woman moves away and two minutes later a large man with an even larger middle appears at their table.

"What's the problem?"

"Jared is looking for one of your employees. Leia Gerron, she hasn't been seen for three days and he's reported her missing to police. We would like to know the last time you saw her."

"Leia hasn't been here since the early shift on Wednesday."

"Did she phone or come in after that?"

"No." The man shakes his head. "Hope you find her. Leia is a good kid."

Brandy nods. "Thank you."

"What good did that do?" Jared asks.

"The more people who know she's missing, the more people who will keep their eyes open looking for her."

Brandy answers.

The waitress shows up with their meals. Brandy eats her soup and sandwich. Jared picks at his burger.

"How's your father?" Brandy finally asks.

Jared shrugs. "He never showed any interest in me and never talks to Grandmother. I sent him my game schedule one year and he never came to a single game."

"Did your grandmother come?"

Jared shakes his head. "She wouldn't know a basketball from a football."

"Then Leia wouldn't know him." Brandy frowns. "Did Marianne know about Leia?"

"I tried the best I could to keep them apart. Not that I think Leia would have embarrassed me but Marianne is as vindictive as my mother." Jared pauses. "If I put a missing poster out at school could I use you as the contact? If I put my phone number down Marianne would notice."

"Or use the police number." Brandy answers.

"I'd have to ask Lang about that." Jared pushes his food away. "The detective says the longer she's missing, the worse my chances of finding her alive and well."

"Put up the posters. Ask people who might know. Neither your mother or Marianne were there the night Leia disappeared. Right now your mother is busy harassing me."

"Mother threatened you!"

"And I ran but she's still here. I didn't make anything better by going so this time I am sticking it out."

Jared blinks. "Thanks."

CHAPTER 5

The alarm rings early. Brandy climbs out of bed. She goes to a coffee shop for breakfast and reads the local paper. She turns to the classifieds under apartments for rent. Pitiful few ads appear and even less that she thought would suit but she phones them to set up appointments to see them.

She comes back discouraged and tired. The man at the desk greets her. "You look like you got the whole world on your shoulders."

"I'm staying until the end of the semester and need to find somewhere to live." Brandy shrugs. "It's the wrong time of year to look for something in a university town."

"I don't know of any place right now. I could ask around."

"Please do and ask around about Leia, the girl that was with me that night. She's gone missing."

"The police asked questions but they didn't give any information."

"Do you know who the man was who was reading the

newspaper in that chair that night?"

"No, he wasn't a regular. I never talked to him. He seemed to be waiting for someone. He looked at the door every time it opened."

"How old was he?"

"Older, I'd say sixty or seventy; almost entirely white and slightly stooped."

Brandy nods. "Did you see when he left?"

"Sometime between when I came and told you about your room and you left for the police station. When I turned around from giving you the map he was gone."

"Thank you." Brandy goes up to her room. She sits on a chair. "Who knew she was coming here?" She picks up a pen and writes down the question.

The phone rings. "Dr. Brandy Hollander."

"Dr. Hollander, this is Beatrice Manley. Are you sending my husband to the sub-Sahara?"

"Dr. Forester is sending him. He's taking my position. A local cleric has threatened the research station if I return. I have a replacement lined up to take his place in June but until then I am afraid that he's going to be living and working in Chad."

"Do you realize just how prejudice he is about other cultures?"

"I understand he will have to make some adjustments to new things but that's better than having the place firebombed." Brandy answers. "Hopefully, the caretaker will keep him from making any fatal mistakes."

"He will have a babysitter?"

"If you wish to see the situation that way," Brandy frowns.

"I do." The woman pauses. "Is there any female students there?"

"A few, but they are outnumbered by the males and

chaperoned by the caretaker's wife."

"Then I might be better off with him there than here."

"That I cannot say, Chad is a Muslim country with Muslin laws."

"Thank you for taking the time to talk to me."

"You're welcome I hope I set your mind at rest." Brandy puts down the phone after Mrs. Manley hangs up.

She goes to shower and change then comes back to her paper. "If he were waiting for me, it might be Norman but his face is on ads all over town the man downstairs should be able to recognize him. It might be Herman Golden." Find a picture of Herman Golden is the next note on the paper.

She doodles a little. Norman's name comes up again and again. "I have to see him but not necessarily have him see me."

In the Mount Vernon Presbyterian Church, Brandy sits in the furthest back row she can get without being surrounded by toddlers, infants, and elementary school children. She wears a business suit with no hat, as she does not own one.

"Let us start with a word of prayer. Please rise."

Brandy stands but merely looks down and does not close her eyes.

The music of the worship time washes over Brandy without penetrating her surface. She watches Norman take his place behind the pulpit. He is neither white-haired nor stooped but stands straight and tall looking like an older version of Jared.

"I know I've been speaking out of Colossians and life in the Spirit but today God has laid a different message on my heart. Today I will be speaking out of the Revelation of John," Pages are obediently flipped, "with side trips into the Old Testament prophets."

"Some people would tell us that we live in end times that the return of Christ draws near and we should be watching the sky. The apostle Paul rebuked the Christians of his day, he pointed out that we have work to do before Christ returns. Christ himself said that it would be good for us to be found working when he comes for we do not know the hour. We are to make the most of every opportunity to share his gospel and his love. God gives the prize to those who complete the task he has given them."

"I shall ask two questions this morning and try to answer them. When shall Christ return? And what will be the state of the earth when he comes?"

"Christ shall come at a time and hour we are not expecting. He shall come in the midst of the final battle between Israel and its enemies. He shall stand on the Mount of Olives, east of Jerusalem, and the mountain shall split in two. There are many prophecies about Christ's coming but only one certainty. When he comes, he will restore all things and bring peace to the earth."

"The last question, what will be the state of the earth when he comes, is the theme of this sermon. Jesus said that we should recognize the signs of the times just as we are know the changes of seasons. There will be earthquakes, plagues, famines, and floods, and throughout history, there have been earthquakes, plagues, storms and floods. Paul described it as the earth groaning with pains like a woman in labor until Christ delivers it from the sin of man."

"He said that his name should be preached to all tribes and tongue. Some have predicted that this goal is in sight. Still new areas where people are almost entirely ignorant of Christ's life and work appear in areas that it was formerly preached do these count as un-reached areas or peoples?"

"The prophet Zephaniah also spoke of Earth being burnt with the fire of his jealousy with all the people coming to a sudden end. Yet he also talks about God sheltering people who seek righteousness and humility."

"The Revelation of John speaks of the four horsemen. The first is bent on conquest. The second takes peace from the earth so men slay one another. The third brings famine through shortages and sends the price of food rocketing. And the fourth brings death to a quarter of the world's population by sword, famine, plague and wild beasts. Then they are further seals that produce earthquakes, the removal of the heavenly bodies and lead to men hiding in caves."

"Still God protects and seals his people with a special seal to cover them before the opening of the seventh seal before the earth is pelted by fire from heaven amid a great storm and earthquake. Before the end comes the death of a third of the earth by fire, first the trees then the oceans, and finally a third of the fresh water is poisoned."

"Then the elect undergo five months of torture. Then another third of people die by fire and smoke, and sulfur. Yet those destined for the pit do not repent even though God sends witnesses who do great miracles. All these things shall happen before the final coming of the Lord."

"There is much in these things and the things that come after that God has not opened my mind to understand. Many would say that much of the language is figurative. We have seen hurricanes and earthquakes in our time what have killed thousands of people. We are told that global warming will do untold damage to the ecosystems, yet at the same time we are told that it would take less than a hundred years to bring on an ice age. Will the earth survive? Will people survive? God says he will create a new heaven and a new earth. He promises us a time, when those who only live to a hundred will be seen as cursed because the average live span will be much longer. The wild beasts will be tame with the lion lying down with the lamb and men will stop fighting each other to live in peace but he does not promise it before times of extreme devastation and war that threatens the existent of all men."

"We need to be aware of God's prophecy but also of his promises. We must humble ourselves before God, submit to his direction, pray for his blessing and do the work he has given us. Those who are saved shall be saved through their faithful love to Christ as evidenced by their love to others around them. Nothing else will save people, not money, not science, not political will, not working together for the common good. God has drawn this line in the sand and we must stand on his side rather than waiting for him to stand on ours."

"We must help people to see that God not only has created this planet but works miracles every day to keep this planet functioning. We read that we could not even take a breath without God's blessing. It is time to give him the glory, it is time to stand up to those who would try to discourage us from teaching our children that we are nothing more than a chance happening. To believe evolution is to believe that all of the creation represents a roll of the dice, when the dice are not six-sided or even twelve or twenty-sided but ten million-sided. We are expected to buy random chance instead of deliberate design by a master creator. I say that is unreasonable. The Bible does not say God tried ten million times to create the earth, it says that he did it in one day."

"Now the word day can be translated as a period of

time but nowhere does it give the impression that God was like Edison and needed a thousand attempts to make a light, nor did he need a committee. No, God knew what he was doing. He spoke and every precise detail was accomplished. His Word never returns to him void, even the salvation he has provided us was done by and through his Word, who become flesh and dwelt among us."

"We must not accept the lies that scientists tell us. They act like they are neutral, and only deal in facts, but their beliefs color everything they do. A new one-celled animal is found in the Sahara and they trumpet that as proof of a theory that even Charles Darwin did not believe. All Darwin said that animals have the ability to adapt to their surroundings. He did not say that all life on earth arrived by random chance."

"Other people wishing to live in disobedience to their Creator used Darwin to create a system of belief that put their own imaginings above God's revealed word. Now we have to refute those imaginings and return the glory to our Creator. We need to pray that God would take the veil that Satan uses to blind them from their eyes so they can see the impact of their disobedience and the destruction they have done to the moral code that we live by. For nothing good happens when people do what is right in their own eyes."

The abrupt end of the sermon causes Brandy to jump.

"Quite an ad for his lecture series," An older man, who is sitting in front of Brandy, remarks to his wife.

"We don't need any more advertisements. The ones we have cost a fortune." She lifts her chin.

"It will draw the university students into the church. We need younger people to continue the work." He shrugs. "We're getting too old to do the Lord's work."

"You're getting too lazy is what you mean." His wife

stands up and starts to leave. Brandy stands then waits for a break in the stream of people going up the aisle. She is carried away by the press of people and deposited in front of a man who approaches with his hand out.

"I'm Rev. Lansing, you are new here." The older man, with mostly white hair and a slight stoop, steps close enough to her that she can smell his aftershave.

"I've never been here before if that is what you are asking." Brandy does not bother to smile but she does step back.

"So what did you think of the sermon?"

"Rather acerbic." Brandy answers.

The man's bushy eyebrow rises. "It was Biblical."

"Arguing the Bible will not convince the scientific community." Brandy answers. "He will need a much better-reasoned argument and more understanding of the facts to do that."

"And you know this how?"

"I am a biology professor at the university. All he did was offend me. Good day." Brandy steps past the man and into the sunny afternoon. She goes to her car and drives away. Her cell-phone rings and she pulls to the side of the road to answer it.

"Dr. Brandy Hollander."

"This is Detective Lang. Could you come down to the station?"

"I will be there in five minutes." Brandy answers.

Detective Lang is waiting when she steps in the door. "Thank you for coming so quickly."

"What did you want?"

He opens the gate and she follows him to his desk. "Recognize these?" He holds up a bottle of pills.

"They are anti-malaria pills."

"What were you doing with them?"

"The sub-Sahara is rife with the world's most deadly strain of malaria. It is in our contract that everyone who works or visits the research station must be taking them."

"You are still taking them?"

"The instructions are to start in advance of arriving and to continue taking them for a period of time after leaving."

"How is malaria transmitted?"

"Mosquito bites. They come out at night and I often worked during the night because my work took me outside and it was too hot during the day. I also wore protective clothing. I take the threat of malaria seriously."

"Do you still need them?"

"For another week."

He hands her the bottle. "Then you better keep that."

"Thank you." Brandy takes the bottle, "Any other leads?"

"No, and nothing on Leia, the Goldens have solid alibis."

"I really didn't expect anything less from them." Brandy answers.

"When do you expect to leave town?"

"I'm not, things have changed at the university. I'm now the acting Dean of Biology until the end of the semester. Dean Manley has been sent to Chad in my place."

"Are you staying at the hotel until then?"

"I started to look for an apartment but this isn't the best time of year to find something. I will phone if and when I move."

"I would appreciate that."

Brandy stands up to go.

"One more question." The detective says.

"Yes."

"Have you contacted your ex-husband?"

"The closest I have come is sitting through his sermon this morning." Brandy answers.

"It might not be wise to be seen publicly with him."

"I have to go to his lecture on Tuesday. Those are direct orders from both Dean Manley and the university president. Changing my schedule to suit Chastity Golden is not on, I did that before and now someone else has paid the price. If she wants to come after me that all I can is prepare myself for the consequences."

"We can't offer you protection."

"I know that." Brandy answers as she leaves the cubicle area. "I don't expect it. The university has security people and the hotel is on the lookout."

Brandy's cell phone rings. "Dr. Brandy Hollander."

"Dr. Hollander, that man is back again." The man from the desk at the hotel comes on the line.

"Thank you." Brandy shuts the phone. "The man behind the rattling newspaper is back at the hotel. He left just about the time Leia disappeared."

"I'm coming with you."

Brandy waits for Detective Lang to enter the hotel before she steps up to the entrance. The darkness of the hotel lobby requires a moment for her eyes to adjust.

"Rev. Lansing. What are you doing here?" Brandy asks.

"I wanted to speak to you."

"Rev. Lansing of the Mount Vernon Church I would like you to meet Detective Lang. He would like to ask you a few questions."

The reverend frowns, "What about?"

"The location of a young woman who disappeared

from this hotel lobby last Tuesday when you were here," The detective answers.

The reverend pales. "I don't know what you mean."

"She disappeared about the time you left here." Brandy answers. "We want to know where she went."

"I don't know."

"Try again." Brandy answers. "You remember the night. Right after my room was trashed."

"You have no proof of anything!"

"Shall we put your face on the evening news and see if anyone remembers you leaving with her?" Brandy asks.

The older man swallows. "You can't do that I am a man of the cloth."

"It's not our business to keep your reputation spotless." Brandy tells him. "Where is Leia?"

"Just what did you come here to tell Dr. Hollander?" Lang signals Brandy to back off.

"She came to the service this morning. Rev. Kettering wants to speak to her."

"Not before Leia is returned." Brandy shakes her head.

"Rev. Kettering knows nothing about this girl." Rev. Lansing frowns.

"You want me to speak to him, give us everything you know about Leia." Brandy answers.

The reverend hesitates until Brandy starts to step around him. "It's complicated."

"So is the rest of life." The detective answers. "You can answer my questions here or down at the police station."

"Please, you must talk to him. I think he is going to do something rash." He turns to Brandy.

"What's his phone number?"

"I-"

"Do you want me to talk to him or not?"

"He's at the church." Rev. Lansing swallows.

Brandy shakes her head then goes upstairs to her room. She picks up the phone, "Directory assistance for the Mount Vernon Presbyterian Church." She writes down the number.

She hands up then picks up the receiver and taps in the number. It rings once, twice, three, four, five, six, seven, eight, nine, ten times. "Mount Vernon, how may I help you?"

Brandy pauses. "The police have just picked up Rev. Lansing in connection with a missing person's case."

"Brandy! Where are you?"

"The Georgetown Hotel," Brandy answers, "but Lansing knew he was here the night Leia went missing."

"Lansing doesn't tell me everything. Who's Leia?"

"Jared Kettering's girlfriend, the one he's been avoiding introducing to Chastity."

"I've got nothing to do with them."

"Either way, a young woman is missing and has been missing for five days. Lansing left when she did and he refuses to co-operate."

She hears a deep sigh. "I need to see you."

"I saw and heard you this morning. I don't think we have much in common anymore if we ever did."

"We have a marriage, a commitment to a life together."

"We had different goals, different dreams only I was too naive to realize it."

"I didn't sleep with Chastity, Jared isn't my son."

"I study genetics. Jared is your son or he's your brother or nephew." Brandy answers. "He didn't get that face out of a cracker jack box."

"I don't have any brothers and my father died before I was born."

"That limits where she got the sperm," Brandy answers, "unless you sold some to the fertility clinic."

"I did not."

"Then don't try to tell me fairy tales."

"You refuse to believe me."

"Give me solid facts and I will consider it. And Norman, you pull Tuesday what you did this morning and the university faculty will bury you." Brandy sets down the receiver.

She wakes up to find that it is quarter past six.

She goes to the restaurant near campus. The waitress comes over, "Such good news about Leia."

"What?"

"The reverend had her stashed away. He thought that having the world find out that his preaching partner had an illegitimate son would cause a crisis this close to the big lecture. Apparently he had her in a closet in the basement of the church, kept her drugged the whole time. The doctors say she'll be okay once the drugs clear her system."

Brandy shakes her head. "I think I need something to eat before I even try to follow that kind of logic, how about something substantial like veal cutlets?"

"We have them tonight, served with potatoes and baby carrots."

"Perfect." Brandy answers.

CHAPTER 6

The university is quiet when Brandy arrives at six the next morning. She spends an hour handling Dr. Manley's questions on the e-mail then she checks on the status of her class. The data from the research station starts arriving. Brandy analyzes it and sends it back to Manley to pass on to the organizations.

She walks into class with all the data and pictures from one of her research projects from the previous year. She starts discussing the problems and questions that the project raised.

After class, she steps out of class to find the hallway full of reports with cameras of all types. "Dr. Hollander, we want your version of that happened to Miss Gerron."

Brandy frowns at the students try to pass to get to class. "Can we take this to the open area outside the cafeteria? I want the students to be able to get to class on time."

Leading the parade, she comes to a halt in a large open

area. "Now what was the question?"

"How were you involved in the Gerron missing person's case?"

"Miss Gerron came to visit me and disappeared from my hotel lobby after we talked. Then the hotel desk clerk saw a man who had been present that night return I received a phone call. Detective Lang came with me to confront the man. After the police had questioned Rev. Lansing they recovered Miss Gerron."

"Why did Miss Gerron want to speak to you?"

"That is a personal matter; it is up to Miss Gerron to make that subject public if she chooses."

"Is your divorce from Norman Kettering legal or not?"

"Honestly, I don't know. I left town twenty-five years ago after being threatened with physical harm by Chastity Golden, who claimed to be pregnant by my husband. Judge Herman Golden presided over the divorce proceeding, which I neither applied for nor agreed to. I never signed any papers but I have been told by the judge that the execution of the divorce decree was perfectly legal. I buried myself in my work then and I am still putting in sixty to seventy hour weeks."

"Are you open to discussing your personal life?"

"I don't think there is much point in discussing something that does not exist." Brandy shrugs.

"Have you talked to Norman Kettering?"

"Once since I returned and that was on the telephone. I phoned to inform him that his fellow reverend was in police hands."

"Do you realize that Rev. Kettering was instrumental in getting Rev. Lansing to give up Miss Gerron?"

"No, I didn't. I didn't talk to anyone after the phone call until hearing the news that Miss Gerron had been freed from one of her co-workers."

"What did you do between those times?"

"I napped. It's been a rough week." Brandy answers. "Now I've answered your questions. I have hours of work waiting for me. So, please excuse, me to do it." She nods to the security men who have appeared while she was talking then she walks away.

At five o'clock Rosemary sticks her head in the door. "Scott told me to tell you that he's left for today and I'm off as well."

"That's fine." Brandy nods.

"A visitor is waiting out here for you. He said he would wait for the end of your workday."

"Does he have a name?"

"Kettering."

"Junior, or Senior?"

"He didn't say."

"I'll step out and deal with him as soon as I send off this e-mail." Brandy finishes typing the reply then hits send. She shuts down the computer and picks up her handbag.

She steps out of her office.

"How long have you been out here?"

Norman Kettering rises to his feet. "An hour."

Brandy pauses. "You could have had Rosemary tell me that you were here."

"And risk you calling security?"

"I still could." Brandy answers. "Only I want a more detailed account of that happened with Lansing."

"What details?"

"Explain why Lansing took Leia."

"He said to protect me from bad publicity on the eve of the lecture."

"It doesn't make sense. Taking her was more likely to

cause publicity that it was to prevent it." Brandy shakes her head.

"Since nothing he said all afternoon was rational, the police have ordered a psychiatric evaluation." Norman pauses. "I have been sent by Jared to invite you to a celebratory dinner."

"Why didn't he ask me himself?"

"Because it would mean leaving Leia's side," Norman answers.

"Aha!" Brandy nods. "He's scared she will be snatched away again."

"He's scared Chastity, or Marianne, whoever she is, will find out about Leia. He is talking about moving to Alaska."

"Marianne is the young woman Chastity has picked out as his bride. He prefers Leia."

"They've started in on him?"

Brandy nods, "Up to and including Marianne bribing her way into his hotel room when he was on a team trip."

Norman sighs. "Solomon was right there nothing new under the sun."

Brandy shrugs.

"Are you coming to dinner?"

"As soon as I lock my office door," Brandy turns back just as the phone rings. "Excuse me a minute." She steps back inside. "Dr. Brandy Hollander."

"How dare you tell the press those horrible things?" Chastity Golden screams in the phone.

Brandy drops the receiver back in its cradle.

"Chastity again," Norman frowns.

"Still," Brandy locks the door. "She showed up the first day I was back."

"You could have phoned."

"Directory assistance told me that your phone number

was unlisted." Brandy starts down the hall.

He touches her shoulder. "My car is out this way."

"Mine is this way. And there is my escort." Brandy indicates the security guard walking towards them. "Just tell me where dinner is and I will meet you there."

"I would rather take you there." He frowns.

"Dr. Hollander, are you alright?" The security guard asks.

"Yes, I am." She turns to Norman. "If you wait beside the driveway I'll follow you."

Norman nods and heads off in another direction. Brandy follows the security officer to her car.

Brandy parks her car behind Norman's at the roadside. Jared steps out of a nearby house. "Good you're here."

"How is she?" Brandy asks.

"Fragile, but the doctors sent her home." Jared kisses Brandy's cheek.

Norman clears his throat. Jared steps away from Brandy to shake his father's hand. "It's good to have both of you here. Come inside and meet Leia's parents."

Brandy glances at Norman before she follows Jared into the house.

"Mr. and Mrs. Gerron, this is Norman Kettering and Doctor Brandy Hollander."

"Rev. Kettering." Mrs. Gerron pauses. "Dr. Hollander."

"Call me Brandy." Brandy smiles.

"I'm Hope and my husband is Jerry." Their hostess seems to relax a little. "Come into the living room."

Brandy stops to remove her shoes then enters the room where Leia is curled up on a large couch. "How are you doing?"

"Still a little dazed." Leia gives a second of a smile.

"Jared refuses to leave my side for more than a minute at a time. Your press scrum made the television news."

"If I hadn't told them something they would have clogged the halls and disrupted classes." Brandy shrugs.

"The Goldens won't like it." Jerry Gerron comments.

"They can fight my proof in court if it bothers them." Brandy answers.

"He's an ex-judge."

"I understood this was a celebration. Herman Golden is not a celebratory topic." Brandy answers.

"I don't see how the Goldens have anything to do with that man." Hope frowns. "And he calls himself a man of the cloth."

"This is about getting Leia back alive." Jared glances at his father.

"For which I thank God." Norman answers and takes the seat next to Brandy.

"I'll get the appetizers." Hope leaves the room.

"So why did they call you the Dean?" Jared asks. "I thought that was Manley's job."

"A slight complication resulting from your questions at the first press scrum; a local cleric in Chad decided that a divorced woman couldn't head up the research station there. Manley had to take my place there until they can find a permanent replacement. I've been appointed dean temporarily while he's in Chad."

"So you're sticking around?"

"Until the end of the semester at least; after that, I'm not certain what is going to happen."

"You really sent Manley to the Sahara?" Jared grins.

"Technically, the university president sent Manley to the sub-Sahara. It was quite urgent that someone stepped into the position."

"So he'll be back next fall?" Leia asks.

"As long as he takes his malaria medication faithfully and doesn't tick off the Muslim clerics." Brandy answers.

"Who's teaching his class?" Leia asks.

"I am." Brandy answers.

"I suppose a week away from my course work is going to put me too far behind to finish." Leia sighs.

"Not necessarily, talk to your teachers they can arrange for some extra tutoring." Brandy answers. "Jared might be able to help if he hasn't lost the last week as well."

"Friends passed on their notes." Jared admits. "You can ask classmates."

Hope returns with a tray of cheese and crackers. "Supper will be in fifteen minutes."

"Your mother and I want you to move back home; going missing for that long before anyone raised an alarm is unacceptable." Jerry frowns.

"I can't dump my roommates. They count on me to help pay the rent." Leia pales even more than she was. "I moved because it took too much time to ride the bus to school."

"Your mother can drive you." Jerry sets his jaw.

"Mom works in the opposite direction." Leia turns to Jared.

"I could lend you my car." Jared offers.

"That would leave you without transportation and you don't live close to the university either." Leia frowns at him. "I'm not moving back here. You knew I was missing within four hours."

"I just want you safe." Jared lifts his hand.

"That's all we want." Hope speaks instead of her husband.

"Even people with bodyguards get kidnapped sometimes. I just want my life to get back to normal." Leia answers.

Her parents frown but back off. A timer goes in the background Hope leaves the room.

An awkward silence descends on the group. Brandy glances around. "So do we have any local teams who are doing well?"

"The varsity basketball team reached the finals this year." Leia answers as she glances at Jared.

"The season's over." Jared leans back. He glances at his father. "You play basketball in school?"

"No, I was on the soccer and rugby teams."

"I preferred baseball myself." Jerry glances at Leia. "Leia played softball in high school."

"How about you, Dr. Hollander, what sport did you play?" Leia asks.

"I concentrated on academics." Brandy answers.

"How did you and Rev. Kettering meet?"

"I had a contract with the rugby coach to tutor his players in the sciences. He didn't want to lose any of them to academic probation."

"So you were his tutor?"

"I think we only had one session together, he didn't really need tutoring in my subject." Brandy answers.

"Half a session," Norman corrects. "Then you got mad."

"We didn't even start dating until a year later when we took an ethics class together and ended up in the same study group."

"Time to come to the table," Hope steps into the living room.

Everyone rises to go into the dining room. Brandy finds herself beside Norman.

"So Dr. Hollander is the world really heating up as fast as they tell us?" Jerry asks.

"Call me Brandy. It's not just the world's temperatures

that are a concern it is a global increase in storms of all kinds and a steady spread in the area of the world's deserts." Brandy answers.

"You know this for certain?"

"I know the data from the four research stations where I've worked."

"Are all of them in the Sahara?"

"No, there are two in Europe and another in Australia."

"None of them is in North America?" Jerry frowns.

"Not run by our university but I do know of a number in North America run by other universities and research organizations. I communicate with them regularly."

"And they all say that the earth is warming up."

"Like any other field of endeavor, we have people with dissenting options. There are differing interpretations of the data we receive." Brandy pauses. "What is it that you do?"

"I work in a manufacturing plant. We make all kinds of things. There's talk at work of new regulations that might shut us down all because some scientist thinks our smokestacks are pushing too much carbon into the air."

"There are methods of decreasing carbon emissions."

"Yeah, but who's going to pay for it. If we raise prices on the goods we make and someone from the third world can make it cheaper, we lose the contract."

"Which they will make by pushing twice as much carbon into the air but there's no political will to enforce the regulations." Brandy answers. "It's not that scientists don't understand the politics it's that we have to start somewhere."

"It's about greed and corporations." Leia answers. "We're learning about it in economics class."

"Greed is a spiritual problem, isn't it?" Jared turns to

his father.

"It is, but unless people are willing to accept that there is a higher moral code of spiritual significance and we have an obligation to each other, there is little the church can do about it." Norman answers. "God has given us the answers but we need to be willing to accept them."

"Yes but the guy who is working to put food on the table has the least say." Jerry frowns.

"Actually, you have a larger say than millions of people. You still have the right to change jobs, vote for your government and access the courts." Brandy answers. "Slavery and dictatorships still exist in the world."

The line of conversation dies. "This is a delicious meal." Norman states.

"Thank you." Hope smiles.

Leia glances at Jared. "Could you give me a ride to my place after this?"

"You sure you don't want a day or two more with your parents?"

"I have to get back to class or I'll lose my semester." Leia frowns.

"Then I'll give you a ride in. I'll stop and pick you up on my way to school tomorrow. We have first class together."

"It's Tuesday tomorrow?"

"Yes." Jared nods.

"Are you going to your father's lecture tomorrow night?"

"I thought I might, why do you want to go?"

"Yes."

"We'll go together." Jared promises. "Are you going, Brandy?"

"I'm going with a group of faculty from the university." She picks at the food on her plate.

"Manley insisted?" Leia asks.

"Actually, Dr. Forester insisted."

"Forester, what else did he say?" Norman asks.

"He wants you to teach an ethics class." Brandy puts down her fork.

"He thinks I'm wasting my life in the church. He wants me to get back into academia."

"Is that why he recommended I read The First Wives Club?"

Hope places a hand in front of her face; then gives in to the giggle that rises in her chest.

Jerry stares at her. "What's so funny?"

"It's a book on how dumped wives get revenge on their cheating spouses." She claps her hand back over her mouth after the last word.

"Apparently his wife made him read it." Brandy adds and the woman starts laughing.

"Sorry." Hope tries to get herself under control.

"That's Jamison," Norman sighs, "The comedian."

"What's this lecture about?" Jerry asks.

"Some scientists are starting to speak up about the possibility that life did not happen through evolution but through intelligent design, everything on earth and in the universe came into being. As a minister of the gospel, I believe that we should give people the facts that support the argument for intelligent design."

"That's your option on that Dr. Hollander?" Jerry asks.

"I am a scientist and deal in what I can verify with my senses. I am not a philosopher, which is the category this sort of thing falls under. I am not even a physicist who researches the beginning of the universe. This is out of my field."

"You are however a biologist who claims to have seen the forming of a new species of one-celled animal," Jared speaks up.

"Only if that animal survives, divides and thrives. Otherwise, it is just a biological accident." Brandy leans back in her chair. "I don't want to jump to any conclusions based on the observations made so far."

"But you said yourself that it's nothing like the parent."

"Evolution theory claims that the creatures should become more complex and/or better suited to their environment. This organism has gone into suspended animation so we have no idea if it can even find appropriate food. The parent needs moisture but we have no idea what this creature needs."

"How long can it stay in this state?" Leia asks

"I have no idea and neither does anyone else. We learn about animals by watching and this little fellow has stopped doing anything. It makes it hard to even hazard a guess."

"So this discovery that Manley was touting is a hoax?" Norman frowns.

"Not a hoax but a premature announcement of a very real scientific observation. One whose meaning is not yet clear."

"You're making excuses." Norman starts to have Brandy slap her hand on the table.

"What I am saying and said at the first press conference that the meaning of the data is up for debate. It is not classical evolution and until it splits we don't know if we have a viable animal."

"That's not that Manley said." Norman starts to be interrupted.

"I suppose you skipped over the fact that I was missing from those interviews."

Norman opens his mouth then shuts it. Jared gives her a thumb up.

Hope stands up. "I'll get the dessert."

Leia closes her eyes.

Brandy says nothing until after dessert is served and she eats enough not to insult her hostess. "Leia looks tired and I have a long day tomorrow. So I think it is time to say goodnight."

"Leia, are you all right?" Jared asks.

"I am tired. Could we go?"

"Yes, get your things and we'll go." Jared stands up and helps her to her feet.

Leia leaves the room.

"She should stay." Jerry glances at Jared.

"I'll see she gets home," Jared says.

"You'll also keep an eye on her."

"I'll do my every best."

Brandy rises to her feet. "Thank you for the delicious supper."

"You're welcome." Hope nods.

Norman stands. "It's time I left too, tomorrow is a busy day."

Jerry stands at the same time and sees them to the door. "Thank you for helping Leia."

Norman sighs. "I am truly sorry for the trouble Lansing has caused. I thought he was sane."

"Too many crazies running around," Jerry comments.

"Goodnight." Brandy gives the man a tight smile then says goodnight to Jared. Norman accompanies her to her car.

"Where are you living?"

"I am still in the hotel."

"You can afford that for the rest of the semester?"

"Finding something decent in this town at this point in the semester is proving difficult." Brandy shrugs as she unlocks her car.

"You could live in my house."

"I don't think so." Brandy opens the car door.

"Your name is on the deed," Norman tells her. "I bought it for you."

"And you want to share it?" Brandy lifts her right eyebrow.

"I don't live there. I sleep on the couch in my office. There is hardly any furniture in the house, and no kitchen stuff. I bought the place then it seemed like too much upkeep to do for just me. It makes no sense for you to stay in a hotel when you own a house here."

Brandy pauses. "Let me think about it for a few days."

"I'll show it to you tomorrow night after the lecture."

Brandy pauses and looks at him. The glow from the streetlight gives his brown hair a slightly golden glow. His chiseled cheeks and firm chin shine next to the hollows that are shadowed. Only a little gray at his temples remind her that twenty-five years have passed.

She takes a deep breath. "I would prefer to see it in the daylight."

"Wednesday, I'll pick you up after work."

"It depends on what else is happening Wednesday. I am working some long hours." Brandy slides into the driver's seat of her car.

Jared and Leia come out of the house. "Good night." Brandy starts the car then drives off with a wave at the younger couple.

CHAPTER 7

Brandy opens her eyes to her fiftieth birthday. She showers briefly then dresses in a new suit. She looks in the mirror squares her shoulders and leaves for work.

Scott is waiting for her at the dean's office. "You never answered when I ask you to come for that drink."

"Sorry, I have to attend a lecture at a church tonight. It would be inappropriate to show up with alcohol on my breath."

"We could go afterward."

"You're young you can stay up late and still get up in the morning; I cannot."

"Okay," Scott frowns, "How about tomorrow night instead?"

"Sorry Scott, I have plans for tomorrow." Brandy pauses, "Anything that requires my attention?"

"Nothing urgent," Scott shrugs. "You sure you don't want to celebrate?"

"Not today, I need to be sharp tonight." Brandy pauses. "You go out with friends and celebrate for me."

"It's not the same without the birthday girl."

"Can't be helped. Have a good time." Brandy leaves him and goes to the dean's office.

She analyzes the daily data and sends it back to Manley. Then she looks up Intelligent Design on the Internet and studies papers on both sides of the question.

"Dr. Hollander?"

Brandy glances over. "What is it?"

"Dr. Forester wants you in his office for a meeting in ten minutes."

"I'll be there." Brandy finishes the article she's reading then closes down the computer. She walks to the president's office. A dozen other people are already there.

"Dr. Hollander." Dr. Forester nods. "Now we are all here. We are going as a group to Rev. Kettering's lecture. I don't want anyone viewing this as an opportunity to cut the reverend down. I want the man willing to teach an ethics class in the fall."

"We can't allow him to take away our funding." One man frowns.

"Rev. Kettering does not control any funding." Brandy frowns. "Those who wish to believe in Intelligent Design will direct their funding based on their personal beliefs. What you have to do is convince them that experiments designed from other points of view can be done in our labs and that personal bias will not affect the outcomes. We have to uphold scientists as objective observers. Once we start to reject experiments or make strong public statements giving the perception of ingrained bias, we have lost."

"That's not so easy in archaeology!"

"If the evidence supports evolution, then you have nothing to hide and if you have nothing to hide, then they can't damage our studies." Brandy answers. "It won't harm anyone of us to start from a fresh perspective."

"You want us to throw out two hundred years of thought!"

"I am asking you to help these people to see the truth by working with them." Brandy leans against the door frame.

"The next thing all archaeological digs will be set up to   prove   Bible   stories."

Brandy smiles. "Christian organizations already fund digs in the Holy Land. Your attitude disqualified you for that money. There's nothing money people dislike more than close-minded researchers when that they want is to hear all the possibilities."

The man frowns then opens his mouth to argue.

"Enough." Dr. Forester frowns. "This is about the give and take of academic debate. I want your comments to support debate. Personal attacks have no place in this situation."

"Manley would fight you on this." The man frowns.

"Dr. Manley is in Chad because he caused an uproar that removed Dr. Hollander from her position. I don't need anyone who can't see past his own preconceived notions attending tonight. If you can't hold a neutral mindset, then stay home." Dr. Forester frowns.

Brandy returns to her office and spends the rest of the day doing administrative tasks. At five thirty, she goes to a restaurant. She pulls into the parking lot at the church at twenty to seven. She enters the church just as the pews start to fill up.

Norman stands at the front of the church. He comes down the aisle to greet her. Brandy blocks any form of physical contact.

"Are you willing to see the house tomorrow night?"

"I am not ready for this conversation. Tonight is about the debate."

"Out for blood this evening?"

"Dr. Forester forbade character destruction. He wants an academic debate with no personal attacks." Brandy shrugs. "Although I must warn you not everyone agreed."

"Did you?"

"Our disagreements are personal and not subject to academic debate over Intelligent Design." Brandy sighs. "I'm surprised you're out here to greet people."

"Lansing's arrest left us short-handed."

Brandy frowns but nods.

"Find yourself a seat. I have to check with my technical people." Norman indicates a pew.

Brandy sits down. "You mind if we sit here."

Brandy turns to see Dr. Forester and a woman. "No, go ahead."

"Martha, this is Dr. Hollander, our new dean of biology." "Dr. Hollander, this is my wife, Martha Forester."

Brandy smiles at the woman, "Nice to meet you, Mrs. Forester."

"Dr. Hollander." The woman nods.

"Call me Brandy." The woman sits next to Brandy leaving her husband on the outside of the threesome.

"How well do you know my husband?"

"Not well, I've been doing field research for twenty-five years. I only returned to town last week. I think we've met twice and talked on the phone once."

The woman seems to relax.

Leia and Jared slide into the pew from the other aisle. "Is the rumor true?" Jared asks.

"That depends on the rumor." Brandy frowns.

"A little birdie told us that it's your fiftieth birthday." Leia whispers in a voice that carries to the adjacent pews.

Brandy sighs. "Unfortunately, yes."

"And we weren't invited to the party?" Jared frowns.

"Considering that I am not attending the party, why would I invite anyone?" Brandy frowns.

"Not going to your own birthday party?" Leia asks.

"I'm too old to get excited about birthdays. My lab assistant wanted me to go for a drink. I told him to celebrate it without me. I just hope he's not hung over tomorrow."

Mrs. Forester chuckles. "That's an unrealistic hope."

"Isn't fifty a landmark?" Jared asks.

"I don't celebrate landmarks." Brandy answers. "I celebrate achievements, and age is not an achievement, it's a fact of life."

"Did Dad take you out to supper?"

"Your father has been busy preparing for tonight."

"Excuse me, but who is this young man?" Dr. Forester asks.

"Dr. and Mrs. Forester, this is Jared Kettering and his friend, Leia Gerron."

"Aren't you the young woman who was kidnapped and held in this church?" Martha Forester asks.

"That's me." Leia retreats to lean back against Jared.

"Showing the world that she has grit and isn't going to flee from life," Dr. Forester looks toward Leia, "That kind of spirit is worth celebrating."

Leia pauses. "Thank you, sir."

Jared puts his arm around Leia. "That's my girl."

Brandy glances at her watch.

"We'll take you out for cake after this." Jared offers.

"It depends on how late this goes. I have to be back in my office early tomorrow morning."

Jared nods.

"Have you started on applications for grants?" Dr. Forester asks.

"Not yet. I thought I would canvas the researchers in the department and see what kinds of projects they are working on first."

"They are responsible for their own applications. You need to get something started for yourself."

"I still have experiments ongoing at three research stations with their attached students." Brandy answers. "Manley has all he can handle with Chad until the situation stabilizes. The information still needs to be compiled and interpreted when the individual experiments are finished. I think I'm covered for projects to work on for a while."

"You want to go to Europe after he comes back and we have someone in place."

"I'll have to see what point the various experiments are in after Manley returns. There's a conference in Sweden in May I want to attend to pick up the latest research that others are doing on the topic of global warming."

Dr. Forester pauses. "Not presenting a paper?"

"Not this year, next year if the experiments can be completed on time." Brandy answers. "They are scheduled to if we can keep Chad operating."

"Are you excited about going to Sweden?" Leia asks.

"It should be a good conference."

"What do you do at a conference?" Jared asked.

"I read all sixty papers ahead of time so I can compose intelligent questions, then I get to sit through hours of technical lectures on each one. Then I get to ask those questions along with the two or three hundred other subject matter experts."

"It doesn't sound like much fun." Leia frowns.

"Afterward, I make the drive to the Arctic Circle in Finland to visit our research station and make certain everything is on track there." Brandy sighs. "I think I feel fifty that sounds like a lot of work."

"When is the last time you took a holiday?" Dr. Forester asks.

"Workaholics don't take vacations," Brandy answers, "Wouldn't know what to do with one."

"Visit family?" Martha Forester suggests.

"They died in a house fire when I was eight." Brandy shakes her head. "I think the lecture is about to begin."

Norman steps behind the pulpit at the front of the room and speaks into a microphone.

"I want to thank everyone for coming tonight. My name is Norman Kettering and I am a minister of this church. For those with academic credentials, I have a master's degree in theology and a doctorate in ethics. My topic for tonight is Intelligent Design.

Intelligent Design is not necessarily a Christian concept. All that Intelligent Design really says is that there are those of us, who believe that the complexity of the universe requires that we admit that there is an intelligent force behind what we see, hear, taste and feel. We believe that natural selection and random chance as postulated by scientists following Charles Darwin's theories are inadequate to explain how a system where one missing element or even a slight change in a multitude of factors would make it impossible for the universe to exist.

Now I am not a scientist. I do not pretend to know and understand all of those factors. What I do know is that scientists have found not only order but also beauty in the largest galaxy and smallest atom. Nothing in nature shows the random nature that some scientists attribute to the creation of the universe. If swilling pools of random molecules were behind creation then somewhere on earth, we should find pools of unaligned atoms ready to produce new creatures or least evidence that such pools once existed. If more complex animals came from less advanced organisms then shouldn't we see that in the world around us? What stopped the creative cycle on earth?

What we actually see is the dying out of species with nothing being created to replace them. Where there once was a great abundance of species we see slight modifications in existing species to take the place of lost species or the loss of whole ecosystems so there is no place to take. We abuse the earth with the expectation that science will find answers to such things as climate change, species depletion, and human suffering.

Unfortunately, even when science gives us answers, they lead to new problems. Antibiotics heal infections then create super bacteria what resist those same antibiotics. We live longer and develop diseases that come from living longer. We learn to travel further faster only to find burning the fuel required is leaving traces of poison in the air, water and plant life. Scientists now tell us our methods of generating energy are endangering our whole civilization through climate change.

We need new perspectives on how the world works; attitudes that extend beyond believing that everything is random and without order until we impose our order on it. We need to respect the systems that are in place and learn about them before we do things that destroy them.

I am not saying that science is evil. What I am arguing is that the philosophy of science limits what they recognize as an acceptable answer and they need to remove the filters that stop them from seeing what is there as opposed to solutions that fit into their predetermined theories. The scientist who finds proof that points in other directions should not find their careers cut short or be cut out of the academic debate as they are now. Many of you laugh at politically acceptable language but scientists as a whole have politically acceptable thought filters that they must keep up or risk being ostracized.

Scientists who argue for Intelligent Design are saying that they have seen things that do not fit with those filters and want the opportunity to research the world without those imposed limits on their results. This is a strike for academic freedom as much as it is for a call for science to admit to the legitimacy of religious thought in the larger debate about what is best for the human race."

There is a stirring in the audience behind Brandy. Dr. Forester shifts his position.

"For those of you wanting to continue this as a dialogue, there are microphones set up in the aisles for you to make statements or pose questions. I will warn you that technical issues are going to have to wait for future lectures when I have arranged for subject experts to join me on the platform."

Dr. Forester stands up and goes to the microphone. "Rev. Kettering, would you be open to a change of format? For those who do not recognize me, I am Dr. Jamison Forester, president of Lakeview University. The members of my staff would like to challenge you and your experts on this topic to formal debate."

"My speakers are not going to be in town all at once. This is a six-week series."

"That's fine. We can handle one topic at a time. No one from our side is going to have to travel."

Norman glances at the audience. "We would have to

come up with a fair question."

"Or a different question each night to suit the evening's topic. We would have to negotiate the details. But the first question is would you be willing to change the format?"

"I would have to consult my guest speakers before I can make that kind of a format change."

"Then I ask you to do so and get back to me." Dr. Forester sits down.

Another man from the far aisle stands up and goes to the microphone. "Does this mean you believe that we should listen to every kook who comes along with a strange theory?"

"I think we need to respectfully listen to people's ideas before we label them as kooks." Norman frowns at the man. "We need to give serious consideration to new ideas from new perspectives. An inventor people called a kook came up with ways to make rubber into tires. Yet who did not drive here on rubber tires tonight? History is full of people that the majority have called kooks whose discoveries and inventions have changed our society. Their ideas may sound strange to you but so would the theory of relativity if you were hearing it for the first time. Until we hear them and give them a chance to proof themselves how do we know whether or not they have something important to give us?"

One of the university staff stands up to the other microphone, "Do we not need a standard by which to gauge these now ideas and inventions?"

"That depends on what you mean by a standard." Norman answers. "What we need is to ask two questions. Does it work or is there a place where approaching this subject from this angle will give us some information we can use to solve problems? To go beyond those questions takes us into a circumstance where we are imposing biased filters."

"We all know of medicines that do nothing yet are touted by those who sell them as miracle cures. Don't we need to have some objective witnesses to decide whether or not the public, who does not have the time nor the resources to check out every claim, is protected from charlatans?"

"I am not suggesting that we do away with regulatory bodies. It would be nice of some of them were more objective and distance from their subjects than they are now. What I am saying is if you teach students to think just like you do then you can't expect new answers to questions that stump you. New solutions need fresh perspectives and sometimes people who have not been subject to your educational process can raise valid issues and solve problems in what your think of as your field of study. Science is getting too specialized and sometimes a broader perspective is necessary to see things clearly."

The speaker glances at Dr. Forester, who shakes his head. The questioner sits down.

A younger man steps to the microphone. "How would you like it if someone used those same arguments to say the Bible?"

"The Bible has been a subject for debate for centuries. Translators have quibbled over exact definitions for words, people have explained and re-explained passages to suit their personal beliefs, different churches have argued for and against the inclusion of parts of the scriptures. Governments have attempted to ban the Bible. If you wish, I can give you dozens of resources for studying the Bible by both believers and unbelievers. God defies man-made boxes, his Word continues in the face of every attempt to destroy it. I will debate you and whatever group you wish to put together on the subject."

The young man sits down.

Brandy stands and slides past Leia and Jared to stand at the microphone. "Rev. Kettering, your argument so far has been a very pragmatic one. You want us to accept everything that works and reject that which does not. If we question that there is an intelligence design behind everything we see how do we prove or disprove it, pragmatically of course?"

"There are things that scientist cannot prove because it is beyond the ability of men to know them. Just as a character in a book cannot prove or disprove their world is fictional."

"If Intelligent Design cannot be proven, then we are to base our pragmatic thinking on what kind of foundation?"

"You are arguing semantics, Dr. Hollander." Norman pauses.

"I am arguing that if we can know only what we can see, hear, feel, and taste, then Intelligent Design fails in the "does it work" category of proof. You cannot prove it works. That leaves us with the does this perspective give us some information that allows us to solve problems."

"I have proof it does work. If we ask if people knowing there is an Intelligent Designer of the universe helps them to live better lives, then I can give you case studies that prove it works."

"Case studies sound more like social science than hard science." Brandy frowns. "Just what measures are you using to gauge whether these people's lives really improved? Are these case studies or merely testimonials? Testimonials are what many wonder drugs seller abuse to pedal their wares."

"The difference being?" Norman frowns.

"Do you have objective observers who agree these people's lives have changed for the better for no other reason than they believe in an Intelligent Designer?"

"In many cases, yes," Norman smiles.

"Then I look forward to hearing and seeing your proof over the next six weeks." Brandy turns and sits down next to Jared.

Jared leans over. "Now you've asked for it."

Brandy just leans back in the pew to await the next questioner. She almost relaxes when the door at the back opens with a creak.

"There she is!" Scott's slurred voice carries through the sanctuary, "One, two, three, happy birthday to you." His voice is joined by a half dozen others, "Happy birthday to you, happy birthday to you, happy birthday Dr. Hollander, happy fiftieth birthday to you."

Brandy curls her head down and hides it with her hands. Jared stands, as do a half-dozen other men, to herd the drunks back outside. Leia scoots over. "Are you all right?"

"Are they gone?"

"I think so." Leia glances towards the back of the building.

"I think we will wrap up for tonight." Norman continues from the front. "If there are any other questions, I will happily answer them if you phone or fax or e-mail them to me here at the church. Contact information is on cards available in the vestibule. Thank you and good night."

Brandy glances up to see him coming her way then leans down again. "They have been sent on their way." Jared speaks from beside Brandy's elbow.

"I hope they had a designated driver." Leia tells him. Brandy raises her head to see Norman's face. It glows with hostile energy.

"What was that about?"

Brandy sighs. "About not being left to get old gracefully."

"Did you deliberately send them to interrupt?"

"No." Brandy rises to her feet. "I did not send them."

"Then how did they know where you were?"

"I only said that I was coming here to make Scott understand that I would not go drinking with him."

"Your lab assistant asked you to go drinking with him?"

"He's into celebrating birthdays."

"And you're not?"

"Why would I want to celebrate getting old?" She steps past Jared. "Good night." She walks down the aisle to the doors then immediately goes out to her car. She checks the back seat before sliding into the driver's seat. She takes two deep breathes and swallows back the tears. She blinks before shoving the key into the ignition and starting the car.

CHAPTER 8

After dropping a handful of files on the desk in front of Scott, Brandy sees him wince.

"Give me one reason why I should not fire you?" Brandy raises her voice.

He rubs his temples. "I have never done anything that stupid in my entire life. I promise no more mess ups."

"You embarrassed me in front of the university president, his wife and most of the faculty if you keep your job I look too soft. I need a better reason than that."

"My head hurts can you give me some time to think about it?"

"How about a week suspension without pay is that enough time to think about it?"

Scott sighs. "Yes."

"If you didn't have an otherwise spotless record I would increase it." Brandy frowns. "Get out of here and I will see you next Wednesday morning."

"I'm going." He takes his coat off the coat rack and leaves.

Rosemary watches her enter her office and shut the door. Brandy only emerges to teach her class then disappears back into the office. Rosemary finally puts her head in at quarter to five. "Rev. Kettering is out here."

"I'll be done here in a minute then I'll come out to see him. You can go anytime you are ready."

"Should I send a termination notice into the human resources department for Scott?"

"No, I didn't fire him. I gave him a week's suspension without pay."

"I'll see the paperwork gets done."

Brandy steps out of her office to see Dr. Forester talking to Norman. "Ah, Dr. Hollander, I wanted a moment of your time."

"I have about one to spare." Brandy pauses. "What is it?"

"Your lab assistant, Scott; I wondered what you intended to do about last night."

"I gave him a week's suspension without pay to think about why last night was not a good career move."

Dr. Forester nods, "Neither too harsh nor too soft."

"But I hope it drives home the message." Brandy grimaces. "He's a good lab assistant when his mind is on his work."

"And the rest of the students who were involved?" Dr. Forester asks.

"Unless you want to take action, I can't say I even know who they are." Brandy shrugs, "Unless the church wishes to press charges for drunk and disorderly conduct."

"That would be up to Rev. Kettering." Dr. Forester pauses. "I will say goodnight to you both." He leaves.

Norman nods to the man and then waits until he leaves. "What's that about?"

"Undoubtedly one of the involved students is someone from an influential family and he's trying to avoid a backlash if he disciplines them." Brandy shrugs.

"That doesn't make you mad?"

"Getting angry would only increase my blood pressure. There's no sense in destroying my health over university politics." Brandy pauses. "So is the offer to rent the house still open?"

"Rent?" He pauses. "The rent is free. Call it atonement for the sin of living off my wife's salary."

Brandy frowns.

"Come and see it before you make up your mind."

Brandy stands by the large French doors in the living room and looks out over a large garden. "Do you plant anything?"

"Like I said it seems to be too much work for one person. You can go out there if you'd like."

Brandy unlocks the doors then opens them. She walks along the stone paths and looks in the flowerbeds. There is even lawn furniture set in a patio encircled with fruit trees so there would be shade in the summertime.

"The trees weren't pruned. You won't get as much fruit this year." Brandy comments.

"I never pick the fruit. The deaconesses from the church pick it and deliver it to needy families." Norman shrugs. "They also come and work the gardens. I think the vegetables go to the same place. The flowers wind up in the church for decoration or are given away to shut-ins; occasionally, the house is used for temporary shelter for guests of the church. All that would change if you moved here."

"You would put them all out for me?"

"I bought the house with you in mind. I was indulging in magical thinking at the time. My thought was that if I bought the house and was perfect in everything, I did for God then he would grant my one prayer and bring you back to me. It took me years to realize that fulfilling my wishes if I followed some sort of ritual wasn't his job. He's under no obligation to play fairy godmother."

"How long have you owned the house?"

"Eighteen years. It was bought in your name."

Brandy shakes her head. "What if I had never returned?"

"That's not magical thinking. Magical thinking says that if I obligate God, then he has to do what I want. If I showed any signs of unbelief, then he wouldn't be obligated."

"It took you seven years to want me back?"

"It took seven years to put together the down payment. You've got to remember I didn't have a job when you left and I still had another three years to finish the doctorate. I finished paying off the mortgage three years ago. I've wanted you back since the second I realized that you had really gone."

"I can't accept the house, not without paying you for it." Brandy turns a corner and starts back towards the house.

"Actually, you already have paid for it. You put at least that much into my education."

"You don't owe me anything." Brandy frowns. "I did that I did because I choose to do so. There is no obligation on your part to pay it back."

"That's where you are wrong. Under Christian theology, the believer is obligated as part of his testimony to right any wrongs he has done before he became a

Christian as a witness to the church and to people around him that he has changed."

Brandy sighs. "I am to believe that you are giving me the house without any strings attached to it?"

"You are still my wife. I want a chance to put our relationship back together." He pauses and glances at the house. "Not that I am going to force you into anything whether you stay here or not. But I do have an ulterior motive, Goldens don't know about this place. I know I have never acted like it but I know Chastity's threats are real. It is too risky for you to remain in the hotel."

"Are you confident that they don't know?" Brandy frowns. "They have lots of contacts."

"I haven't had anything to do with them or my mother in twenty-five years."

"Jared seemed to know where you were even if you didn't contact him." Brandy frowns. "He said he sent you information on his games."

Norman sighs. "You like the kid, don't you?"

"He is the victim in all this." Brandy answers. "The kids usually are."

"I did not sleep with Chastity." Norman frowns. "It will always come back to this, won't it?"

"It's part of it." Brandy pauses before opening the door to the house. "You hid the greater part of your life from me. When the accusations came, I had no ability to make a stand against them because everyone except me knew the truth. I felt like I had been a victim of a fraud. I was ashamed that I allowed you to play me that way. I probably would have committed suicide had I been forced to stay. Now you're asking me to take your word and trust you again. It's not a simple thing."

"I'll show all the paperwork that relates to the house. I would really feel better if you weren't living in the hotel.

They might have caught Lansing but I still don't trust Herman or Chastity."

Brandy frowns, "Even if we have no hope of ever getting back together?"

"I'm still praying Brandy. I don't believe he has any obligation but I keep throwing myself on his mercy." Norman opens the door for her. "Come I'll show you those papers."

Brandy's cell phone rings. "Dr. Brandy Hollander."

"Dr. Hollander, this is Jim Turner. We think we have some information that you should know."

"What is it?"

"Rev. Lansing isn't who he claims to be. It's complicated maybe you should come down to the station for a full explanation."

"Just who is he?" Brandy asks as she glances at Norman.

"He's a medical doctor and researcher by the name of Joseph Conroy-Hamilton."

"Conroy-Hamilton," Brandy frowns. "Where did he practice?"

"The university, he used to work at the medical clinic for students."

Brandy pauses. "I used the clinic."

"No reason for you to see him." Detective Turner answers, "Unless you were willing to pay to get pregnant. He also wasn't very successful. He killed a patient."

"What is it?"Norman asks.

"Lansing is a doctor who used to work at the university clinic as a researcher. He killed a patient."

"I don't remember that." Norman frowns.

"I've got to go down and talk to the detectives."

"You left your car at the university. I'll take you."

Brandy nods and follows him out of the house. They

get in the car. Norman pulls into traffic. "I don't remember you being sick and going to the clinic."

"You were off on one of your varsity trips. It was happened and I dealt with it." Brandy answers.

"What else did you have to deal with?"

Brandy shrugs. "Nothing that didn't get magnified once I got to the desert. Maybe you better drop me off at my car. I can manage the police station by myself."

"I think you've managed enough by yourself." Norman turns in the direction of the police station.

Brandy says nothing as Norman escorts her to the police station and asks for the detectives. Det. Lang comes to get them. "Rev. Kettering, we've been looking for you."

"Good, then maybe we can get this cleared up." Norman guides Brandy through the gate.

The detectives find a chair for Brandy but leave Norman standing. "What is this about?"

"We ran Rev. Lansing's prints and came up with another identity. Dr. Joseph Conroy-Hamilton. Dr. Conroy-Hamilton was arrested twenty-two years ago for the death of a young woman who went to him for an abortion. She died because he tried to harvest the child for transplant into the womb of an infertile woman. He left her to bleed to death while he concentrated on the embryo." Lang starts the story.

"He was charged with premeditated murder but disappeared while out on bail." Det. Turner finishes. "He underwent extensive plastic surgery before resurfacing as Rev. Lansing about a year later."

"So our question for you Dr. Hollander is could you have been pregnant when you went to see Dr. Conroy-Hamilton?"

Brandy frowns and glances at Norman. "Things were

crazy between my job and my studies. I went to the clinic because I couldn't afford to take time from either one."

"But is it possible that you were pregnant?"

"I was on the pill but that isn't foolproof." Brandy answers. "I just didn't consider the possibility at the time."

"Dr. Hollander, what were you told was wrong with you?"

"Appendicitis."

"Could we ask you to do to a doctor and have it confirmed that your appendix was taken out?"

Brandy nods. "I have to know."

"If she was pregnant what would have happened to the child?" Norman asks.

Lang flips open a file. "It seems Dr. Conroy-Hamilton tried to develop methods of moving a child from one womb to another. He was staunchly anti-abortionist."

"So he would have some woman lined up to take the baby?"

"He had a long list of women wanting children. He was a fertility specialist."

"So we may have a child out there somewhere?"

"I don't want to give an opinion on that until Dr. Hollander sees a physician."

Brandy stands to her feet. "I need to find an appropriate medical facility and a doctor."

"We will make a phone call for you." Det. Turner answers.

Early the next morning, Brandy shivers under the thin hospital gown. The radiation technician arranges a sheet across her hips. A silence hangs heavy as cold jelly is smeared over her abdomen. Brandy says nothing as a pressure across her skin.

"You want the results before I give them to the detectives?" The technician asks.

"If you wouldn't mind," Brandy pauses. "Yes."

"You still have an appendix but your right Fallopian tube has been mutilated."

Tears spill down the sides of Brandy's face to dampen her hair. "I see."

"I'll just clean this up then you can go to the bathroom and get dressed." The technician starts to clean and falls silent again.

Norman turns from the window then she comes out of the cubicle. "So?"

"I still have my appendix." Brandy wipes tears from her cheeks. Norman comes over and hugs her.

"You got him to give up Leia. Do you think you could get him to tell us what happened?" Brandy asks.

"Thinking about this makes me want to throttle him. I am not certain I can." Norman rubs her back with his hand. "Maybe the detectives can get him to talk."

"If I was pregnant why would he assume that I would want to abort my baby?"

"I can't answer. I thought I knew the man after working with him for twenty years." Norman sighs. "I wonder if he drew me into the church to find you."

"Why? It sounds like he did this to other women?" Brandy frowns.

"Let's go talk to the detectives and find out." Norman answers.

"We've got his notes but they seem to be some kind of code." Det. Lang sighs.

"Would another fertility specialist be able to read them or are they written in another language?" Brandy asks.

He hands her the file. "You tell me."

Brandy stares at the writing for a few minutes before she manages to make any sense of it. "Latin, or at least, some of it is."

"Latin, as in ancient Rome?" The detective asks.

Brandy nods. "I recognize a few phrases. Latin and Greek are both used in the sciences. I can't read it well enough to understand this."

"You wouldn't have a Latin scholar at the university?"

"I don't know." Brandy frowns. "I don't know who we have in the linguistic department."

"Let me see it." Norman holds out his hand.

Brandy passes him the file.

"It's Latin all right but I can only pick out a few words."

"Can you phone someone from the university?"

"I should show up there soon." Brandy picks up her cell phone. She hits the buttons.

"Rosemary, this is Brandy Hollander. Sorry, I am going to be a little late but I have a question. Who at the university would be an expert in Latin?" Brandy asks her secretary then listens to the answer. "Could you find out for me and call me back quickly?" Brandy closes the phone.

"Have you questioned Lansing-Conroy-Hamilton?" Norman asks.

"He refuses to speak. He refuses to eat. We've got him under suicide watch." Turner frowns.

"You want to try to talk to him again?" Lang asks.

Norman shakes his head. "I might throttle him."

"Can't say I would blame you if you did(.) I can't let you do it but I understand the sentiments." Lang nods.

Brandy's phone rings. "Dr. Brandy Hollander." "Yes, Rosemary." "Okay, thank you for trying." She closes the phone. "The university does not offer Latin. Neither the language department nor the English department has anyone with qualifications in Latin."

"A university where no one studies Latin!" Det. Turner frowns.

"There's a Latin professor at the seminary. I can call him."

"I have to get to the university." Brandy stands. "Call me if you find out anything."

Det. Turner walks her to the door. "Are you going to be all right to drive your car?"

"I think so."

CHAPTER 9

Brandy spends most of her day analyzing data and sending the results back to Manley. She is just getting to the administrative work when her cell phone rings.

She fumbles with it for two seconds before getting it to her ear. "Dr. Brandy Hollander."

"Are you sitting down?" Det. Lang asks.

"Yes." Brandy answers.

"It seems you were the only success Dr. Conroy-Hamilton had in his experiments. The zygotes he took from you had not yet attached themselves to your uterus so they had no trouble being transplanted. The rest were, further along, had already settled in the womb so they were destroyed when he tried to remove them."

"Zygotes, as in plural."

"Apparently you were targeted. He found someone to slip you fertility drugs so you released more than one egg."

"Does it say how many?" Brandy asks.

"Not from what we managed to get translated so far."

Brandy closes her eyes. There is a moment of silence. "We will keep you informed."

"Please do and thank you." Brandy manages before closing her phone. It rings immediately.

"Dr. Brandy Hollander," Brandy answers on automatic.

"Dr. Hollander, you sound strange somehow." Leia is on the other end. "Jared and I wanted to take you out for that birthday celebration. We thought if you had a day or two to calm down."

Brandy pauses to think. "Can I bring someone along?"

There is a slight hesitation. "Sure."

"Where and when?"

"At the restaurant where I work about six tonight."

"I'll meet you there." Brandy answers.

"Then we will see you later." Leia answers and ends the phone call.

Brandy reaches for the telephone directory. She's flipping through the pages when the phone on the desk rings. "Dr. Brandy Hollander."

"It's Rosemary. Rev. Kettering is out here."

"Send him to the office and hold off everyone else for a while."

"Gladly," Rosemary answers.

Brandy gets up to open the door but Norman enters before she can reach the knob. "I take you've heard from Lang." She sinks back into her chair and motions to a second chair.

"I was there when he phoned you. You scared him."

"He shocked me so I think we might be even." Brandy pauses. "Leia just phoned, she and Jared want to meet me for supper. I hoped you would come with me."

"Why?"

"I want to talk Jared into a DNA test."

"I told you that I didn't sleep with Chastity."

"Not for paternity, I want to know if Chastity Golden managed to get one of the stolen zygotes." Brandy answers.

Norman's jaw drops and stares at her. Finally, he recovers enough to say. "That's crazy."

"The detectives think I was targeted. Your mother sided with the Goldens and accepted Jared as her grandson."

"That nuts!"

"Nuts or not it would explain why twenty-five years later both of them would still try to run me off." Brandy answers. "It would also explain why Jared looks so much like you."

"How were you going to approach him?"

"I don't know. I need your help." Brandy runs her hands up and down her upper arms. "All I know is I have an opportunity tonight."

"It would be too easy to alienate him from the Goldens but if they are all he has for a family it might not be the best." Norman sighs. "I could ask him to go for a paternity test then add the maternity test afterward."

"Do you think he would go for it? It might cost him his inheritance from your mother." Brandy frowns.

Norman takes a deep breath. "We can only ask."

Dr. Forester knocks on Brandy's door and sticks his head in early that afternoon. "Can I speak to you Dr. Hollander?"

"Come and sit." Brandy motions to the chair. "What can I do for you?"

"Convince Norman Kettering to teach an ethics class."

Brandy takes a deep breath, "Why do you want him to teach this ethics class?"

"He's a brilliant man in his field. I want the best professors I can get. Small universities have to compete with larger ones for good teachers; with good teachers, we can attract more students. Paying students are what keeps us out of the poor house."

Brandy leans back in her chair. "Right now is not the right time to put extra pressure on my relationship with Rev. Kettering."

"You have until the end of July surely you can manage it before then."

"I can talk to him about it. Right now they are one reverend short at the church." Brandy pauses. "He's also got this lecture series to finish; unless you managed to convince him to make it a debate series."

"Not yet, I would argue the point but it's almost impossible to get him on the phone these days."

"Next time I see him, I will tell him that you are trying to contact him."

"Soon please." He stands up. "What's this I hear that Lansing was an alias?"

"He was a doctor and a researcher here twenty-five years ago. He was charged with murder and disappeared. The police are investigating further."

"If you need counseling, we have a psychologist on call to provide our faculty and staff with mental health care."

"I might take you up on that later when I know all the facts." Brandy answers.

"There's no shame in admitting we can't handle everything that life throws at us." Dr. Forester pauses. "Everything I've heard about your work is excellent, I don't want to lose you to stress."

"I'll remember that." Brandy answers. "I need a few more answers before I know how to explain what has happened to anyone else."

He nods.

Brandy goes down to the cafeteria for an afternoon coffee. She turns from the coffee urn to see Scott sitting at a table. "I didn't expect to see you here." She starts the conversation.

"I've got a class." He glances up from his books. "Can we talk for a minute?"

"Just let me pay for my coffee." She nods. She takes it to the cashier and offers her pre-counted change then turns and walks to where he is sitting.

"How's the hangover?"

"The headache disappeared last night; my conscience is still prodding me." He pauses. "I didn't really mean to do anything other than take you out for a quiet drink. It's not like I was hitting on you or anything."

"It just got out of hand."

"I usually don't drink that much, honestly, I don't. I just thought I had lost my chance to talk to you about something."

Brandy leans her head slightly to look in his tipped forward face. "What did you want to talk about?"

"It's personal really." He pulls an envelope out of the back of his binder. "My mother drank herself to death. Her marriage ended years ago. After her funeral, I found this letter she had sent it to my father but he returned it unopened. I couldn't throw it away without reading it. It blew my mind. I want you to read it and tell me if she was crazy or not." He holds it out to her.

Brandy takes the envelope and slips out a one-page missive. She opens it.

Dear Scott,

I know you believe that I had an affair. I did not. When no baby came after ten years of marriage and your family started to urge you to leave me, I went to a fertility specialist. Dr. Conroy-Hamilton told me that he was doing an experiment that might help me get pregnant. He transplanted a fertilized embryo into my womb.

Your mother just told me that everyone knew it was not your baby all along because you can't father children. I cannot believe you could put a woman you love through this kind of torment. So now I realize I love you but you don't love me. I would kill myself but then who would look after your namesake.

May you burn in hell for this!

Mona

"Tell me that she was crazy."

"Why did you bring this to me?" Brandy asks and sits across the table from him.

Scott rolls his eyes toward the ceiling in a gesture Brandy immediately identifies. "I broke into the medical clinic archives. You were the only patient that got surgery the day my mother had her final appointment with Dr. Conroy-Hamilton. It was a weekend and the place was closed except for emergency services. Since he was your surgeon, I thought you might know what he was doing. "

Brandy reaches for her cell phone, "Det. Turner or Lang please."

"Det. Turner here."

"I think I just found another piece of the puzzle. Could we meet?" Brandy answers and then puts her hand over the mouthpiece. "Is your class just starting or just over?"

"It starts in twenty minutes." Scott frowns.

"When is it over?"

"Four."

"Can you come to the university at four o'clock? You

need to meet someone." She speaks back into the phone. "We will be in the cafeteria."

Lang and Turner came directly to the table. Brandy hands Turner the letter since he arrives first. The detective finishes it then hands it to his partner. Lang checks the zip code then reads the letter.

"Detectives, this is Scott Parker. He's a student here and my lab assistant. Scott these are detectives Turner and Lang."

"How did you get this letter?" Turner asks.

"My mother died five months ago. It was in her things." Scott frowns. "She was crazy right? I mean she drank a lot and suffered deliriums."

"We have reason to believe that Dr. Conroy-Hamilton did try to perfect this type of baby swap and that Dr. Hollander was involuntarily involved."

"She really could be my biological mother?" Scott turns to stare at Brandy.

"Yes. She really could." Detective Lang answers. "I wouldn't rule it out until DNA testing is done."

Scott leans his elbows on the table then places his head in his hands. He takes several deep breaths then looks up at Brandy. "Then who is my father?"

"Rev. Kettering, we were married at the time." Brandy states. "You have some of his mannerisms now that I look for them."

"Why would he target a married woman?" Scott asks.

"I haven't figured that out." Brandy frowns.

Brandy phones the church. A secretary picks up. "Mount Vernon Church, how can I help you?"

"Is Rev. Kettering in?"

"Who's asking?"

"Brandy Hollander."

"I'm transferring you now." The woman announces and there's more ringing.

"Rev. Kettering." He sounds distracted.

"Norman, it's Brandy. I have news."

"What now?" There is a note of impatience in his voice.

"One of our children may have found me."

"Where?"

"He works here at the university. His name is Scott Parks."

"The drunk!" His tone hardens.

"I'm not going there. The detectives are setting up a blood test. Contact them to find out when and where." Brandy hangs up.

She arrives at the restaurant a few minutes early to find Jared waiting for her. "Where's Leia?"

"She's in the back. She gets off shift in five minutes." Jared rises at her approach. "I thought you were bringing someone."

"I asked Norman but then we had some harsh words. We'll have to see if he shows up." Brandy sits and he sits back down.

"So that's new?" Jared asks.

"There's been sort of a break, Lansing was using an alias." Brandy pauses then glances to where she thinking Leia will appear. "If I asked would you submit a DNA test to establish the identity of your parents?"

"You mean to find out officially if Norman Kettering is my father?"

Brandy takes a deep breath and nods.

"Is this a private conversation or can anyone join in?" Norman asks from behind Brandy. She places her hand on her chest and takes a deep breath.

"Please join us." Jared gives a wave of his hand.

Norman takes a seat beside Brandy. "How far has this conversation gone?"

"Brandy asked me if I minded doing a DNA test for paternity. Have you decided not to trust Chastity?"

"I trust Chastity, alright, to lie and cheat." Norman answers. "The question is, does Brandy have a reason not to trust me?"

Jared leans back in his chair. "Sorry Brandy, I didn't realize I was hurting you."

"It's not your fault, but Chastity did a lot of damage before I left town." Brandy glances at him.

"If it will help in any way, I'll go get the blood test done."

"I would appreciate it." Brandy offers him a smile. Just then Leia comes over to join them.

"So is fifty any different than forty-nine?" Leia asks.

"In my case, yes," Brandy glances at Jared. "It seems I've waited to turn fifty to become a mother."

Silence meets this announcement. Jared's mouth starts moving but nothing comes out. Leia stares at her.

Norman frowns. "I thought we were going to leave that announcement until we knew for certain."

"I considered it but I don't want Jared finding out from anyone else." Brandy answers.

"Finding out what?" Leia asks. Jared reaches over and gives her hand a squeeze.

"Twenty-five years ago, a doctor stole fertilized eggs from my body in what I thought was an appendectomy. There's a good chance I have children I never knew existed."

"Wow!" Leia waves a hand in front of her face to cool herself. "How did you find out?"

"Rev. Lansing turns out to be the doctor who operated on me only he had a different name and different face at the time. The police are investigating." Brandy answers.

Jared looks at his father. "How will you find your children?"

"The doctor was a researcher. He left notes." Norman pauses. "I just don't want to destroy these people by turning lives upside down."

"Why would a doctor do something like this?" Leia frowns.

"He's refusing to speak so we don't know." Norman shrugs.

"That's got to be really mind blowing, finding out you have kids you've never known."

"I don't know that would be any worse than finding out your parents aren't your parents." Norman glances at Brandy.

The waitress arrives to take their order.

Brandy kisses Leia then Jared on the cheek. "Thank you for supper."

"You're welcome. I hope I look as good at fifty." Leia smiles.

"You ready to go?" Jared turns to Leia.

"I just have to go grab my stuff from the back room." Leia heads off.

"Has Chastity or Marianne given you any trouble?" Brandy asks.

"Not a peep. But they will about the time they think I've let down my guard."

Brandy nods. "Take care of each other."

Norman is waiting and walks beside her when she leaves.

"We need to talk." Norman starts.

"On what subject? The fact you think I'll go charging in and destroy people's lives to satisfy my curiosity?" Brandy keeps walking to her car.

"You took it on yourself to find this Scott."

"Scott found a letter written by his mother that more or less outlined what happened. He came to me not the other way around." Brandy unlocks the door of her car.

"Which might be a scam? This could open up my mother's will and challenge Jared's right to inherit."

"We'll know when the tests come back." Brandy opens her car door and sits in the seat she starts to close it but he reaches out to stop her.

"I said we have to talk. I want to show you the papers concerning the house."

"No tonight." Brandy shakes her head. "My brain is in shock. Legalese requires a fresh perspective."

"I'll bring them to your office tomorrow." Norman steps back allowing the door to close.

CHAPTER 10

Scott is sitting outside the dean's office the next morning. Brandy stops at the sight of him. "Can I speak to you for a moment?" He asks.

"Come in." She nods towards the office.

Brandy places her purse in a drawer then turns to the young man. "What did you want to say?"

"I'm changing jobs. I'm not coming back next Wednesday."

Brandy nods. "I hope you found something that pays the same or better."

"It doesn't matter." Scott frowns.

"Yes, it does. I know yesterday was bizarre, and if you need some time and space to think about how this news changes your view of yourself and the world, I'll deal with it. What I do know is that destroying your career because of it is incredibly foolish. I can find a professor willing to trade lab assistants. There is no problem with the caliber of your work. I won't have any trouble recommending you."

"What about my drinking?"

"Lots of university students drink not all of them become addicted to alcohol. It depends on why you drink and in what amounts. You managed to make it to work every morning. I saw no sign that it was interfering with your ability to do the job until the incident at the church. I will write you a reference."

Scott pauses, "Just because I might be your son?"

"No, I would do so for all good employees." Brandy answers. "Being biologically related has nothing to do with it."

"You would help me find another position here at the university?"

"If that is what you wish." She nods.

"Are you going to introduce me to Kettering too?" Scott frowns.

"No." Brandy shakes her head. "I think it would be best if you to attend one of his services if you wish to meet him."

"Why?"

"My relationship with Norman Kettering is quite turbulent. You need to start fresh."

"Is he abusive?"

Brandy shakes her head. "Not abusive, argumentative. He wants me to believe his version of that happened twenty-five years ago and I want him to see my point-of-view. We've got a lot of things to work out. You shouldn't be burdened with our problems."

Scott frowns. "I don't think I'll go until I learn the outcome of the tests."

Brandy nods.

"Can I ask you one thing?"

"What's that?" Brandy leans back in her chair.

"When did you find out that there might be someone

like me out there?"

"Yesterday, the police also told me that Lansing-Conroy-Hamilton had someone feed me fertility drugs so you might have siblings."

Scott shakes his head. "This is incredible."

"They are still trying to translate his notes. He wrote them in Latin." Brandy bites her bottom lip. "I think you might have a brother. I can't say any more until we get the DNA tests done."

"I guess it was good I didn't show that letter to you Tuesday night. You wouldn't have had any idea what it was about."

Brandy pauses. "Who talked you into coming down to the church?"

A blush rises in Scott's cheek. "Marianne. She's a psychology major. I shouldn't have listened."

"I'm sure she was very persuasive." Brandy answers. "She wouldn't happen to work at the library?"

He nods. "Yeah, you know her."

"I've heard about her. She's a friend of Chastity Golden."

Scott hits the center of his forehead with the heel of his hand. "Now I really feel stupid."

"Do you want me to find you another job?"

"Can I have a few days to think about it?"

"Until next Wednesday at least, the paperwork has already gone to the human resources department and if I try to change it now things will be mixed up until after you graduate."

"Okay." Scott stands.

"Stay in touch."

"I will." Scott leaves.

The phone rings as Brandy is working on her analysis.

"Dr. Brandy Hollander."

"Dr. Hollander, this is Marianne Gilford."

"And what can I do for you, Miss Gilford?" Brandy leans back in her chair.

"Stay away from Jared Kettering."

Brandy laughs. "Any particular reason you feel you have the right to give me orders?"

"He's none of your business."

"According to Jared, he's not yours either. He stated for the police records that you have been harassing him."

"I am going to marry him."

"If you're going to pursue him, I hope you like the cold."

"Cold?"

"He said he would run away to Alaska before he would marry you." Brandy tells her. "Chastity is steering you wrong just like my mother-in-law steered her wrong. Neither one of you will marry if you insist on chasing men who have said no."

"He'll come around." Brandy can almost see the pout.

"Just like his father did? Are you willing to wait thirty to forty years for him to do so?" Brandy catches the gasp and manages to move the phone away from her ear before the receiver on the other end smacks against plastic as the line clicks off.

Brandy is e-mailing the analysis when the phone rings again. "Dr. Brandy Hollander."

"How dare you-"

Brandy sets the phone down, "Easily, Chastity."

The phone rings immediately. Brandy waits for the third ring to pick it up. "Dr. Brandy Hollander."

"I'm suing you."

"Go right ahead." Brandy sets the phone down a

second time then picks up her books and goes to class. She steps outside her office.

"Rosemary, if Ms. Golden calls again. Report her for being a nuisance."

"She must have figured out your extension. I haven't been letting her calls past me. Don't worry I'll deal with it."

"That would be appreciated." Brandy gives the woman a smile. "I'm off to class."

Rosemary nods.

Norman was waiting outside her office when she returns. "Where have you been?"

"Teaching, it is part of my job around here." Brandy shrugs. "Did we have an appointment?"

"I brought the house papers."

"You could have left them with Rosemary. She's trustworthy."

"I wanted to talk to you over lunch." He frowns.

"If you don't mind the cafeteria, I'll be with you as soon as I pick up my messages." Brandy answers and opens her office door. She picks up the slips Rosemary has left on her desk. She frowns.

"Is something the matter?"

"I have to go down to the police station." Brandy picks up the phone and punches out the phone number.

"Detective Lang, tell him it's Brandy Hollander."

She waits. "Detective Lang, what happened?" She listens without making a comment. "I'll be right there."

Norman frowns. "What's going on?"

"I have to go down and bail Scott out." Brandy answers as she hangs up.

"He's old enough to be responsible for himself." Norman puts an arm across the office door to block her from leaving.

"Unless you want me to call security, you will move your arm." Brandy frowns.

He drops it. "You're not his mother."

"No, I am his employer and he has no family." Brandy picks up her purse. "Besides all he's guilty of is accessing records to find me." She walks past him.

Norman rubs his face with his hands then follows her.

Scott sighs. "I really messed up this time. The police found evidence I accessed the clinic's old files."

"I've put up your bail." Brandy tells him. "Just not more hacking until this is cleared up."

"I wish I could say I could pay you back."

"They will give me my money back when you show up for your court appearance. It wasn't doing anything except sitting in the bank."

"You're not mad?"

She shakes her head. "I'm not mad."

The guard gestures with his head. "Let's go finish the paperwork so you can leave."

Scott follows Brandy out to the sidewalk. "I gave the detectives the names of the women who came to the clinic that day. I think some of them gave false names. I couldn't find them."

"I wouldn't be surprised." Brandy answers. "You want to be dropped off somewhere?"

"I don't think so, you know what guy who is coming at us?" Scott nods.

Brandy glances up to see Norman advancing on them. "Norman Kettering."

"I don't think he likes me." Scott frowns. "I never have any luck with fathers. I'll see you on Wednesday."

Brandy nods and then turns to face Norman. "So you rescued him."

"Nothing I haven't done for students and employees other places." Brandy answers.

"I hope you fired him this time."

"No, and I don't intend to." She starts to walk away. He grasps her arm and turns her around.

"He's engaging in destructive behavior and you are aiding and abetting."

"His mother killed herself with booze leaving behind a letter that's gone off like a bomb in his life. Where's your compassion?" Brandy frowns. "Or is this jealousy because I'm not spending every second with you?"

Norman frowns. "This has nothing to with us."

"Go lie to someone who hasn't heard it before." Brandy rips her arm out of his hand and stomps off to her car. "You can forget about me moving anywhere." She gets behind the wheel and drives off.

Scott is waiting for Brandy after work. Brandy glances at him. "Is something the matter?"

"I talked to Norman Kettering."

"And what did he say?"

"He offered to let me move into his house if I would persuade you to become my housemate." Scott answers.

Brandy sighs. "He's persistent."

"He thinks you are in danger."

"Are you hungry?"

"He fed me a big lunch." Scott shakes his head. "But I'll sit with you if you want to eat."

Brandy nods and walks with him out to her car. They get in and she drives to a downtown restaurant. "Are you considering taking up his offer?"

"It's a good house. He's not living there. I'll be around

to do the heavy work and keep the Goldens from the door."

"He wants to control me." Brandy shakes her head.

"I think he'd settle for knowing that you're safe for the moment. He's scared you're never going to talk to him again."

"I'm making progress I recognized the lie this time." Brandy closes her eyes for a moment. "I told you that you didn't want to get mixed up in my relationship with Norman."

"You need some food." Scott opens the door and comes around to help her out of the car. "My mother used to drag me into her problems all the time. I worked odd jobs to pay her rent when I was ten. She would have never bailed me out of jail. She wouldn't even have reached the police station if there was a bar between her and me. She would have been in the drunk tank trying to phone me to come bail her out."

"I'm sorry." Brandy frowns. "You shouldn't have had to live that way." She walks with him to the restaurant.

"Instead, I have the offer of free rent, two offers of meals, and someone who cares that I keep my career going. I think I might just be coming out ahead."

"Is the free rent important?"

"It could cut thousands off my student loans," Scott admits. "It took everything I earned last year to bury my mother."

Brandy nods and enters the restaurant.

Brandy calls the church when she gets to the hotel.

"North Vernon Presbyterian Church," This time it is Norman who answers.

"Norman, it's Brandy."

"You talked to Scott." Norman comments.

"Why did you make him the offer?"

"He probably told you why." Norman pauses. "Except I lied to him, I didn't tell him how much I want to share that bed with you."

"I knew I should never have come back."

"You're still scared."

"Of course, I'm terrified that you will use me again. Just when I think you want me to be a permanent part of your life, I'll find out it's all a lie again. Some woman will phone up and tell me that truth about the man who is supposed to love me. The world isn't big enough to keep running especially if you're running away from what you believe about yourself."

"I promise this time will be different."

"I think you believe that but Chastity is still calling me; still trying to warn me away from you. Still threatening to sue me or kill me."

"I didn't marry her. I wouldn't marry her. I married you for a reason."

"I think it is called lust."

"Lust doesn't make a man want to put his fist through the wall when he finds out just how rotten a husband he was. Lust doesn't endure quarter of a century separations. Call it what it is."

"I can't. To call it what it is means, I have to admit it matters. If it matters, then I have to respond. If I respond, I set myself up for humiliation. If I am not dignified, then I hurt too much to bear."

"Please, I won't touch you if you don't want me. Scott couldn't withstand losing another mother that way." Norman's voice lowers. "My life wouldn't be worth living without you."

"Are you trying to talk me into moving into the house or moving in with you?"

"Both if you want honesty."

"You'd be a poor example to your flock sleeping with your ex-wife."

"I don't believe our divorce is legal." Norman answers. "I never wanted it. You never signed it. How can it possibly be legal?"

"I don't know, but Herman Golden says it is." Brandy sighs.

"Who gave him the right to decide?"

"The law of the land, apparently," Brandy answers.

"That leaves me only one choice, doesn't it?"

"What choice is that?" Brandy closes her eyes.

"To marry you again."

Her eyes spring open. "Marry me again?"

"As many times as it takes for people to accept it; only, this time, it will be in the church with everyone watching you come down the aisle in a long gown."

"The church will object if I am not a believer?"

"The church cannot stop me from renewing my vows."

"This is too much for me to consider tonight, I'm tired." Brandy places her free hand over her eyes. "I'm going to take a bath and consider your offer to Scott."

"Scott's moving in tomorrow with or without you." Norman pauses. "It would be easier for him to keep his sobriety pledge if you are there to support him."

"You got him to agree-"

"He told me that the scene at the church reminded him of something his other mother would have done and he decided on his own to quit drinking. I did not coerce him into anything. I just believe it would be easier for him to keep his promise to himself if he has our support and lives outside the dorms."

Brandy takes a deep breath. "You are certain it was his

idea?"

"Yes, you can ask him if you don't trust me."

There is a short silence. "I still have the contents of our apartment. I don't know how well it stored or whether any of it would be of any use."

"Where is it?"

"In a storage locker, I gave the detectives the key so they could find the answering machine tapes with the messages Chastity left me. I haven't I got it back from them."

"Phone tomorrow and ask. Scott has a few days off we could move it to the house and sort it out."

"You're really going to give him a chance?"

"We are going to give him a chance." Norman answers.

"You are making it impossible to say no to moving, you realize that?"

"That's part of my plan."

"What if it backfires and Chastity finds me?"

"Then Scott and I will be your protection."

"And who will protect you?" Brandy asks.

"My heart protects me. I gave it to you and I refuse to take it back. She can't marry me without my consent, I proved that twenty-five years ago."

"That just leaves Scott."

"Scott knows the enemy now. I doubt they will pull another fast one on him."

"You know this how?"

"I spend the greater part of this afternoon talking to him. We ate lunch and went through the house together. We talked about a lot of things. He reminds me of you."

"I thought he was much more like you in his mannerisms."

"But not his thought patterns, he shares your quirky

sense of humor. He liked the blue mouse joke."

Brandy pauses long enough for Norman to ask. "Are you still there?"

"Yes, I just haven't thought of that joke in years."

"Then you should hear the one about the-"

"Norman, it's late and I'm tired."

"Let me come over and I'll give you're a nice massage then we can both get a good night's sleep."

"How would that give you a good night's sleep?"

"I'd know you were safe."

"Safe, from my perspective is something else. Having you here is anything but safe. If Chastity is watching, she will burn down the hotel over our heads if she thinks we are within touching distance of each other."

"I think it's time I dealt with that woman once and for all."

"That could be understood as a threat."

"I am not going to kill her. I just would like to see her behind bars for the next twenty-five years so I could spend the time with my wife."

"First you have to deal with your mother, or she will just find another Chastity." Brandy yawns. "I have to say good-night."

"Goodnight, Brandy."

Brandy hangs up the phone.

CHAPTER 11

Dr. Forester is waiting in Brandy's office when she arrives the next morning. "I finally reached Dr. Kettering. He has agreed to change the lectures to debates. I think my deans need to face off against his subject matter experts."

"I am not sure that would be a good idea in my case." Brandy frowns.

"What is going on between you and the reverend?"

"We were married once."

"You did not seem to think that mattered only last week."

"Twenty-five years ago, someone operated on me for what I thought was appendicitis but really they harvested already fertilized eggs and implanted them in other women. We have children in common that we did not know we had until two days ago. I don't even know how many."

The university president pauses. "Children?"

"Young adults really; two of them are students here

at this school."

"Lansing-Conroy-Hamilton, the man is going to cause us grief."

"You have the files. Where did his funding come from while he was here?"

"I will look it up and send the information along to the police. Still the genetic debate is the fourth one and I wish you to take the stage. I have no one else as qualified in the subject matter as you are."

"I cannot herald my discovery. It hasn't proven its viability."

"It's not required all you have to do is rebut his so-called expert."

Brandy nods. "That I may be able to do, it all depends upon the argument."

"That is all I can ask."

Brandy goes to the library to check the availability the resources for a paper she plans on assigning her students . A clerk behind the desk stares at her while she waits to talk to the senior reference librarian. Brandy is just finishing the consultation when she sees the young woman put her cell phone back in her pocket.

Jared picks that moment to come past. He puts his arm around Brandy's shoulders and kisses her cheek. "Hi, Mom."

"It's not smart to rile the bee's nest," Brandy tells him without glancing at the young woman.

"Then I will walk you back to your office so you don't get stung."

Brandy shakes her head. "I think I can find my own way back."

"Dad phoned and asked if I would keep an eye out for you. He is riling the queen bee and he wants you protected. He also wanted me to point out the advantages of you moving in with my younger brother. Birth order is so important among siblings."

Brandy laughs. "So is brotherly love."

"I really should get to know him." Jared pauses. "You can invite us over when you get settled."

"I have to get back I have a class to teach."

"Deans are very busy people." Jared keeps his arm around her to walk her out of the library. He stays with her until she gets her books and then walks her to class.

Jared winks and leaves. Brandy enters the classroom.

Scott is waiting when she gets out. "Jared called he had to go deal with something to do with a friend."

"I hope his friend is all right." Brandy frowns but allows Scott walk her back to her office. "Have you decided what you want to do regarding your job?"

"I want to keep it if I may."

"You may." Brandy answers. "You are still off until Wednesday."

"I know. The reverend said you had some furniture."

"I have to phone the detectives and get my key back." Scott enters the office with Brandy.

Brandy picks up the phone to call the detectives. She pauses and looks at a paper on her desk. She shakes her head then pushes buttons. "Detective Lang, please." "Brandy Hollander." "I'll hold." "Yes." "I will expect his call." She sets the receiver down. "I am afraid that I won't get it back this afternoon. The detectives are out of the office."

"Tomorrow will be soon enough." Scott answers.

"Out of here, you can't come back to work until Wednesday."

Scott starts to argue but notes the piles of work

waiting for her. "I will see you later."

Scott is not gone more than five minutes before Marianne Gilford pushes her way into the office. Brandy picks up the phone, "Security to Dr. Hollander's office." She sets it back down.

"You cougar!"

Brandy sighs. "What is your problem?"

"First you have Jared hanging all over you and now Scott. I could report you for sexually harassing students and employees."

"Go ahead if you think you have any clue as to what is going on," Brandy leans back in her chair, "Knowing that I will sue your pants off if you are wrong."

Marianne pouts. "I am going to the university president."

"The door is that way." Brandy motions with her hand. The woman walks out and slams the door behind her. Brandy glimpses a security guard.

Brandy goes back to work on the pile of papers.

Ten minutes later the phone rings. "Brandy Hollander."

"Dean Hollander, what is this about you and two male students?"

"I told you about them the other day. We are waiting for the tests to come back to prove whether or not they may be my sons."

"Miss Gilford seemed to think-"

"Jared and Scott were acting on Norman Kettering's orders to keep a close eye on me. He fears the reaction of his mother, Miss Golden, and Miss Gilford should the news get out before the tests are done and the police deal with the receivers of the pilfered zygotes. It is really a personal matter which I do not want public."

"Ah, I see. You can count on me not to release the

news prematurely."

"Thank you, Dr. Forester."

Brandy works in her office until seven before sending off her daily e-mails and locking her classified documents away. She opens the office door to find Norman Kettering waiting for her.

"You could have told me you were here."

"I didn't want to interrupt your work."

"How did your session with your mother go?"

"Mother is not about to change either her mind or her preferences. She is threatening to disinherit Jared if he does not come up to snuff and marry Marianne soon."

Brandy just shakes her head and locks her office door.

"You don't think she will carry through with the threat?"

"So long as she can get you and Jared to react to the threat she's getting what she wants, power over you."

"I agree."

Brandy stops short and stares at him.

"I walked away from her twenty-five years ago. Today I saw what a pitiful creature she really is."

"Pitiful?"

"She's clinging to the assumption that she controls my life."

"Don't be so confident that she does not have some influence. If Chastity got a hold of one of our children and did so through Lansing-Convoy-Hamilton, she might have more influence than you think."

He pales. "What?"

"Why would a fertility specialist with even warped Christian principles agree to give a baby to an unmarried woman with the morals of Catherine Medici? Someone either paid him off or blackmailed him. I wouldn't put either past your mother."

"You hate her that much?"

"I think this conversation is over for this evening." Brandy answers. "Good night."

"I am offering to buy you supper."

"To talk about your mother, sorry, but my stomach is not that strong."

"Even if I promise not to mention my deluded mother or her insane pick for daughter-in-law for the whole evening?"

"To what purpose are we having supper?"

"Friendship, companionship, an update on what the lawyer said when I consulted him on the state of our marriage," Norman gives her a half smile.

"You consulted a lawyer?"

"I am only having this conversation over dinner."

Brandy pauses to count to mentally count to ten. "Alright, we will go to dinner to discuss the state of our marriage."

Norman immediately claims her arm and leads her out to his car. "What about my car?"

"I will bring you back after supper to get it." He opens the passenger door. Brandy takes the seat. He closes the door and comes around to the driver's door.

"Do I need to go back to my hotel to change?"

"No, you are fine just the way you are." He starts the car and puts it into gear.

Brandy leans back against the seat then glances out of the window. "I am not what I was."

"No one expects you to be after twenty-five years. I know I am not."

"I managed to ignore the years until this last week, now I am starting to feel old."

"It's just the mid-life doldrums. Once you get used to the idea of being fifty, then you will realize it has its compensations."

"Like what?"

"You have enough of your life behind you to be able to figure out who you are and enough ahead of you that it's possible to make any corrections you need to get comfortable in your own skin."

"Is this the start of a get right with God speech?"

"Just a reflection of what has happened to me since I turned fifty last year. Are you this cynical about all of life or just me?"

She glances in his direction then back at the scenery. "I'm just realistic."

"No, you are scared."

"There is nothing unrealistic about scared. You convinced me to take a chance once and it ended badly."

"You could have talked to me."

"To hear what? It was intercollegiate soccer season. You are barely home and had told me once that whatever my problem was it could wait until the finals were over. You had your friends and I obviously wasn't one of them."

Silence falls between them.

"Take me back to my car. I don't think I can do this a second time."

"What if we are still legally married?"

Brandy closes her eyes. "Please don't do this to me. I should never have married. I should have known better."

"You are overreacting."

"Just like I overreacted twenty-five years ago? You convinced me to marry you without your family's approval. It caused nothing but pain. I buried all that pain under eighteen hour days. What am I going to do with it this time?"

"You could try giving up the pain so you can live again."

He stops the car and Brandy opens her eyes. "Where are we?"

"Somewhere we can talk. This time, you are not in control."

Brandy undoes her seat belt and starts to open the door. "No, this time we are going to talk this out." Norman reaches over and grabs the door handle. "You are going to listen. That divorce cannot be legal."

"It doesn't matter." Brandy drops her voice.

"I don't agree. We are husband and wife. I want my wife back." He leans forward to kiss her.

Brandy pulls back as far as possible and asks. "Or what?"

"Don't play with my feelings Brandy. If I didn't matter to you, you wouldn't feel anything."

"What about my feelings? You promised me the sun, the moon, and the stars but dropped all pretense of having a marriage when your friends showed up and wanted you to go out and play. You hid me from your family like some embarrassing mistake. I did everything I could think of to keep the bills paid and my studies current. Your friends treated me like dirt and your mother sicced Chastity Golden on me. Now you want to kiss and make up like none of the past has any place in the present. Well, it does."

"When are you going to let go?"

"When the threatening phone calls stop being a daily occurrence. When you realize that I am not going to fit in your church-going lifestyle because I don't believe the same things as you do. When you stop thinking that everything will magically fix itself on the strength of sex and a marriage that has kept me in nightmares for the last twenty-five years."

Norman closes his eyes.

"Think of it this way Norman, God got me out of your life so he could claim you all those years ago and this is a test to see if you will continue to choose him."

"God values marriage, Brandy. A believing husband is to stay with his non-believing wife." Norman opens his eyes.

"And the non-believing wife?"

"Is free to go and the husband is then free of the marriage."

"I left, Norman. Twenty-five years of no contact has to count."

"If you had filed for divorce, I would count it but you never did. If you want me to believe you want to end this relationship, then divorce me, Brandy. Don't hide behind Herman Golden's nonsense."

Brandy's cell phone rings. Norman moves back so she can answer it. "Brandy Hollander."

"Yes, Detective, I need my key back for the storage locker." There is a slight pause. "I will stop by tomorrow." Brandy closes the phone. "Take me back to my car."

"Only if you remember one detail," Norman answers.

"What's that?"

"I never, and will never accept that divorce. I have filed a complaint against Herman Golden's handling of our so-called divorce."

Brandy sighs then nods.

'Retired Judge Under Investigation for Corruption.' Brandy reads the headline in the paper sitting on top of everything on her desk.

Brandy steps into the outer office. "Rosemary, did you leave a newspaper on my desk?"

"No."

"Has anyone been in my office this morning?"

"Not since I got here." The secretary frowns. "Why?"

Brandy goes into her office and checks the locks on all her drawers. Rosemary comes to the door of the office and looks into the room. "Is anything missing?"

"None of the locks seem to be broken. Just the paper left." Brandy answers.

"I will check with security." Rosemary leaves.

Brandy glances at the article as the phone rings. "Brandy Hollander."

"Dr. Hollander, this is Jeffery Winters of the Daily Courier. Have you read the paper this morning?"

"Someone left it on my desk but I have not had time to read it."

"Can I get your statement about Herman Golden's handling of your divorce?"

"My statement is this. Herman Golden's daughter came to me claiming to have had an affair with Norman Kettering to whom I was married. She told me she was pregnant with his child and threatened me with bodily harm. I left town. I never filed for divorce but Herman Golden contacted me saying that he had officially divorced us so his daughter could marry Norman Kettering. It was only when I returned to town less than two weeks ago that I learned that Norman Kettering neither applied for a divorce nor signed the papers. Reverend Kettering never married Miss Golden, who phones me regularly to threaten my life. That is all I know for certain."

"Wow! Are you suing the Goldens?"

"I have taken no legal action but I have not ruled it out."

"Then who filed the complaint?"

"I will leave that piece of information up to your detective work." Brandy tells him.

"Come on this is too good an opportunity to miss."

"If you print my statement, I will get phone calls threatening to sue me. I do not view that as a pleasant opportunity."

"Can I record them?"

"It would break the university's confidentiality rules. As dean, I sometimes deal with highly sensitive matters. You could, however, sandbag Chastity Golden by mentioning my name in her hearing which may set off a tirade especially if she has read this morning's paper."

"Thanks for the tip." The phone line goes dead.

The phone rings again. "Brandy Hollander."

"Did you read the paper?"

"Someone left a copy on my desk but I have not read it, Dr. Forester."

"I left it there. You understand that Judge Golden has donated significant funds to the university over the years?"

"I did not file the complaint, Norman Kettering did." Brandy sighs. "He's trying to convince me that I should give him a second chance and part of that is convincing me we are not legally divorced."

"You will attend the first debate in the series on Tuesday, the creation of the universe debate."

"I will be there." Brandy answers.

"Dr. Hollander, don't forget that there is counseling available."

"I haven't."

CHAPTER 12

"Mom?" The voice on the other end of the phone is masculine. Brandy takes a half second to recognize it.

"What is it, Scott?"

"Where is the key?"

"I picked it up from the police station this morning. I will meet you at the storage place at lunch."

"Why don't I just pick it up?"

"Marianne Gilford laid a sexual harassment complaint against me because Jared walked me to class and you walked me from class to my office."

"Marianne Gilford, what right did she have to do that?"

"Ask the university president," Brandy sighs. "I will see you down at Seal and Save shortly after twelve."

Both Scott and Jared are waiting for her at the storage place. Brandy pays the end of the storage fees then opens the locker for them. "I have to get back to the university. Handle that stuff gently, after all, some of it might count as antique."

Brandy manages to make it bedtime without hearing from Chastity Golden. She is closing her eyes when the phone rings. "Brandy Hollander."

"Mom."

"What is it, Scott?"

"I found a photo album with press clippings about this little girl who lost her family in a house fire. Why would you keep track of anything this horrible?"

"I was the birthday girl. It was my family who died."

There is a lengthy silence. "I understand why you wouldn't want to celebrate your birthday."

"It was a long time ago. Nothing anyone should remember." Brandy feels the tears running along her temples. "Just set it aside and I will deal with it later."

"Does Dad know about this?"

"In sort of an abstract way, I refused to join his jock club. Not being able to join him put a damper on some of the things he wanted us to do together."

"He really was a jerk."

"We were badly matched, still are, but it's not all his fault. I will come over tomorrow night and sort through the personal stuff just set it aside."

"He's still in love with you."

"My attacker thought he was still in love with his wife too. Good night." Brandy sets the phone down. She struggles to stay awake as long as possible before she falls asleep.

It is nearly dark the next night before Brandy arrives at the house. She rings the bell. Scott arrives at the door to let her enter.

"I have a key for you." He goes to get it.

"Thank you." Brandy takes it and adds it to her key ring. "I will just go through some of the stuff."

She starts with the things Scott has put aside. She breaks it into three piles. Then she phones Norman.

"Norman, this is Brandy."

"What's going on?"

"Scott asked me to go through the boxes of personal items. There are things I don't remember and other things I know are yours."

"Brandy, where is Scott?"

Brandy looks up and around. "He must have gone to bed."

"Brandy, it's two in the morning and you have to be to work in five hours. Why haven't you gone to bed?"

"Sorry, I did not realize it was so late." Brandy closes up her phone. She stands and glances around her. She packs everything of hers back in a box and tapes it shut.

Brandy stops to lock the front door with the key Scott had given her. "I warned you to stay away from Scott."

Closing her eyes and counting to ten before turning to look at her accuser, Brandy frowns.

"Does Scott know you are stalking him? I thought you were after Jared."

Marianne Gilford glares at her. "Scott is too kind for the likes of you."

Brandy pauses. "You are getting tedious. Scott gets to choose his own friends. You do not get to choose them for him."

"Friends!" Marianne Gilford charges at her. Brandy feels the first collision with her back but it is the collision of her head with the door of the house that causes her to black out.

Brandy wakes up in an ambulance with sirens shrieking. She opens her eyes every briefly then closes them again.

"Mom, Brandy." It is Scott's voice.

"I'm here but I don't want to be."

"The police are holding Marianne."

"Until her family bails her out of jail." Brandy answers.

"It doesn't matter you aren't going to be left alone. I am moving your things to the house tomorrow." Scott tells her.

"Phone the university and explain why I will not be in to work."

"I have to wait until someone is there."

The ambulance stops and then backs up.

The next voice, Brandy hears, is Norman's. "What happened?"

Scott tries to answer as the stretcher gets whisked away.

Detective Lang is one of Brandy's first visitors. "We held Marianne Gilford until the court opened this morning. The judge ordered a full psychological assessment so she was moved to a hospital. Scott gave us a full statement of what happened. I need yours as well."

"I had gone over to the house to sort out some boxes of personal belongings that were in with the old furniture and things from the storage locker. Marianne Gilford was waiting when I left the house. She told me to stay away from Scott. I told her that she had no right to choose Scott's friends and she charged at me. I hit my head on the door and blacked out. I woke up in the ambulance."

"Does she know that there is a possibility that Scott is your son?"

"No, and until we get the test results back, I won't tell anyone."

"We did get the doctor's notes translated. Six women got eggs implanted that day. We managed to figure out that Mona Parker was one, Chastity Golden was the second. The third woman's name was Nancy Allen. She was killed in a domestic dispute less than six weeks later and the last three women were identified only by first names. We are searching his files to see if we can link them to last names."

"And the doctor?"

"Refuses to open his mouth. Herman and Chastity Golden have been brought in for questioning but their lawyer refuses to allow them to say anything useful. I think this is about all you can handle for now."

"I am tired."

"I will keep you informed about the file. I will get your statement typed up and be by to get you to sign it."

Brandy nods and then falls into a slumber.

Someone holding her hand when wakes Brandy she opens her eyes to see Norman sitting beside her bed. "What are you doing here, Norman?"

"The doctor wants to speak to you but he did not want you to be here alone when he did."

Brandy glances down at his hand. "What's the bad news?"

"The doctor will be here in a moment."

"Just tell me."

"All he said is that he wants someone with you when he gets here. How's your head?"

"It still aches. Norman, did Detective Lang stop to talk to you?"

He pauses then sits in a chair beside the bed. "Why?"

"Detective Lang thinks we may have as many as three more children out there."

"Did he say who they were?"

Brandy frowns. "Just that the mothers are written into the doctor's notes just by the first names only. They are double checking his files to see if they can identify them."

"Ah, here you are." The doctor appears at the door.

"Dr. Rowe, why did you send Rev. Kettering ahead?"

"Miss Hollander, this is a little delicate."

"You found a brain tumor?"

"No other than the injuries you received last night you are in good health."

"Please be blunt. Is there something wrong with my head?"

"No. Your concussion is relatively mild and as long as you are not alone for the next twenty-four hours it is not an issue."

"What else did I injure?"

"Your back, technically it is a re-injury."

"How bad is it?"

"We won't know until the swelling goes down. We are going to ask you to return to using a wheelchair until we can do x-rays."

"Until when?"

"That depends on the rate at which you heal."

"I never used a wheelchair much. They didn't want the muscles to atrophy." Brandy answers.

"We will loan you one until we can get a definite diagnosis. I will have the physiotherapist come in and show you how to use it before you leave."

Brandy just nods.

The doctor leaves.

"When were you in a wheelchair?"

"After my eighth birthday but like I said it was only until my spine healed enough." Brandy answers.

"How did you break your back?"

"I went through a second story window and landed on   a   paved   walkway."

"Why didn't you tell me?"

"I was trying to forget it." Brandy answers. "So long as I was careful not to expose my back to damage, it was just old news."

Norman frowns at her but says nothing before the physiotherapist arrives.

"I need to put in a few hours at my office," Brandy tells Scott as soon as Norman drops her off at the house. "I have reports that need analysis and information to send out."

"Only if I can sit there with you," Scott answers, "Otherwise I will lose my new digs."

"You can come. I'm not certain my arms are strong enough to push myself that far or get in and out of the car by myself."

Scott nods but goes off to answer a knock at the front door. He comes back with Jared and Leia.

"Hi." Jared kisses Brandy's cheek. "How are you doing?"

"Itchy, she wants to go back to work," Scott tells him.

"I find solace in working." Brandy frowns at Scott.

"I was going to take her over to the university and stay with her."

"After we take you both out for supper," Jared

answers, "Considering the age of the kitchen supplies around here, I don't think you should try to cook."

Brandy works through the files on her desk then locks the confidential stuff away. Scott is sitting in the pulled away office chair reading a textbook from the shelf.

"It's time to go," Brandy tells him.

"Do you mind if I borrow it?" He holds up the book.

"What is it?"

"Genetics, the Map of Life."

"Not so long as it is returned." Brandy answers.

Norman is waiting for them at the house. "Goodnight Scott."

Brandy hears the deadbolt click as she waits for Scott to disappear into his bedroom. "Why are you here Norman?"

"I am saving my son from the embarrassment of having to help his mother undress." He takes the handles of the wheelchair and pushes her into the bedroom. "I am not going to have very much time during the day for the next six weeks but I can handle the nights and mornings so Scott can get some rest."

"Once I get used to this chair, Scott can get on with his life."

"And how long will that take?"

"With any luck the x-ray will come back and they will let me get back on my feet again. If I am told to stay in the chair, it might take a while to build up arm strength. I am not going to turn him into a servant. I know what Mona Parker did to him."

Brandy falls silent for a minute then Norman starts

looking through the drawers and returns with a nightgown. He helps her undress in silence. He lifts the nightgown over her head before scooping her out of her chair carrying her into the en suite to wash up and use the bathroom. Finally, he brings her to the bed. Brandy says nothing as he strips and slides up to against her back and puts an arm around her waist.

"Disappointed?" The word slips out of her mouth.

"In your body, no, in your lack of trust twenty-five years ago, yes."

Feeling the wetness of her pillowcase against her temple, Brandy controls her breathing to stop them from turning into sobs. The phone rings. Norman rolls over to pick up Brandy's cell phone.

"You slut, you are faking this to get Norman's sympathy." Brandy can hear the shrieks from her side of the bed.

"Chastity, one would think after twenty-five years of rejection you would understand the meaning of no. Just so you get it, this time, I am laying stalking charges." Norman answers then sets down the phone. He rolls over and pulls Brandy close.

"Now you were going to tell me that happened to your back."

"My parents allowed a woman and her two children to move in with us. Her husband showed up on my eighth birthday. He got their attention by throwing me through a second story window and out onto a concrete patio. He murdered my parents and older brother before setting the house on fire. Then he disappeared with his wife and children and as far as I know he's still out there somewhere."

The arm around her waist tightens.

"I might have gotten away with lesser injuries but the

firefighters had to move me out of danger from the fire without a backboard." Brandy sighs. "The doctors managed to wire my back together and get me walking. Then it was foster homes and a name change just to lessen the chance of my assailant finding me."

"What was your name?"

"Brandy Hollander, I changed it back when I became an adult and realized that he probably was long gone and wouldn't be back."

"The nightmares did not go away." Norman's voice drops.

"Please, can we talk about something else? It has been forty-two years and I just want to forget. Must I be tortured forever for his crime?"

The phone rings. Norman rolls over and picks it up without speaking. "I told you to stay away from Scott."

"What kind of prank call do you think you are making?"

The phone is slammed in his ear.

Norman turns off the phone. "I think you need a new number." He slides back into his place in bed. "Hush now and get some sleep. I will keep the nightmares away."

Exhausted, Brandy closes her eyes and allows the lie to lull her to sleep.

Brandy wakes up and lays there for a moment. Lines of sunshine decorate the opposite wall, "Ready to wake up?" Norman asks in her ear.

"I made it through the night without a nightmare."

"All it takes is a little faith," Norman tells her as he throws back the covers.

"Faith?"

"Acting on something because you believe in it," He

answers.

"What if I didn't really believe?"

"Then you wouldn't have acted on it, shower or bath?"

"Bath, if you help me into the tub then I can manage on my own."

Norman glances at the nightstand clock. "Shower it is. I have to be to work in forty-five minutes."

Brandy pushes herself up to a sitting position, "Anything to get your hands on me."

"You forget I had to prove that you were much more to me that just a pair of breasts before you would agree to marry me. I will not be branded a dirty old man because I have natural urges for a woman I believe to be my legal wife. On the other hand, you are under a doctor's care and I want you to get well. You do not have to worry about me acting on any urge until I know the state of your back."

Swinging her feet off the bed, Brandy gingerly runs her hands along her back. "It still feels sore."

"A warm shower might help."

"So would a hot bath."

"All right, a hot bath." Norman goes and runs the tub.

CHAPTER 13

Scott delivers Brandy to her office all the while continuing to read the textbook. He takes her to class and sits there reading the book. He leaves her in Rosemary's care while he goes to class but returns right afterward and opens up the text.

Brandy pauses. "What is so interesting?"

"Genetic testing for diseases in unborn babies." Scott answers.

"Human testing?"

"Just think of all the suffering we could alleviate."

"Not my field." Brandy answers and reaches for her computer. "If that is what you want to get into then you need a different mentor." She stops a moment before picking up the phone. She presses a quick set of buttons.

"Yes, Dr. Buford, this is Brandy Hollander. We meet" She breaks off for an instant. "It is nice to be remembered." She smiles. "Yes, I have a hard, working lab assistant who has voiced an interest in human genetic testing to prevent disease. I was wondering if you would consider speaking to him and assisting him in finding an appropriate program."

Brandy listens for a minute. "His name is Scott Parker and yes, I will give him an excellent reference."

"Hold on and I will put him on the phone." Brandy hands the receiver to Scott. "Good luck."

"Yes, Dr. Buford." Scott smiles before he answers. "I picked Genetics, Your Map to Life, off Dr. Hollander's bookshelf and yes, I am very interested in getting into this field."

"I understand there are ethical questions about treating people too young to give consent, with or without parental consent but if we could turn off triggers for genetic diseases and predispositions to addictive behaviors then the world would be a much better place."

Brandy tunes out the rest of the conversation as she places her attention on analyzing the newest information from Chad. She only hears the click of the receiver being set back in its cradle.

"Can I ask a question?"

"What?"

"How badly do you need me here?"

"If you are thinking of turning down Dr. Buford to push my chair around for the next twenty years, I will get out of it long enough to send you packing."

"I have to apply to another university and he wouldn't have work for me until the fall which gives me time to deal with my legal difficulties. I was upfront about having to stay at least until the charges can be heard."

"Good for you."

"You are certain you don't need me here."

"I hope to be out of this contraption before you go."

Scott pauses. "You want me to go."

"I want you to be happy and studying something you

can turn into a satisfying career. It's not like you can't text, e-mail, and visit."

"First I have to get accepted. I need to go online and apply."

"There is a computer lab somewhere in this building. I will be right here waiting when you get back."

"Thank you." Scott kisses her cheek and leaves.

Brandy gets back to work.

The phone rings. Brandy picks up the receiver. "Can I take my wife out to dinner?"

"Is there any specific occasion?"

"They brought in a new minister to take over some of the work. I have the evening off."

"Don't you have a debate to prepare?'

"That's the subject expert's responsibility. All I have to do is moderate. The new minister is preaching Sunday just to prove he can so I don't have to prep that either."

"Feeling fancy-free are you?"

"Only if I can get my favorite lady to come along so I can celebrate by having good conversation while looking at her."

"Looking without touching could be considered torture."

"A feeling that I suffer gladly after all those years of emptiness. I know it scares you but once you accept that it is about feeling alive, then it's worth the discomfort. Besides good conversation is a form of mind to mind touching."

"Cerebral sex?"

"Only if you will let me whisper sweet things in your ear I have a public reputation to uphold."

The door opens. Scott sticks his head inside. "Mom, do you have a problem if I go out to celebrate tonight without you?"

Brandy tosses him her keys. "Norman will pick me up."

"Thanks." He pauses. "You will be okay here until he comes?"

"Tell him I am on my way," Norman says into her ear then sets down the phone.

"He says he's on his way. Have fun." Brandy answers.

"See you later." Scott closes the door.

Brandy goes back to e-mailing for another fifteen minutes when Norman knocks and then enters her office.

"Ready to go."

"One last e-mail to send." Brandy finishes then closes down her computer.

"Where did Scott go?"

"He didn't say. He has been reading and he may have found his niche. I will let him tell you the details." Brandy locks files into the bottom drawer of her desk.

"Then what if I take you home and change your clothes so I can take you out some place fancy no one will see my misdeeds."

"No. On the other hand,I didn't buy any clothes after they were trashed that would make such an event look like much of a misdeed." She sets her wallet in her lap.

"Every woman needs a little black dress."

"I am not going shopping on an empty stomach," She states as he navigates her out of her office.

"Then I will have to feed you before I take you shopping."

"For something black and clingy, I don't think so."

"Brandy, if I buy you something black and clingy it won't be a dress and no one will see it but me." Norman leans down so he is speaking directly over her ear and in a low voice.

Brandy glances up at him then back just in time to see Chastity coming. "Look out."

Norman reacts a second too late to push Brandy completely out of the way. He does, however, drop Chastity where she has thrown herself against him and goes to Brandy to check on her.

A security guard comes running. "I saw the whole incident on the security camera. Are you all right Dr. Hollander?"

"Just a little bruised." Brandy frowns, "Nothing worthy of fussing over."

"I will decide how much fussing is required," Norman tells her. "How does your back feel?"

"No worse than usual, it was my shoulder she hit."

"I will take you out for dinner and if you are in pain I will take you to the emergency ward."

"What about me?" Chastity moans.

"The police are on their way, Miss Golden." The guard walks over until he is standing above her. "And phoning your Daddy won't do you any good this time we have everything on tape."

"I need an ambulance."

"To the psych ward." The man tells her.

She glares at him.

The police insist that Norman and Brandy go to the hospital to get checked out. The doctor insists on x-raying Brandy's back before he will release her. "Stay in the wheelchair, there is a good chance that you may need an operation to fix fractures of your vertebrae."

Brandy frowns but nods.

Norman comes to look for her a few minutes later.

"You ready to go find some supper?"

Brandy blinks and then looks up at him. "Yes, we should go."

"Brandy, what's wrong?"

"The doctor thinks I am going to need surgery on my back. It may interfere with my trip to the conference in Sweden."

"Is the trip to the conference that significant?"

"It would keep me current with the research and allow me to talk to other researchers. Let me know if the paper I'm writing is still up to standards."

"You can take someone with you. Scott could help you."

Brandy shakes her head. "He would need the court's permission to leave town. Besides, he's just found his niche and needs to get current by reading the latest papers in his field and getting his life in order so he can change universities."

"You haven't taken the time to think this through." Norman commandeering the handles of the wheelchair. "An empty stomach isn't helping you concentrate let's go to dinner."

"Surgical practices have changed in twenty years, it might not be as long a recovery as you envision." Norman reaches out to take her hand after the waiter take her still full French onion soup plate.

"Sorry, I don't seem able to make good conversation."

"You are in shock you hoped the news would be better."

"Still it is no excuse for rudeness." Brandy frowns. "You said that the church hired someone new."

"Hubert and Anne Mueller, they are here to

candidate. An elder is taking them around to meet the members. Hubert will preach Sunday morning and evening. Then they will go home Monday. Next Sunday the congregation will vote on whether to give him the job."

"And they don't want your opinion on him?"

"I have already given it before they offered him the chance to candidate. I worked with Hubert when he co-ordinated our children summer day camps about five years ago."

"Wouldn't the rest of the congregation know him then?"

"Some better than others, he still has to go through the process." Norman answers. "It would be unfair to the other applicants if he didn't."

"And where are the other applicants?"

"Churches hire differently. They rate the candidates and call them to candidate one at a time. If the congregation decides against Hubert, the next one on the list gets a phone call."

"Is there a chance he won't get the job?"

"Yes, none of us questioned him intensely on his beliefs and how he intended to put them into practice when he was doing children's camps. Since then he has married and we know nothing about his wife. There are questions about what role she expects to have as a minister's wife. There are many issues which may break the deal."

"Are you hoping he will get the job or not get the job?"

"It's better if I just wait and allow the congregation to pray over their decision."

"You think I should do the same with the surgery?"

"No, surgery is much more personal than the identity

of a co-worker. This time, the decision belongs to you and not someone else."

"So what do you do?"

"I pray that God would guide the congregation in making their decision and enjoy having a few hours of freedom to spend with you."

Brandy half-smiles. "What if your church decides it doesn't want me as a minister's wife?"

"Twenty years too late, they knew I was separated from my wife when they called me. I told them I would remain celibate or reconcile with my wife. They accepted my statements then and fully expect that I will keep my word."

"Did you tell them who I was?"

"They know you are an unbeliever that is all they needed to know."

"Dr. Forester has asked me to rebut your subject matter expert in the field of genetics."

"That should make for an entertaining evening," Norman smiles.

"Yes, but will your congregation think the same way."

"One way or another they will have to deal with it."

"I don't want to get you fired."

Norman laughs. "I doubt any of them would go so far. They might gripe about the cost of advertising for the debate series but they are not ready for another change in their clergy."

"You are married to the enemy."

"I am married to a lost soul who needs to find the kingdom of heaven."

"That is not funny, Norman."

"From their point of view, you have to understand. That is their point of view."

"And what is yours?"

The waiter interrupts their conversation by bring their meal. Norman turns his attention to his plate.

Brandy waits through the meal and then through the Crème Brule for Norman to answer her question. It is not until they are back at the house and he is in bed with his arm wrapped around her that he answers.

"I love you, Brandy. I want what's best for you. We may not agree on what that is but I want you to feel secure knowing that I am not going to force you to convert or to have sex with me if you object to reconciling."

"Norman."

"Hush, those are my feeling and I have no right to impose them on you or expect you to react to them in a favorable way. It's been a long emotional day and you need some rest."

"This must be torture for you."

"No, I can sleep this way. Torture was laying wondering if you were dead or in love with another man. This is heaven compared with those options."

"I've put you through hell."

"And I've caused you nightmares. What we have to decide now is if we can change things or whether we are going back there."

"We don't agree in so many areas of life."

"We are individuals in personality and opinion that does not mean we can't love each other."

The cell phone rings. Norman reaches for it before Brandy. He opens it and listens.

"Just because I've retired does not mean I don't still have friends on the bench."

"Then I will just have to make sure that politically none of them have the guts to allow you to play your little games."

"Who is this?"

Norman pushes the end call button then turns the cell phone off. "Remind me to bring my mini tape recorder home from the office so I can record those calls." He cuddles into her back. His hand takes up a subtle caress of her stomach. "Good night Brandy."

"If I said yes would you have sex with me?"

"Not until I know it would not hurt your back, and you quit using the word sex and start calling it making love." Norman's hand stops its movement. "Even most atheists know that difference. Good night Brandy."

Contrary to her expectations Norman curls even tighter around her before he falls asleep. Brandy lies there thinking for a long time before slipping off into blissful nothingness.

Brandy and Norman are up having breakfast when Scott unlocks the front door and enters as quietly as he can.

"Good morning Scott," Norman says in a loud voice.

Scott comes into the kitchen. "Sorry about the hour."

"You don't sound drunk," Norman says.

"I'm not. I meet a girl who was having trouble with the computers yesterday. I took her out for some supper. She had way more problems than I could handle so I suggested that she go home and talk to her mother. I opened my mouth and told her I would drive her there not knowing it was a five-hour drive each way. She took me up on it. Mom, I know I should be helping today but-"

"Go get some sleep." Brandy tells him. "I wouldn't want you driving right now."

"Thanks."

"And Scott, you need to stop allowing women to take advantage of you."

Scott comes over and kisses Brandy's cheek. "Thanks, Mom." He heads for his bedroom.

Norman shakes his head. "I'd nearly forgotten what young men will do to get a woman's attention."

Norman leaves Brandy at her office when he goes to play his small role in the candidating of Hubert and Anne Mueller. Rosemary being off and Scott being asleep, Brandy was surprised when the door opened and Marianne Gilford steps inside.

"Where's Scott?"

"Scott is none of your business." Brandy answers.

"But he is yours." The words did not ask a question.

"What do you want Marianne? You are the reason he was suspended from his job for a week wasn't that enough damage?"

"Suspended for what?"

"The drunken scene at the church last Tuesday, a week was the least I could give him with the university president and most the deans in the audience."

"You…"

"Scott's my lab assistant. Your parents can make a phone call and get the university president to overlook your breaches in good manners but Scott has no one ready to make significant donations to atone for his misdeeds."

"He's sleeping with his boss."

"Even if he offered, which he hasn't, my career means too much for me to throw it away on stupidity. Scott just happened to need some place to stay since he lost a week's pay and my house has an extra bedroom. You used him and he knows it. I don't think he is interested anymore."

Marianne's cheeks stain red. "You are living in the same house."

"Scott is none of your business. If you give him any trouble after he comes back to work even your daddy's money won't buy you out of the trouble I will make for you. The security guards are probably walking towards that door and if you don't leave now, I will have them call the police and have you put back on the psych ward." Brandy tells her.

"You hate me."

"I am facing major surgery because of you. Now leave." Brandy picks up the phone.

Marianne leaves.

CHAPTER 14

The phone rings. Brandy reaches out for it with her mind on the information she is reading. "Brandy Hollander."

"Dr. Hollander, it is Manley. Can I ask your advice?"

"About what?"

"Would exposing this creature to water wake it up?"

"Where are all the people who are supposed to be watching it?"

"The Chad government has ordered us to evacuate. Local churchmen have decided that all this science is against Allah."

"What did you say to them?"

"It doesn't matter it is all water under the bridge. The rest are getting on the bus. I only have one chance to prove that this little guy is viable. How do I do that?"

"You don't, you get on that bus before it departs." Brandy tells him. "Those clerics don't play games."

"Tell me how!"

"It could take hours even if you did put him in water.

Get out while you still can."

There is the start of a loud sound and then the line goes dead. Brandy sets down the phone and picks it up again. She calls a long-distance number.

"I would like to speak to-"

"Dr. Hollander, I thought it might be you. The station is bombed out and your Dr. Manley is dead. Your claim that there is no God is de-bunked.

"I never claimed there was no God."

"I thought that Dr. Manley lied about that one. You were always more diplomatic than that."

"What about the students?"

"On their way to the nearest international airport, your Dr. Manley refused to leave. Now he is a martyr for your cause."

"A fool is more like it." Brandy frowns.

The man laughs. "I should have known that he was acting on his own accord, you were always more intelligent than that."

"I have to inform people. I must go now." Brandy sets down the receiver as she reaches for the telephone directory for the university. She sighs and phones Dr. Forester at home.

The media gathers at the university's entrance. Brandy sits in her wheelchair beside Dr. Forester and the rest of the deans. "Is there a Mrs. Manley?" A member of the press asks.

"My wife and I gathered Dr. Manley's family together two hours ago and explained what happened or at least as much as we know happened. We have contacted our government's ambassador to Chad and he is looking into the situation."

"How did you find out?"

"Dr. Manley phoned Dr. Hollander. He was speaking to her on the phone when the bombs hit the building. Then she phoned someone she knew there to get confirmation."

"Who exactly did you phone, Dr. Hollander?"

"The Muslim cleric from the local mosque, he admitted that he ordered the people onto a bus to go to an international airport."

"What about Dr. Manley?"

"Dr. Manley was trying to finish off a scientific experiment. He asked for information on how to push the end of the experiment."

"And you told him?"

"To get on the bus," Brandy answers. "He obviously did not have time to complete the experiment and it would have been wisest for him to flee with everyone else."

"Did the cleric tell you why Dr. Manley was killed?"

"He mentioned something about statements Dr. Manley had made and others Dr. Manley attributed to me."

"What was Dr. Manley doing in Chad?"

"Dr. Manley was an emergency replacement and was scheduled to return in May. Unfortunately, he was not always the most diplomatic of people when he felt religion was given greater prominence that science." Dr. Forester breaks into the conversation.

"What will happen with the experiments that were going on at the station?"

"Dr. Hollander has agreed to help us work with those organizations that we had contracts with to see if there is any way of completing the work. Unfortunately, the famous new creature was destroyed in the bombing and that discovery is irreplaceable."

"Dr. Hollander, is it true that you and Dr. Manley had some disagreements?"

"We held differences of opinions on many subjects. I know of no one who sees the world exactly as I do. I am sincere when I send condolences to his family. I never wished him dead and I truly thought I had given him enough warnings and provided him with staff who would keep him out of trouble. The phone call was utterly shocking."

"We shall have psychologists on campus to speak to any staff member or student who feels the need for grief counseling on Monday. Dr. Hollander has been through enough for today. I will answer the rest of your questions."

"How long had Dr. Manley been in Chad?"

"About a week."

Brandy leans back in her chair and closes her eyes. She lets the words drift past her as the questions keep coming. She knows the instant someone touches the handles of her chair.

"Are you all right?" Norman's voice is soft and comes in her right ear.

"No." Brandy answers. "I sent a man to his death."

Norman catches Dr. Forester's eye and signals. A sharp nod is the reply and Norman slowly extracts Brandy's wheelchair from the crowd.

"Where are your things?"

"In my office."

He takes her inside only long enough to get her purse then back out to the car. He lifts her into the passenger seat. He folds up the wheelchair and places it in the trunk. He comes and gets into the driver's side.

"How did you know?"

"Mrs. Forester called me."

Brandy nods. "I phoned the cleric. He said that Manley told him I said things which I had not. I cannot go back to Chad now to set things right."

"The man was in idiot."

"Which begs the question, why would I send a fool into a delicate situation?"

"And the answer is."

"He put me in a position where I could not go back. Once the cleric heard I was divorced." Brandy shrugs. "I couldn't find anyone to take over until June but does not make it right to send someone so clearly unsuitable."

"Or the cleric was looking for an excuse and Manley gave him one. You are not responsible. Dr. Forester sent him not you. Manley would have had to consent to go. Brandy, he made your job impossible and then destroyed your life's work. There is no defense against people like that."

"Tell that to his wife and children."

"What did you have for lunch?"

"I didn't have lunch."

"Then we need to find some food." He makes a turn. "Tell me that you did not warn him of the dangers."

"I did, I made certain he knew to take anti-malaria drugs. I explained the contracts and the situation as well as I could. I put him in touch with the native overseer. I thought I had covered everything."

"Then he's responsible for his own actions if they lead to the firebombing of this place."

Brandy rests her head against the back of the seat and tears start falling. Norman parks the car and goes inside. He brings out a bag and two drinks in to-go containers that are stuck through holes in a cardboard holder. He hesitates but drives the car back to the house.

He takes the food in before getting her wheelchair

and delivering her to the bedroom. Stripping off all but her underclothes he puts her to bed then goes and gets a tray with the Chinese takeout set out on two plates.

"Sorry, if I interrupted your day."

"You rescued me from a grilling about how Rev. Lansing managed to remain undetected for so long."

"By Hubert Mueller?"

"No, the candidate's wife it seems Mrs. Anne Mueller has strong opinions on these things."

"A young woman?"

"Mid-twenties give or take a year."

"She still doesn't know how much she doesn't know."

"I hope you will allow me to refrain from telling her that."

Brandy laughs. "It would not be tactful."

"You are going to get past this?"

"Manley was a jerk and a fool. He sacrificed himself for a hopeless cause. I heard the start of the blast. He should never have been allowed out of academia where his opinions and bluster were insulated from people who throw firebombs instead of words to make their points."

"Eat up and take a nap."

Brandy obediently finishes her meal before settling down for a nap.

Brandy wakes up to a quiet house. She sits up and looks around. The wheelchair is pushed out of reach. The clothes she was wearing are hanging in the closet. Her phone rings.

She opens the cell phone. "Brandy Hollander."

"Dr. Hollander, this is Mrs. Manley."

"I apologize for thinking that he could handle the Chad station even temporarily."

"They said you talked to him last."

"He phoned and wanted to know how to wake up a one-celled creature."

"He did have a fixation with it."

"I don't think Dr. Manley understood the power of the local clerics. Once the cleric said something his followers would sacrifice themselves to carry it out."

"He did not pass along any messages?"

"No, but as I said I do not think he realized the danger he placed himself in by staying. I tried to tell him that he should be on the bus rather than dealing with the creature. Then the phone line cut out."

There is a long drawn out sigh on the other end of the phone line. "He always did have a one track mind when it came to certain ideas."

"I am sorry I cannot be more consoling." Brandy frowns. "I called the cleric and it had sounded like they had had a public argument."

"That's no surprise."

"I truly am sorry."

"No need to beat yourself up. I knew him better and I did not stop him. He grumbled about all the precautions. I should have known he would ignore them. Like a little boy if you said no, he did it."

"Once I find out where the students and staff of the facility went I might be able to get you more information."

"I would appreciate that."

"Then I shall make some phone calls." Brandy promises. They say their goodbyes and Brandy disconnects the phone.

After swinging her feet over the side of the bed, Brandy looks at the wheelchair and then at the closet. She takes a deep breath and starts to rise as she does the pain in her back intensifies and she eases herself back down. She lies back on the bed and stops long enough to wrap herself in a blanket before she calls. "Is there anyone home?"

No one answers. Brandy sighs before glances at the position of everything again. She is about to move when the phone rings.

"Brandy Hollander."

"Dr. Hollander, this is Dr. Rowe. I have looked over your x-rays. I think you need to come to the hospital immediately."

"It will take some time to get there. My wheelchair is out of reach and no one is answering my calls."

"Did you try to stand up?"

"Yes but the pain intensified."

"I am sending an ambulance. I don't want you to move until it gets there."

Brandy sighs. "The door may be locked."

"The emergency crew will handle it. You just stay calm, and give me the address."

Brandy gives him and address before she hangs up.

Less than ten minutes later someone pounds at the front door. Brandy hears Scott get up to answer it. He's still dressed just in pajama bottoms then he lets the ambulance attendants into Brandy's bedroom.

"Mom, what's happening?"

"The specialist looked at my x-rays and wants me in the hospital."

"I should come with you."

"Not before you get dressed." Brandy answers. "Besides I need you to get in touch with appropriate people, I might not get to work for a while."

"I'll be there as soon as I dress and make a few

phone calls." He disappears into his room.

Brandy is tucked into a hospital bed before Scott gets there. "They will operate tomorrow. They want to make certain there's nothing in my system to choke me before they put me to sleep."

Scott nods. "I tried to phone Dad but the woman who answered the phone at the church insists that he is not there. Jared and Leia are on their way over."

Brandy nods before she remembers to ask, "Did you call the university?

Dr. Forester said not to worry about anything. He will appoint a temporary dean."

"Thank you."

"Where do you think Dad went?"

"I don't know he came and got me from the university, fed me lunch and told me to take a nap."

"Young man, I am afraid you are going to have to leave." The nurse comes into the room. "We are going to start to give her drugs to prepare her for surgery."

"I will go see if I can find Dad." Scott kisses Brandy's cheek.

"Dr. Hollander." Dr. Rowe stands over her bed about three hours after she comes out of the anesthesia.

"Yes."

"We had some trouble with your surgery."

"Am I paralyzed?"

"No, you just have a very, very fragile spine. We fused six vertebrae together and there are others which will not take any abuse without cracking or worse. You will be able to walk but a fall of any kind will cause further medical problems. I strongly recommend that you consider using the wheelchair unless it is an emergency."

"Is there no chance for strengthening the bone?"

"There is, of course, calcium supplements, but it will take years for them to do enough to get you back on your feet. I am afraid that your diet should have been monitored especially for calcium."

"I did not live where fresh foods were readily available."

He pauses before he says. "I thought it might be something like that. However it came about this is the state of things. Like I said you should be able to walk and we will have you up before the end of the week but you need to be very aware of the stress and strains you put on your back."

Brandy nods.

Scott and Jared come to visit her immediately after the doctor leaves. "Hi, Mom." Scott kisses her cheek while Jared kisses her other cheek.

"What's the bad news? That doctor looked grim." Jared asks.

"My backbone is fragile. He wants me to remain in the wheelchair."

"I will phone Dr. Buford-"

"You will do no such thing." Brandy frowns. "I have insurance to cover long-term medical expenses. I want you to stay on track. Nothing short of a doctorate is going to get you into your field of choice."

"Mom."

"No, I am not going to allow you to throw your life away when I can deal with my own problems."

"Speaking of problems Dad's missing." Jared frowns. "We have searched everywhere does anyone knows that he would go."

"Did you contact Detectives Lang and Turner?"

"We did. They are investigating." Jared nods.

"We contacted the church. They allowed a search of their building. Hubert Mueller said he would stick around to moderate the debate but other than that no one has seen him." Scott adds.

Brandy frowns.

"Mom, what happened?" Jared asks.

"Your father has been answering my cell phone late at night. He didn't want Scott to be responsible for helping me go to bed or get dressed in the morning. He dropped me off at the university yesterday morning. Marianne Gilford came to see me but I talked her into leaving. Then Manley phoned. Your father came and got me from the press conference. We stopped and picked up some food. He took me back to the house and made sure I ate. He told me to take a nap. He was gone when I woke up."

"Marianne, what did she want?" Jared frowns.

"She was upset that Scott was living in the same house as me."

"Scott, my poor boy, you are doomed." Jared smiles when he says it.

"It's none of her business." Scott frowns.

Brandy just sighs. "She's sure that I am trying to seduce you. She has no idea that it is entirely likely that I am your mother."

Scott shakes his head.

"You need to get to class."

"Mom," Scott starts.

"I gave Dr. Buford a reference for you. You're not going to let me down now, are you?" Brandy frowns at him.

"If you promise to take a nap we will both go to class." Jared tells her.

"I promise."

"Then I will take him with me." Jared pulls his brother out of the room.

CHAPTER 15

Brandy wakes to find Detective Turner in the room. "Dr. Hollander."

"I don't know where Norman Kettering is."

"We found him locked in a room on the Golden estate. He's downstairs in detox for the drugs that were forced on him."

"Anything else I should know?"

"He didn't go there of his own free will."

"Were any arrests made?"

"Herman Golden was arrested. Norman Kettering's complaint about the divorce was causing the retired judge major legal trouble and he thought it would go away if Norman disappeared. The judge was using street drugs to discredit the reverend by getting him hooked."

Brandy shakes her head. "How is Norman?"

"Alive, I need to know if Norman Kettering took any drugs in the past."

"If he did it wasn't around me. I was a serious student and Norman was serious about both his studies and his sports. He tended to sidestep the offers for that kind of parties when we were together. He limited his drinking to one glass of wine with supper." Brandy frowns. "He had friends who were into booze by I never smelt it on Norman."

"Why do you think that was?"

"Norman was into ethics, morality. Those were his fields of study."

"Yet you thought he was having an affair on you."

"Norman Kettering committed sins of omission, Detective, he hid the fact that his mother was using her fortune to try to break up our marriage and that she was actively convincing a woman of no morals to stalk him and scare me off. I had been victimized as a child and knew the horror that such people caused so when bad things started to happen I ran."

"But you were convinced?"

"Chastity Golden was pregnant with his child. How else was I to explain that to myself? Transplanting of embryos was cutting edge science and not an explanation that was likely to pop to mind."

"Norman would like to see you."

"I can't move from this bed without my doctor's permission. You have to set it up with Dr. Rowe."

"You are not willing to bend the rules a little?"

"I can't bend, they fused my spine."

The detective blinks. "What?"

"I have had major back surgery. You will have to borrow a wheelchair and bring him up to me."

"When did this happen?"

"Saturday the specialist finally saw the x-rays. Sunday I think they operated. I woke up Monday morning."

The nurse steps through the door. "Doctor's orders, Dr. Hollander can only have five minutes worth of visitors every hour. Your time is up."

Brandy wakes up the next time to see Norman sitting by her side in a wheelchair. "How are you, beautiful?"

"Sleepy but I will get over it. How are you?"

"Buzzed. The detective said I had to be subdued or I wouldn't get to see you until they manage to clear the drugs out of my system."

"It doesn't sound like I am going to be leaving for a few days. You have time to get clean."

"Promise you won't leave without telling me first."

"I promise." Brandy answers. She waits for a few seconds then says. "I may be stuck in that wheelchair except for the occasional stroll. It seems I forgot to drink enough milk and now my spine is fragile."

"We will figure it out as soon as my head is clear." Norman tells her. "You go back to sleep and I will go back to detox and do as they tell me."

Brandy reaches out and squeezes his hand. "I will be waiting."

"No kiss for good luck."

Brandy drags his hand up to her mouth and kisses the back of it. "The only part of you I can reach."

"Close your eyes."

Brandy closes her eyes and she feels his lips touch her forehead. "Sleep tight." And then he leaves.

Dr. Forester comes to visit Wednesday morning. "You missed a good lecture last night."

"Sorry, but the doctor is keeping me in bed a few more days."

"It was a lively discussion."

"Who won?"

"Very much a draw I am afraid."

Brandy nods slightly. "I don't know when I will be back to work."

"You have about five years of sick leave to use up. I am giving you until the fall semester. Norman Kettering was absent."

"Norman Kettering is right here." Brandy turns her head slightly to see Norman standing in the doorway. He is still dressed in hospital clothing with a robe thrown over the gown.

"Dr. Forester was just telling me about last night's debate." Brandy manages half a smile.

"Yes, sorry I missed it. How was Dr. Newly?"

"Excellent, as I was telling Dr. Hollander I judged it to be a draw."

"Considering the difference between the two points of view is philosophical rather than an actual measurable one, it is up to the persuasive power of the speakers to determine who would win a debate of this type." Norman pauses. "How are you today?" His eyes meet Brandy's.

"In need of a good book to keep my mind busy," Brandy answers. "I don't seem to be in any pain."

"Scott said something about needing someone to discuss ideas for his major paper in genetics. He will visit later today."

"Dr. Hollander is on medical leave."

"Yes, but that does not stop our son from visiting his mother." Norman comes and kisses Brandy on the forehead.

"How about you?" Brandy asks.

"The doctor thinks I can safely be released today. I have a project to make the house wheelchair friendly before you leave here. Scott said he would be on hand if I need any help."

Brandy just nods.

"Have you given any thought to teaching an ethics class next year?" Dr. Forester asks.

"No yet. Other things have kept me occupied." Norman squeezes Brandy's hand.

"You realize this lecture series was your cry to get back to a place where people understand three syllable words without endless explanations."

Norman laughs. "Then teaching might not be the best way to scratch that itch."

"We have faculty who can meet that need."

"I have a wife who can more than meet that need. If I have to leave town because certain people make life here unpleasant for us, then I don't want the promise to take a job hanging over my head."

Dr. Forester frowns. "You are serious."

"I have an itch to see northern Europe. Brandy would make an excellent tour guide since she's traveled more in the last twenty-five years than I've managed in the last fifty."

"Dr. Hollander has a teaching contract."

"Which she has fulfilled, quite brilliantly, without stepping onto your campus for twenty-five years, you still have three research stations out there."

"What would it take to get you to agree?"

"I already told you, the ability to live with my wife without interference."

Dr. Forester frowns.

"It is not something you have the ability to promise. We are just going to have to see how the investigations turn out." Brandy tells her boss.

Detectives Lang and Turner arrive after Scott stops to get Norman. "The DNA tests have come back on Scott Parker and Jared Kettering. There are no surprises in the result. They are both your sons."

"Charges have been laid against the doctor and Miss Golden."

"Have you found the other women?"

"No, they do not seem to be in the doctor's files so we have started to investigate his personal life."

Brandy nods. "Have you told anyone else about the results?"

"The clinic will phone both of the young men and Rev. Kettering this afternoon. We could stop downstairs if you want."

"Rev. Kettering was released from the hospital half an hour ago. Scott came to take him back to his house." Brandy answers.

"They will all be told today," Lang tells her.

Jared and Leia are the first to arrive after learning of the news. "Hi Mom," Jared greets Brandy. "It's a immense relief to know that Chastity Golden is not actually related by blood."

"The detectives told me that she is facing charges." Brandy answers. "What did your grandmother say?"

"I haven't spoken to her. There was some suggestion that she was under investigation and I didn't want to do anything that might tip her off to what's coming." Jared answers.

Leia frowns. "You or someone else is going to have to tell her sometime. I refuse to marry you until I've met all of your family."

"I promise I will introduce you to Grandmother. Chastity hasn't been part of that I considered my family for a long time." Jared answers. "I just thought I would let the detectives do their job without worrying about Grandmother fleeing town."

Leia sighs. "When?"

"Just as soon as the detectives decide whether she is to be charged with anything." Jared promises.

Scott shows up shortly afterward. "Dad will be here in a little while he was called to the church for a meeting with the elders and Hubert Mueller."

Brandy nods but says nothing more on the subject. "Have any of you been questioned by reporters?"

"No, and until there is an announcement of charges against Lansing-Conroy-Hamilton or Chastity Golden they probably won't bother us." Jared answers. "We would offer to take you out to dinner to celebrate but the nurse will be in to kick us out any moment."

"I say we should put birth announcements in the newspaper." Scott answers.

Brandy smiles and shakes her head. "It might get Marianne Gilford off my case."

"Now I know for certain, I will tell her myself." Scott answers.

The nurse appears at the door. "Time's up."

Brandy nods to her sons and Leia and they leave together.

It is well past the next hour before Norman arrives. His facial expression is tight as if he is uncomfortable with what he has to say.

"Jared and Scott were here, they acted as if having me for a mother was good news." Brandy glances down at her hands.

"Finding out I have sons is not bad news." Norman answers. "It's something else entirely."

"Your mother is under investigation for her participation." Brandy continues.

"My mother doing jail time is not the issue."

"Then stop looking like you are delivering a eulogy."

Brandy answers.

"I think our other three children have found us." Norman answers.

"Is this bad news or good news?" Brandy asks.

"Lansing-Conroy-Hamilton was part of a small fundamentalist congregation where women were shamed for being barren. Three of these women came to him wanting him to heal them so they could have children otherwise their husbands had threatened to have their marriages set aside so they could remarry women who could have children. They did not know a child could be taken from one woman and transplanted into another."

"Are you blaming me for that?" Brandy asks.

"No, that's not the point of the story. The three other women were older women all of whom have since died. They all had daughters who looked like each other. Lansing-Conroy-Hamilton was forced to answer to the church elders when the women confessed how they came to be pregnant. That was about the time he was charged with manslaughter when one of his experiments went wrong and he disappeared."

"Did this church know where he went?"

"No, but they have been waiting and watching for some news about him. When his name hit the news, one of the daughters came to get as much information as she could find." Norman sighs.

"Anne Mueller?" Brandy asks.

"Yes, and apparently there are two more exactly like her." Norman answers. "But there is more."

"You are alright with two sons but not with three daughters?" Brandy frowns.

"They have heard about your health issues. They are prepared to come and look after you for the remainder of your life." Norman warns.

"As I told Scott I have extended health insurance to cover whatever help I need." Brandy answers. "These women owe me nothing of the sort."

"These are God-fearing young women whose parents taught them that family are required to look after each other."

"But Anne has a husband. Shouldn't he get her attention?"

"He recognizes that her mother has a right to call for her time." Norman answers. "I am sorry to put it this bluntly but I don't want to have daughters married or otherwise under foot to get between us."

"Is the church likely to hire Hubert Mueller as a pastor?" Brandy asks.

"They have already hired him." Norman nods. "They held a special meeting after the last debate."

Brandy closes her eyes for a moment. "When do the girls arrive?"

"Tomorrow, if they did not arrive today. Brandy, please tell them to go away." Norman says. "So far Anne and Hubert have refused to listen to anything I say that is contrary to their church's teachings."

"How am I to stop them if you can't, as a pastor?" Brandy answers.

Norman leans forward and places his forehead on her arm.

"Go home and get some sleep. The doctors are still refusing to spring me for another few days." Brandy tells him. "I need you sharp if we are going to think our way out of this one."

Norman rises a little and kisses her nose. "Just don't go home with anyone else."

"I am not going anywhere," Brandy tells him. He kisses her lips.

"I will be back tomorrow." With that, he leaves just as the nurse appears at the door.

Brandy wakes up feeling like she is being watched. She opens her eyes to find three young nearly identical women standing around her bed.

"Hello," Brandy speaks slowly. "And you are?"

"Anne Mueller." The woman on the right says.

"Mary Anderson." The woman directly at the foot of the bed says.

"Ruth Jameson." The woman to the left answers. "You are our mother."

Brandy smiles. "Your father warned me you were coming but I did not expect you so early in the morning."

"You mean Rev. Kettering." Anne answers.

"If I am your mother then Norman Kettering is your father." Brandy answers. "And you have brothers, Jared and Scott."

"Our other fathers are still alive but our mothers are in heaven." Ruth answers.

"If you claim me as your mother then you have to listen. Norman Kettering was my husband when you were conceived that makes him your father. I understand Anne is married, what about you two?" Brandy asks.

"Ruth is married to David. He's a carpenter. I'm not married." Mary answers. "But I am engaged."

"Congratulations when is the wedding?"

"It's on hold, you need us."

"I am afraid that I do not hold the same views as you do. There is nothing in my beliefs that lead me to accept aid from you when that help threatens to derail your life plans." Brandy answers. "I suggest that you go back and speak to your fiancé. You have a wedding to plan."

"But...who is going to look after you?" Mary frowns.

"I have health insurance through my employment as a university professor and your father, Norman Kettering, has offered to make his house wheel chair friendly so I can be as independent as possible. I am on medical leave until the fall semester but then I will return to work." Brandy answers. "The three of you have husbands and a fiancé who need you much worse than I do. Do I have any grandchildren yet?"

Anne, who is giving her a serious frown, shakes her head.

"Since I did not get to enjoy your childhoods, I would hope you would not deny me the pleasure of visiting with grandchildren in the future. Go spend time with your husbands." Brandy tells them.

"The Bible says that believers must look after their own families." Anne's frown deepens.

"I am a scientist and not a biblical scholar; I am neither helpless nor without resources. I have modern medical devices to help me live without putting undue stress on your marriages." Brandy shakes her head. "I would rather have the chance to get to know you as people and to get to know your husbands, and children when they arrive."

"What kind of scientist?" Mary asks.

"I do research in the field of climate change but my formal education is in environmental ecology and genetics." Brandy answers. "I really don't have time to sit back and have someone wait on me."

"I am afraid your time is up." The nurse comes to the door.

"But we want to help look after her," Anne says.

"The biggest help you can be right now is to let her rest as per doctor's orders." The nurse answers.

The three women leave but Brandy does not think

they will simply give up.

Two hours later Scott comes with the outline for his paper, when the nurse interrupts the discussion Scott leaves the outline with her so she can read is over to give him a response. She is doing so when Marianne Gilford arrives.

"Scott says that you are his real mother." Marianne frowns.

"I have five biological children. Scott is one of them." Brandy answers and feels around for the call button for the nurse. "Jared Kettering is another."

"Chastity stole him from you." The girl frowns.

"Then she used her pregnancy to destroy my marriage to Norman." Brandy nods.

"But Scott's mother was a drunk, why would she steal a baby from you?"

"It was a misguided attempt to save her marriage," Brandy answers, "Helped by the same crazy man who kidnapped Leia."

"Jared hates me." Marianne frowns. "Chastity ruined him for me. Scott is nicer."

"Scott has to make up his own mind about you," Brandy tells her.

Marianne frowns. "You are sending him away."

"Scott is leaving because he has decided to study a specialty with a world renowned subject matter expert and he cannot do that at this university." Brandy answers.

"What subject?"

"Using genetic therapy to treat possible future disease in fetuses," Brandy answers, "the field is somewhat controversial."

Marianne frowns. "You are still living with him."

"Scott required some stability after an unsettled time in his life. Now he has a clear direction and is actively pursuing new goals, he won't be there long."

Marianne frowns and shakes her head. "What about Chastity?"

"My understanding is that she is being charged with her part in stealing my eggs, harassment and stalking Norman Kettering." Brandy answers. "It would be good for your mental health to stay away from her."

There is a long silence before Marianne step towards the door. "Are you going to be all right?"

"The underlying damage was done before you pushed me; a lack of calcium over twenty-five years following breaking my back as a child and not enough weight bearing exercise to rebuild the bone." Brandy answers. "It was going to happen sooner or later even a bad fall or a jarring in an auto accident would have caused the same end."

"You are not mad?"

"It is the life I choose by running from Chastity instead of taking my evidence to the police." Brandy answers.

Marianne nods. "I am sorry I listened to Chastity. I am sorry about being so nasty but I am not sorry for feeling I had to protect Scott."

"Perhaps you should ask Scott what he needs protecting from before charging ahead."

Marianne just nods and leaves. The nurse enters after the young woman is gone. "I was away from my station. Did she harm you?"

"No, we just talked." Brandy answers. "She made no threats this time."

"Thank goodness." The nurse answers.

CHAPTER 16

Norman came just before lunch. "They have kicked me out of my own house."

"Who?" Brandy asks.

"Those women and their husbands," Norman answers, "They have decided that they know better than I what needs to be done to make it wheelchair accessible."

"Ruth's husband David is a carpenter he probably knows what he is doing." Brandy answers.

"You are not taking this seriously."

"I had hoped that you would bend a little and not try to block them out of our lives completely."

"I just want…"

"We have children and that should expand the family circle."

"These are grown adults, not babies." Norman frowns.

"Who need us to show them that this new family is not going to be the same as the last one where their mothers died and they were expected to take her place, making meals, doing housework and being expected to put family demands ahead of their personal lives." Brandy answers.

"You know this how?"

"They visited me first thing this morning. One of them is willing to put off her wedding to look after me. I told her to go plan her wedding." Brandy answers. "Obviously, they have been trained to defer their life plans if their parents need them. We need to make it obvious that while we accept them into our lives, we expect them to build their own." Brandy reaches out to take his hand.

"This is from the woman who works sixty hours a week."

"I see me in them. I know how serious I was about wanting to do the right thing." Brandy answers. "These three women are living by rules handed down to them but life is not always going to let them do that as in this case where I am refusing to let them help me. Building a few ramps in exchange for emotional growth seems a fair."

"I want to look after you." Norman frowns.

"I am not a child I don't need to be treated like one." Brandy frowns.

"I am not talking about taking away your right to make decisions or stopping you from working. I am talking about helping you in and out of that chair. I'm talking about all the little things one spouse would do for the other if they had limitations." Norman answers. "I'm talking about traveling with you so you can get to the research conference in Sweden and helping you to reach your other goals."

"You have a career and a life. It wouldn't be any different than…"

"No, I have a job but I've spent twenty-five years

waiting to get my life back." Norman answers. "You are the life I want and if I am pushing too hard, it is because you've never reciprocated and said that marriage to me is part of your plans."

Brandy frowns. "I'm afraid. This time, instead of your mother ,there's your congregation to say no."

"If my church family thinks it can change my mind I can go teach ethics at the university. I am not asking you to be anything but a university professor who works well with young adults and argues for what she thinks is right." Norman answers.

"Norman, if we try again, will Chastity and your mother interfere? I can't run again or they will make Jared, Scott, Mary, Ruth and Anne miserable." Brandy shakes her head.

"Once the investigations are over, they will be standing in front of a judge." Norman answers. "If there is any justice, what will follow is jail time."

Brandy reaches out and takes his hand. "I know you are going to argue but it has been my experience in this life that the rich buy their way out of trouble rather than serve time for their misdeeds." She rubs his knuckle.

"I am not going to preach to you," Norman answers, "in this life, I agree that justice is rarely done. I am not pleading for justice in an afterlife, I am hoping for a chance to spend every day of this one by showing you my love by being the one who is there to do whatever you need to be done."

The nurse appears at the door. "She needs some rest now."

Norman sighs. "I will go." He stands and kisses Brandy on the forehead. "Please don't fear me, Brandy. I never meant to hurt you." Then he leaves.

After he leaves, the nurse gathers all the papers off

the bed. "You need sleep. The doctor wants you to stand up tomorrow and you need to gather your strength."

Brandy tries to close her eyes but instead of sleep memories creep into her head. The surgery was during the first weekend of spring break and Chastity was visibly pregnant by August. Those weeks leading up to her leaving with the constant phone calls from Chastity and the lack of her usual supportive study groups because it was summer. She thinks back to the study groups and who was in them. Who was she tutoring that spring? Her mind searched for anyone who fed her anything that they didn't eat. She frowns but no one stands out. The only prescription she was taking at the times was the birth control pill which she got from the health clinic on campus. Only it was not Lansing-Conroy-Hamilton who prescribed it, it was another doctor but it was filled through the pharmacy on campus. The prescription was also unfinished since Brandy did not take any after she left for Chad. Brandy reaches for the telephone and calls Detective Lang.

After the detectives came for a visit to take a new statement from her, Brandy sleeps. She wakes to find Norman at her side.

"The police came and took all the boxes of your personal items from the house."

"I told them they could." Brandy answers. "I wanted to figure out how Lansing-Conroy-Hamilton fed me hormones to get me to release six eggs at once. I couldn't remember anyone feeding me or anytime I ate meals that I did not cook. I thought it might have been the birth control pills I got from the pharmacy."

"Why?"

"Unless someone tampered with my groceries it was the only prescription I was taking." Brandy frowns. "I didn't finish the whole prescription. I didn't need them after I left for Africa. I don't remember tossing them out so they should be in one of those boxes."

"What did you do in Africa?"

"Research and finished a pair of doctorates," Brandy answers, "keeping busy is the best antidote to what ailed me."

"Is that how you got over your parents too, just forget about them and move on?"

"My parents left me." Brandy frowns.

"They died." Norman frowns. "They didn't have a choice."

"At eight, all I knew what that they didn't come. The nurses, the doctors, the foster parents acted like my parents and brother never existed. I didn't exist either not as the same person. They gave me a new name. The only thing I was to remember from that time was not to do anything that might do more damage to my back."

"What do you remember about your parents?"

Brandy pauses before answering. "Not much, my father worked a lot and mother spent her time pacing and preoccupied. My older brother resented looking after me. I was a brat who was in everyone's way."

"That can't be all you remember."

"I didn't want anyone living with us. After that woman and her children had come I wasn't nice to them. The woman latched onto my mother's every moment, she talked and cried and whatever her problems were my mother banished me to my room just about all the time. Her children got to play with all my toys. That's why I was in my room when the attack came. I refused to let them play with my birthday present." Brandy frowns.

Norman frowns. "You had a right to your present."

"My parents didn't think so." Brandy answers. "I

need a rest. The doctors are going to come and want me to stand in a few hours."

"Brandy, what was your birthday present?" Norman asks.

"I don't remember." Brandy closes her eyes. "I never got to play with it."

The doctors are there when Brandy awakes. She follows their advice knowing that after that length of time in bed her blood pressure needs to adjust to standing. She manages a few steps before returning to the wheelchair.

"We are going to set up appointments with the physiotherapist to help you strength the remaining bone." Dr. Rowe tells her. "Other than that you will be released from hospital tomorrow morning. I want to know that the effort you made today isn't going to cause a delayed reaction. Report any pain to the nurse."

Brandy waits for the doctor to leave before phoning Norman. "You asked me not go home with anyone else. The doctor said I would be released in the morning. I need some clothes to wear home."

"I will be there with everything you need." Norman tells her.

Norman arrives at the hospital with a bouquet of primroses. "Here's a little posy to celebrate leaving the hospital."

Brandy takes the flowers. "Is there some message in the choice of flowers?"

"They were blooming in the garden." Norman tells her. "Ruth picked them."

"Clothing?"

He hands her a bag. "Anne chose them for you."

"What happened to I want my wife to myself?"

Brandy asks.

"You asked me to bend a little." Norman answers. "I decided not to get between you and your daughters."

"They are your daughters too."

"Unfortunately, they don't see it that way." Norman answers.

Brandy opens the bag and lays out the clothing.

"You need any help?" Norman asks.

"Only if she sent any clothing that does up down the back." Brandy answers.

"You want me to leave?" Norman asks.

Brandy just shakes her head and changes into the underwear, blouse, and slacks. After she tries to lean down to put on her shoes, Norman insists on helping her with them. Then he helps her into the wheelchair.

"Shall we get you out of here?" Norman smiles at her.

"A change of scenery would be good." Brandy nods.

Once done at the nurse's station and the admissions office, Norman drives her back to the house. Brandy rolls through the door before she realizes that all their children plus others are waiting for her.

It is two hours before everyone goes home and Brandy is exhausted. Norman helps her to bed. "What do you think of being a mother of five plus in-laws and in-laws to be?"

"Was there really only ten people here?" Brandy asks.

Norman laughs. "I think it is going to take some time to get used to the crowd. Although I am surprised Scott invited Marianne given the history between her and Jared."

"I don't know if Scott's serious about Marianne or he's out to scare her." Brandy answers. "I've made my peace with her."

"I don't understand the appeal." Norman frowns.

"Marianne is not looking for a servant." Brandy answers. "She wants to take care of him." She closes her eyes.

"Sleep well," Norman tells Brandy.

The ringing of her phone awakens her. Brandy reaches for it only to find Norman gets there before her.

"Yes." He flips it open and answers. He listens for a long time before he shuts it without saying another word.

"Who was it?" Brandy asks.

"No one you wanted to hear out." Norman answers.

"Don't treat me like a child." Brandy frowns.

"It was a man by the name of Abraham Russell." Norman answers. "He said he had information about your parents."

Brandy pauses for a long time. "I don't remember the name."

"Then we will ask Lang and Turner to investigate. You go back to sleep." Norman tells her. Brandy lets her mind drift but little remains of the memories of that day. Finally, she feels Norman slide in beside her. She stirs.

"Sh. Sleep." Norman whispers in her ear.

"I've slept the day away." Brandy answers. "Questions are floating through my mind."

"Like what?"

"How will I handle it if they all give us grandchildren?"

"By visiting each of our children's families one at a time," Norman answers,

Brandy chuckles. "Maybe they will wait a few years."

"No one has said anything about expecting a child in my hearing." Norman buries his face in her neck.

"Has anyone ruled on whether or not our divorce is actually legal?" Brandy asks.

"No, but I expect it to come before a judge soon," Norman speaks into her ear. "Now go to sleep."

Brandy sort of drifts off again. Norman curls around her and sleeps.

The phone rings early and Brandy reaches for it before Norman stirs. "Brandy Hollander," She answers it.

"Dr. Hollander, it is Detective Lang. Norman Kettering phoned us about a telephone call you received yesterday from an Abraham Russell."

"Yes, but he spoke to the man, not me."

"Using that name we have tracked down your parents' and brother's killer. We wanted to warn you before you saw it in the press."

"He has to be an old man." Brandy frowns.

"In his late seventies, and not exactly repentant," Detective Lang answers,

"I don't remember much about him anymore. I couldn't positively identify him." Brandy frowns.

"It is not necessary for you to identify him. His son is convinced your parents' actions caused the attack." Detective Lang answers. "We are dealing with mental illness."

CHAPTER 17

Norman awakens by the time her conversation with Detective Lang is over. He makes her breakfast before taking her out to sit in the garden. "Mary spent some time planting it before she returned to talk to her fiance. She said she would send out wedding invitations." Norman tells Brandy.

"I don't suppose she left a plant list or plant map." Brandy frowns.

"Sorry, she's not a trained botanist." Norman shakes his head. "What did Lang want?"

"To tell me they found my parents' killer and are charging him." Brandy answers. "He wanted to do so before it made the news."

"You want me to take you off on an extended holiday until the court cases are over?" Norman asks.

"I might be called as a witness. The judge might toss cases if I am not here." Brandy answers.

"I just hate to see you victimized all over again." Norman frowns.

"I doubt there is much they could tell me that would shock me." Brandy answers.

"You might be surprised." Norman frowns.

Brandy shrugs. "I became numb to the whole episode years ago. No one acted like their deaths were important. The past was not important as getting good grades and winning scholarships so I had some place to go when the government money ended which was what was important because I couldn't stay there."

"Is that why you put so much effort into that apartment when you were already over your head in studies?" Norman asks.

"I thought I was building a home." Brandy answers, "For both of us."

"You did, I just didn't appreciate it enough." Norman answers. "It was certainly a shock when I came back to an entirely empty apartment. You didn't even leave my clothes."

"I panicked. The threats were escalating, the chance to join the research team had an immediate deadline, the rent was due and I was short. The medical bills had eaten my financial cushion. I had to act fast if I was going to get away. So I threw everything into storage and went." Brandy frowns.

"You could have phoned at least." Norman frowns.

"Phoned where?" Brandy frowns. "You had left off leaving me any information on where you were. I felt like I was being laughed at over Charity flaunting her pregnancy and telling everyone it was your baby without having to ask someone where my husband was because I didn't know."

"I really was a jerk."

"Don't ask me to say that, you were doing what you always did, your background caused you not to question the roof over your head or the food on the table. I never forced you to face the realities that marrying me and turning your back on your mother actually meant." Brandy frowns. "I was far too accepting of the situation and too proud to ask for help."

"That hardly helps my ego." Norman frowns.

"We were too different." Brandy shakes her head. "You needed some time to finish school and change your focus before you were ready to concentrate on anything domestic. I had emotional needs I was hiding. Our timing was wrong."

"How many excuses are you going to make for me?" Norman softens his voice.

"Enough so I don't have to face the truth about how badly I wanted someone to put me before everything else in his life." Brandy pauses.

Norman watches the wave of pain flow over her face. He reaches over and places his hands on her shoulders. "I never meant to hurt you."

Brandy swallows. "I was already broken I just assumed I had healed."

Norman lifts her out of her chair and holds her on his knee. He puts his arms around her then starts to rock her gently in his arms. "Cry if you need to," He holds her head against his neck by running his hand through her hair, "For that little girl who never got to play with her birthday present."

"Why her?" Brandy asks.

"She didn't feel loved. We all need to be loved, Brandy, especially when we feel we don't deserve it." Norman answers.

"I was a brat."

"You were a young girl whose very real needs were dismissed by preoccupied people who had no business being parents." Norman answers.

"You don't really know that." Brandy answers. "I didn't see life from their point of view."

"You are making excuses for people who hurt you." Norman frowns. "You needed them and they let you down. It's not you, Brandy, you are lovable. I love you."

Brandy says nothing but Norman continues to rock her. When she starts to fall asleep, he carries her to bed and lies down with her.

The house is quiet when she wakes. She turns her head to see her chair right beside the bed. Brandy gets herself into her wheelchair and goes to the other room. Scott is there reading his textbook.

"Dad got called to the church." Scott tells her. "Leia and Jared are bringing supper over."

"Is there any mention of charges being laid in my parents' and brother's deaths in the news?" Brandy asks.

"There was in the newspaper that came this afternoon." Scott frowns. "I left it on the table."

Brandy rolls her wheelchair to the table and looks at the headline. Suspect arrested in forty-two year old murder. She reads the story. No surprises jump out at her. She pushes it away.

"How is the paper coming?" She looks up at Scott.

"Thanks for your help, I am well into it." Scott answers. "Mom, if I said I was taking Marianne with me would you be unhappy with me."

"If living with Marianne would make you happy then take her with you." Brandy tells him. "I am not going to make it an issue between us. I will do what I can to get along with her."

"Thanks, Mom." Scott hugs her.

"Do yourself a favor and talk to her about what you are doing and who you are working with so she doesn't derail your career over you spending time with someone she doesn't trust."

Scott kisses Brandy's cheek. "I really lucked out when I found you."

"Go study, it's time I cleaned out the kitchen so I can cook and don't have to be feed by my children." Brandy tells him. She spends the afternoon going through the cupboards she can reach.

Norman arrives home about the same time as Jared and Leia get there and the five of them sit down to supper. Norman says grace and they start to eat.

"Jared took me to meet his grandmother." Leia starts. "I don't think she is going to accept me."

"My mother is not an accepting person." Norman answers. "Never has been."

"Well as of today I am looking for some place to live," Jared answers, "And a job. She can keep her money and her house, I refuse to be bullied."

"What type of a job are you looking for?" Scott asks. "I try to keep my contacts fresh in case I need to make some extra money."

"Right at the moment anything. I need to get started." Jared answers.

"What's your major?" Scott asks.

"Business, with an emphasis on finance," Jared frowns, "I'm not certain what's out there for jobs without at least a bachelor's degree."

"If you've got an hour tomorrow I can introduce you to a few people." Scott tells him.

"I will make the time." Jared tells him.

"Is the investigation into your grandmother over?" Brandy asks.

"No, but Marianne told Grandmother that she had changed her mind about marrying me. Grandmother was going to start looking for a replacement and I said I had found my own girlfriend." Jared frowns. "Chastity called me and threatened me but I told her I had proof that she wasn't my mother and I wanted nothing more to do with her. She blew her stack over the phone. I called Detective Lang and he gave me some advice about dealing with her."

"So what are you going to do?" Norman asks.

"Once the semester is over we are getting married and then transferring to an out of state university. Leia's grandparents are willing to rent us a small house they have in Florida." Jared answers. "Leia's parents seem to like the idea."

"My grandparents are talking about moving into a senior's complex nearby where they don't have to cook all their meals." Leia answers. "Grandfather was worried about selling the house and then not having the option of moving back if he hated the complex."

"What if he decides to move back?" Scott asks.

"I doubt he will. He is just a very cautious person." Leia answers. "He has been complaining about grandmother's cooking ever since she had a mini stroke last year."

Brandy just nods.

"My parents are insisting on paying for our wedding." Leia pauses. "My grandparents won't rent to us unless we are married."

"Why don't you set up a meeting between your parents and us? You can tell us just what kind of wedding you want." Brandy answers. "We can discuss who pays for what then."

Norman nods. "We can help."

"With all your medical expenses," Jared starts.

"I am covered by a medical plan through my

employer, I am far from bankrupt." Brandy answers.

"Neither one of us is. There will be limits but we can afford to help pay for a wedding or two." Norman answers.

Silence falls over the table for a few minutes before Brandy asks. "Are you ready for exams?"

"I hope so." Leia answers. "It helps that I am only taking three courses."

"I still have to finish my thesis but no exams this semester." Scott answers.

"I am keeping on top of my studies." Jared answers.

"How are the debates coming?" Brandy asks Norman.

"I've got every speaker to agree to the debate style. A week from Tuesday is the one on genetics. Do you think you can still handle it?"

"Yes."

"Dr. Forester offered to find someone else if you didn't feel up to it but I am glad you still want to debate." Norman smiles at her. "The congregation is ready to meet my wife."

Brandy returns his smile but it is a little stiff.

The next morning after Norman leaves for the church, Brandy gets a phone call. "Sorry for the short notice, the court date for the complaint concerning Judge Golden's handling of your divorce from Norman Kettering is this Monday at ten o'clock in the morning." The sheriff tells her. "Mr. Kettering's lawyer has requested a subpoena in your name."

"I will be there," Brandy tells the man.

Norman comes home about a half hour later. "The court date is set."

"I have been subpoenaed as a witness." Brandy

answers.

Scott brings textbooks from Brandy's office at the university. "In case you want to bone up for the debate."

Brandy shakes her head at him but skims through a few to see if there is anything new that might help her. She breaks off to get Scott to take her grocery shopping. Scott tells her that he has a date and leaves after he brings in the food. She makes a simple meal of soup and biscuits for Norman when he gets home.

"It's just you and me for supper tonight. Scott has a hot date." Brandy tells him when he comes in the door.

"You didn't have to cook." Norman tells her.

"Yes, I did. I need to know just how independent I can manage to be." Brandy answers, "Unless you need something fancier."

"No, I don't need anything fancier." Norman shakes his head. "I just don't want you in pain when takeout would satisfy my hunger for food."

"I didn't attempt anything difficult and I rested between tasks." Brandy frowns. "I am not a child."

"Sorry, I don't want you in pain." Norman answers.

"It helps if I can keep a little bit busy; it soothes the workaholic in me." Brandy wheels herself to the table and places a plate of biscuits beside the soup pot.

"Okay, I admit I am overprotective." Norman answers as he takes his place at the table. He takes her hand and says grace. They are just about to start when the doorbell rings.

"Excuse me." Norman says before he rises to get it. Brandy moves to where she can see who is at the door. A tall woman with a stiff bearing and expensive clothing gives the house a haughty look.

"This is what you are reduced to." She says to Norman.

"I chose it." Norman answers.

"I want to speak to you about Jared." The woman says.

"Rebuilding a relationship with your grandson is easy, accept his choice of bride or he will never speak to you again." Norman answers.

"He will come around if I stand firm." The woman frowns.

"As I did," Norman answers. "Your money did not buy me and it will not buy him."

"You will not speak to me that way." The woman snaps the words out crisply.

"I think you have worn out your welcome." Norman tells her.

"Jared simply cannot marry that creature." A hand reaches out to grab his forearm.

"Jared will marry whom he pleases. I happen to like Leia and I think she will make Jared an excellent wife." Norman answers as he pulls the woman towards the door.

"Marianne is much more refined."

"Then you will be pleased to know that she is dating Jared's brother, Scott." Brandy answers. "You might still get her as a granddaughter-in-law."

"Scott is not my grandson." The woman lifts her nose as she turns away from Brandy to cut her out of the conversation.

"Actually, he is." Norman answers as he reaches out to open the door. "They all are your grandchildren. And they are all Brandy's and my children."

"Chastity-"

"Is mentally unstable and morally bankrupt," Norman frowns. "Whatever made you believe that such a person would be acceptable to me?"

"She is of your class."

"I hope not, I hold a doctorate in ethics. There is nothing ethical about either her or her father. They are completely amoral." Norman frowns. "But then you have shown little talent for moral living. Now you have been asked to leave."

"I am your mother." The woman glares at him.

"You have chosen through your demands to push me away. As it is, you are not welcome in my house." Norman frowns at the woman.

"Jared-"

"Has made his decision, you didn't accept it and he turned away." Norman escorts her out the door. "He loves Leia and you rejected her."

The woman frowns. "I will leave my fortune to my dog."

"Good." Norman tells her. "Do that."

The woman stares at him for a moment he closes the door in her face.

Norman comes back and rolls Brandy's chair back into its place at the table. "Sorry for the interruption."

"What did she think to accomplish by coming here?" Brandy asks.

"I don't know, she never makes much sense to me." Norman frowns. "I don't want to discuss her."

"You've dug into my family but I'm not allowed to dig into yours."

"My mother drove my father off early in their marriage with her attempts at social climbing. He went mountain climbing in Alaska and fell down a crevasse. She got his money as well as her father's fortune. She had a thousand demands that she treated as absolutes when I was growing up and all of them were rubbish. She hated religion because a family member used to tell her everything she did was wrong so I studied it and that led to ethics. I came to the conclusion that she knew nothing about right and wrong. Then I fell in love with you and chose to separate myself from her insanity. Once you left, I went into the church because God called and she rejected that choice too."

"Do you remember your father?"

"No, he died months before I was born." Norman answers. "My paternal grandfather made certain that I did not get caught up in my mother's version of reality. He died when I was a teenager. Now I don't want to waste the soup you prepared."

Brandy nods and they eat.

Anne comes over the next morning to help Brandy clean the house. "This is something you cannot manage on your own."

"Scott keeps it picked up." Brandy answers. "He does it of his own accord."

"What happens when he leaves?" Anne asks.

"Then it will be up to Norman and me." Brandy answers. "If it gets too bad we will hire a cleaner to come in one day a week."

"That's expensive." Anne frowns.

"Nothing I can't afford." Brandy answers.

"My father would like to meet you."

"As far as I am concerned your father is Norman Kettering." Brandy answers.

Anne frowns. "Why do you insist on saying that?"

"I am no more your mother than he is your father. He hasn't suffered any less than I have over the events of twenty-five years ago." Brandy answers. "Just because the man you think of as your father is still alive does not mean that Norman was any less involved than I was."

Brandy answers.

"He doesn't want us here." Anne frowns.

"Norman wants us to put our marriage back together which takes time and privacy. You, Ruth, and Mary acted like you intended to be here every minute of every day. Jared and Scott have other interests that keep them from overwhelming us with attention. Norman needed me to set some boundaries with the three of you." Brandy attempts to explain. "Last month he was living alone with his only commitment to his church discovering he has five children is a big change."

"It's a big change for you too."

"For the last twenty years, I had students, mostly graduate students, about your age to oversee. Had this been discovered ten years ago or twenty years ago when you were teenagers or young children I would have no more idea what to do than Norman does." Brandy admits.

"You don't have to do what he wants. You are divorced, right?"

"There is a hearing on Monday to decide whether our divorce was legal. Neither of us filed for it. When things started going wrong, I did not talk to your father. I just ran." Brandy answers.

"How could you get a divorce without filing for it?" Anne frowns.

"Other people who thought they had an interest in wrecking our marriage had legal connections." Brandy answers. "Norman is contesting their right to do what they did."

"Other people tried to come between you?"

"Jared's surrogate mother told everyone she was pregnant with Norman Kettering's child," Brandy answers, "that he intended to divorce me and marry her."

"Did you rip her eyes out?" Anne asks.

"No, I ran to Africa and stayed there for twenty-five years." Brandy answers.

Anne frowns. "If anyone tried that with Hubert I would rip their eyes out."

"I wasn't up to the fight." Brandy answers.

Anne shakes her head. "You have to fight for your man."

Brandy pauses. "I need to study genetics according to Intelligent Design so I am ready to debate against it."

"Mom, if you really want to stay with Norman, you will fight for him." Anne says before going off to find the mop.

That sentence stays with Brandy all through her internet research. She thinks about what happened and goes through her belongings for the letter Judge Golden had sent her. It had come like a bullet falling from the sky about the time she was reconsidering contacting Norman. It had killed any hope that Norman would do anything but what his mother wanted. Brandy sets the letter aside. Scott phones to say he is going out.

"I told you I didn't expect you to do any fancy cooking." Norman frowns at the table.

"I didn't Anne came and cleaned. She insisted on leaving us a meal." Brandy answers. "I spent my afternoon researching possible angles of argument for the debate."

Norman nods. "How did it go?"

"It's likely to be based more on philosophy than hard science." Brandy frowns. "Not my strong suit."

"You will do fine." Norman answers.

"And what do you base that opinion upon?" Brandy frowns.

"I don't even remember you being unprepared for

any test."

"I flunked the biggest one. I didn't stand up to Chastity. I didn't fight for my marriage." Brandy shakes her head. "I didn't confront you or do any of things a normal wife would do. I didn't believe I could truly be happy that life would allow it. I know you didn't really need me. I just messed things up for you."

Norman crouches beside her chair to get to eye level. "Brandy, it was all lies. I needed you. I was barely breathing until God called and I knew which direction to go. Chastity Golden was nothing more a nuisance."

"Even with Jared in the picture?"

"As far as I was concerned Jared couldn't be my son, I never had sex with Chastity," Norman answers, "and before you try to correct me, I couldn't make love to her because I am in love with you."

"I am not certain I deserve it." Brandy answers.

"Deserving love is not as important as accepting love, there are days when none of us deserves love but we need it and if we accept it as the gift, it is then it can work its healing power in us." Norman tells her.

Brandy's tears overflow. Norman pulls her into his arms and rocks her. He takes her to bed and holds her as she cries. It is a long time before Brandy can speak.

"This isn't very dignified."

"Tears might not be dignified but they can heal." Norman answers. "I shed enough of them bargaining with God for your return."

"I've caused you a lot of pain."

"No more than I have caused you." Norman answers. "Why didn't you move on, find someone else to love?"

Brandy answers. "I decided to devote myself to my studies and my research they seemed more reliable than the people in my life."

Norman kisses her, softly, gently but intensely. There was a pause in the kiss as if he is waiting for her reaction before he takes it any further. Brandy holds her breath for a second before she manages to kiss him back only her kiss is tentative. He pulls back and starts again still gently and softly but with less intensity. She is still tentative.

Norman pulls back. "Am I pushing too soon?"

"It's been a long time, I am out of practice." Brandy says.

Norman kisses her again but this time, there is more play as he kisses her not on the mouth but the cheek, the chin, the nose, the eyelids and the forehead. The next kiss on the lips is a teasing kind of kiss. "Do I have to tell you the blue mouse joke again?"

Brandy smiles. "No one else ever bothers to tell me jokes."

"Which is why I was always looking for ones I thought would appeal to your quirky sense of humor," Norman answer, "You need to leave room for fun in your life."

"Fun, as in drinking and parties?"

"Fun, as in doing something that you enjoy for the sake of relaxing, drinking does not necessarily enter into it. Telling you jokes was the only thing I found that relaxed you."

"And what have you been doing for fun these last twenty-five years?" Brandy asks.

"I play chess with a group who meets at the public library once a week, coach youth soccer during the spring and fall, read detective novels, and am part of a group of men who at the church who meet to socialize and keep each other accountable for our actions." Norman answers.

"Do they know that you are cuddling with me?"

"They know I am attempting to put my marriage back together." Norman answers. "They are praying for us. I know between my mother, Chastity, and the commitment I had to the varsity teams it seemed like everything was against our marriage last time but my life is different now. No one is going to hurt you."

"You can't promise that pain is part of life." Brandy frowns.

"Brandy, you have to decide between living life in fear, and relaxing so that joy and love can push the pain into the background where it isn't in control of you."

"And my choice will change whether you stay or not?" Brandy frowns.

"No, I will be here either way. I want you to be happy Brandy." Norman pauses. "You've had your work but have you been happy these last twenty-five years?"

Brandy gives this some thought. "I am not certain I know what it feels like to be happy. I thought I did for a few weeks so long ago I've forgotten the feeling."

"I want to correct that mistake." Norman kisses her again this time on the forehead. "I will go as slow as necessary so you can adjust to the changes."

"What kind of life do you want for us?" Brandy asks.

Norman pauses. "I want us to enjoy each other in bed and out. I know you are not going to give up your work and I am not asking you for that. What I am asking that you acknowledge me as your husband and commit to living with me as my wife."

"Trusting is not an easy task." Brandy frowns. "I double check everything when I am working with students or other researchers. I have other people double check my work when I work alone. You want me to assume the world is a safe place, that Chastity's threats aren't real, that your mother will stay out of our lives, and my parents killer won't try to get rid of the only witness to his crime."

"No, I am asking you to trust me to stand beside you so you don't have to face their threats alone." Norman shakes his head. "I don't want you to have to live in hiding. I want you to know that someone will be here to stop them. It's one part of being a husband I completely missed the first time around and I want to make up for the oversight."

Brandy looks into his eyes. Norman looks back but there is no shadow in his eyes, no glancing away, no reason to disbelieve him. She feels something inside her relax but somehow it doesn't reach her brain intact. "I'm a scientist. I believe in what I observe that's reproducible."

Norman laughs. "Okay, so long as you give me enough time to show you time and time again that I mean every word I am saying."

"You are not upset that I didn't give you a commitment?" Brandy frowns.

"You just agreed to give me a chance, that's more hope than I've had in a long, long time." Norman smiles before he kisses her on the lips. Brandy kisses him back with much less hesitation.

CHAPTER 18

Brandy continues with her research the next day but this time, the Christian perspective comes up in the papers and she spends time investigating that the Bible says about genetics and the environment. Norman comes home to no supper but so Norman orders take out.

"What have you been doing today?" Norman asks.

"Research into the Christian theories surrounding genetics and environmental science," Brandy pauses, "Which do you subscribe to that the earth is for the plundering because God will produce a new world or man's primary task on earth is to steward the gift of God's creation?"

"I think I lean towards stewarding. He asks us to steward everything else why not his creation." Norman answers. "You think you know what you are going to say?"

"I think I have a whole lot of new information to work with and I haven't had the time to make any decisions." Brandy answers.

"I will answer any questions I can but this is not my field of expertise." Norman tells her.

"No, I think I will break off for the day." Brandy answers. "Give my mind time to think about what I've read."

Norman nods. "Do you need to get out of here for a while after supper?"

"Why?"

"I thought we might go to the library and you can decide whether or not chess is a game you want to try to play." Norman answers.

"I played chess briefly as a teenager. A teacher thought it might help with my logic skills." Brandy answers. "I can come and see whether what I remember is right."

"Then that's what we will do." Norman smiles at her. "See what you can remember."

The next day is Saturday, Norman takes her to his team's soccer game. They actually play two games but Norman makes certain she has something to drink and a place out of direct sunlight not far away from the sideline where he stands.

Scott and Marianne show up for the second game and sit with her.

"How is it going?" Scott asks.

"They lost the first game and are one goal up in the second." Brandy answers.

"I mean with you, not the soccer game."

"Norman takes me places so I am not housebound." Brandy answers. "How are you?"

"Marianne and I are getting married in eight weeks."

"Congratulations." Brandy answers.

"You really are alright with this?" Marianne asks.

"Yes, do you need any help with the wedding?"

Brandy asks.

"My father said we didn't have to worry about anything. He is just happy we didn't just run off and elope."

Brandy looks at Scott. He gives her a smile and a wink. "Marianne's father welcomed me into the family. They asked if you and Norman could come to dinner tomorrow night."

"I will have to ask him once the game is over." Brandy answers. "Do you want to stick around and make your announcement to him directly?"

"We can." Scott answers. "Then I have to get back to work."

"How deep into wedding plans are you?" Brandy asks Marianne.

"I'm not yet. Scott has convinced me to make the effort to finish the semester out so I can transfer schools with the best grades I can get." Marianne smiles, "He's looking after me."

"I am glad to hear that." Brandy nods.

They watch the game which ends with the one goal advantage for Norman's team. Norman comes directly over after he has congratulated his players.

"What brings you out?" He asks Scott.

"Marianne and I want you and Mom to come to dinner tomorrow night at her parent's house." Scott answers.

"Any particular occasion?" Norman asks.

"We are getting married and her parents want to meet my parents." Scott answers.

Norman glances at Brandy. "What do you say?"

"I have nothing planned." Brandy answers.

"Then we will come. What time?"

"Six-thirty," Marianne says, "Dinner will be served at

seven on the dot."

"I will stop by later and give you the address." Scott says. "Right now I have to finish my paper."

Marianne smiles, "Thank you for coming."

Brandy smiles back and Norman nods. "We will see you tomorrow. Right now we have to go meet the team for pizza."

Scott takes Marianne's hand and draws her away. "We will see you later."

Norman bends down. "You don't seem surprised."

"I knew she intended to follow him when he transferred schools." Brandy shrugs. "Marriage might be a little sudden but I knew it was headed towards at least living together."

Norman stands to take the handles of the wheelchair. "The next question is going to take deep thought."

"Okay." Brandy says.

"What kind of topping do you like on pizza?" Norman asks.

"Pizza, I haven't had pizza in a long, long time." Brandy answers. "What are my choices?"

"For that, you have to wait until we get to the pizzeria to read the menu." Norman tells her.

Brandy laughs.

Norman wakes Brandy up the next morning, "Sorry but I need to get to church so if you want my help to get dressed before noon you have to get up now."

Brandy sighs and opens her eyes. "I will get up."

"Bath or a shower?" Norman asks.

"Can I change my mind?" Brandy asks.

"About whatever you want, except living with me." Norman answers.

Brandy shakes her head. "You will get yourself into

trouble if you mention living with me in front of your congregation."

"My congregants are not ogres." Norman frowns. "They are normal people who just happen to believe that this universe has a creator and that he wants to be involved in the daily life of his people."

"There's no proof of that."

"You are not looking in the right places if you can't see the evidence. You think by dissecting the created matter you should find the creator."

"There should be a signature of some kind."

"It is in the genius of the genetic materials you study and the millions of interactions large and small that allow the earth and life to exist." Norman answers. "It's there if you open your eyes to it, Brandy, all around you."

"I think I will stay in bed, I've had my sermon for today." Brandy frowns.

"It's in my love for you too. I was too selfish to truly love you before God showed me what real love was, Brandy. I am not afraid to love you Brandy because real love casts out fear even the fear of living the next twenty-five years alone if that's what it takes to convince you I mean it."

Brandy frowns and rolls onto her side to sit up. "I am getting up then you can go."

"I am sorry I promised myself that I would not put pressure on you." Norman frowns. "I apologize for the sermon. Bath or shower?"

"Whichever one is faster." Brandy answers.

"Shower, it is." Norman answers.

Brandy is sitting out on the patio overlooking the garden when Scott comes out. "Where's Dad?"

"He went to work, Sunday morning service." Brandy

answers and stares at the still brown soil.

"Something happened."

"He preached an early morning sermon before he left." Brandy answers.

"Actually, I was wondering when the preacher in him would come out. I was sort of scared it would be yesterday when I announced I was marrying Marianne." Scott answers. "Considering everything I would say he's been quite restrained."

"This morning was not restrained." Brandy frowns.

"Mom, you fall into the wise professor mode on me all the time, you don't think it's hard for him to ignore twenty years of being expected to argue his faith with everyone he meets."

Brandy sighs. "Are you leaving soon?"

"I thought I might stick around until Dad gets back." Scott answers.

"Isn't Marianne going to get upset?"

"She has finals to study for this morning and afternoon. So long as we show up on time this evening she will be fine."

"So are you planning a society wedding or something smaller?"

"I am leaving all the wedding planning in her mother's hands, I am concentrating on getting everything together to change universities and make things right with the law."

Scott answers. "You can ask her tonight."

"Just do me one favor." Brandy starts.

"What's that?" Scott asks.

"Make sure that you and Jared and Mary aren't picking the same wedding date. I don't want to have to choose whose wedding I am going to attend."

"I will check with them." Scott promises.

Brandy looks out over the garden. "You wouldn't know what was planted."

"Seeds," Scott shrugs, "I was out when Mary was working here."

"How am I supposed to weed it if I don't know what she planted?" Brandy frowns.

"I don't think your doctor would approve of you getting down on the ground to weed."

Brandy closes her eyes for a few seconds. "Scott, go find your textbook."

Scott frowns at her. "You want to be left alone."

"I need to think." Brandy answers.

"I will be inside if you need anything call. Just please, don't do anything like try to get down and weed without assistance."

"There is nothing to weed." Brandy looks out over the bare ground. "Weeding comes later after my back is healed."

Scott nods and goes into the house.

Brandy sits there for a long time before she hears footsteps. She turns around. The man she faces is slightly familiar but much older. Brandy calls. "Scott!"

"There is no one here to save you this time." He pulls a large knife from behind his back.

Brandy spins her wheelchair around and puts as much distance as the backyard allows between them. She also puts the man between her and the house so he cannot see what is happening behind him. She sees Scott in through the glass patio doors.

"Your parents deserved what happened to them." The man says. "Their interference stole my wife and hurt my children."

"Your wife did nothing but cry on my mother's shoulder for the whole time they stayed there," Brandy frowns, "Perhaps if you treated her better."

"My wife would never have left without your parents' urging. She wasn't a strong woman."

"I know nothing about that. What I knew was I was forced to share my room and my toys without so much as a minute of my mother's time or attention. I wanted you to take them away" Brandy answers.

"What you wanted wasn't important. My children told me that your parents thought you were just a brat."

"Actually, I was important. My surviving forced you to change your identity and your place of residence. You might have hung on to your feelings of victimization but you knew what you did was wrong, very wrong. There was no reason for you to kill my parents."

"I had to get my family back." He raises the blade and takes two steps towards her.

Brandy frowns, "If you were in the right then you should have went to the authorities and gotten a custody order and got the law to remove your children from my parents' home." Brandy pauses. "You could have sued my parents. There were lots of other solutions rather than attempted murder, murder, and arson."

"The courts favors mothers even when they are under the influence men like your interfering preacher father." He takes another few steps forward as a firearm comes around the side of the house.

"Hold it right there." A deep voice commands.

"What!" The man turns to see four uniformed police officers step out from the side of the house all of them have guns trained on him. "Who called-"

"Throw down your weapon." The voice commands again.

Instead, the man turns to charge at Brandy who spins her chair but the man never reaches it. He crumples under the first bullet.

Seconds later, Scott comes to Brandy's side. "Are you okay?"

"Yes, thank you for calling the police."

"I wanted to come out here myself but the 911 operator discouraged it." Scott frowns. "Dad will be upset with me."

"You got help before he hurt me." Brandy places a hand on his arm. "That's the important part."

"Who is he?"

"Mr. Solberg, the man who killed my parents." Brandy answers.

"Why would he come after you now?" Scott asks.

Brandy doesn't seem to hear him. "I will come into the house there is something I need to do." Brandy goes inside to the computer and starts researching the people of her distant past.

When Norman comes in from church, Scott pulls him aside and tells him in a quiet voice what happened.

"Good thing you were here."

"Mom's been pouring through her research and has said nothing." Scott frowns. "I get the feeling that she's not here."

"Trauma," Norman says. "I will stay with her and call Harry, a counselor I know, to see what we can do."

"I will be in my room, call if you need me." Scott says.

"You still have school work?"

"I've got to stay up-to-date on Dr. Buford's latest research when if the judge asks me I can show that I am serious about turning things around." Scott answers.

Norman nods. He goes and leans down to kiss Brandy on the forehead. "How is the research going?"

"This isn't about the debate. This is about who my

parents were." Brandy answers without lifting her eyes from the page.

"And who were they?" Norman asks.

"My father was the pastor of an inner-city church according to these records. He was known for taking abused women out of their situations and finding new lives for them. His supporters called him a saint and his detractors suggested that he seduced the women involved." Brandy frowns.

"I warned you about emotional shocks over your family." Norman rubs her back with the ends of his fingers. "Do you want to talk to a counselor?"

Brandy frowns. "No wonder my mother worried. People threatened his life."

"Perhaps she believed he innocently rescued these women at risk to himself. Some women love hero types." Norman answers.

"So how many women have you rescued from abusive men?"

"None, what's not quite true but if I do so I do it by sending them to the police or a professional counselor. I believe in law and order and I don't have the qualifications to do personal counseling but I have a friend who runs a Christian counseling service."

"Did you ever go to him for counseling?" Brandy asks.

"No, knowing Harry he would ask to see your picture and when I showed it to him, he would tell me that I was an idiot for letting you out of my sight never mind running off every weekend to play games." Norman answers. "I know I was an idiot, I don't need Harry to confirm it."

"How come if my father was a pastor do I not remember going to church or Sunday school?" Brandy frowns. "Am I just remembering what I want to remember?"

"Where was his church?" Norman frowns.

Brandy turns the screen to where Norman can see it. Norman writes out the name of the church before doing a search. Then a web page pops up for the church he picks up the phone and calls the number on the screen.

"Yes, I would like the name of someone who attended your church during the time when Ned Hollander was a minister there."

Brandy waits for the answer.

"No, I am not a member of the press. My name is Norman Kettering and I am a minister of the gospel. I am sitting with Ned Hollander's daughter who would like information on her family."

"She's been through enough without answering a dozen questions." Norman frowns. "Her attacker showed up here today. He has unsettled her mind about what she thinks she remembers. All I want is someone she can talk to who knew her parents."

Norman writes down a name and number. "I will give you twenty-four hours to speak to him before phoning him." Norman turns to Brandy. "There is an elderly gentleman who is still known to the staff at the church but they want to inform him that you are looking for information rather than his just receiving a phone call out of the blue."

Brandy nods and then glances up. "It is time to start lunch."

"You seem a little preoccupied. Scott or I could make it." Norman answers.

"Didn't you get an invitation to lunch with a church member?" Brandy frowns.

"I didn't accept. I wanted to get back here." Norman

answers. "I am being paid to preach sermons not necessarily to accept invitations to lunch."

"I've interrupted your life yet again." Brandy frowns.

"No, you are my life." Norman answers and places his hands on her shoulders. "I wish you would truly, truly believe that."

"You need to spend time with your adherents."

"I will accept invitations to Sunday lunch if you will come with me to church. That I will not do is to leave you home alone while I go out." Norman answers.

"I thought I told you I would not play the minister's wife."

"I do not expect you to accept my sermons without honest comment. I expect you to be yourself and to stand up for your personal beliefs. All I ask is that you socialize with members of my congregations as you would anyone else." Norman answers.

Brandy sighs. "I don't handle sermons well."

"I doubt I could handle philosophical lectures on evolutionary sciences without some negative reaction. I understand your dilemma but it would go a long way to healing the breach between us if you would attempt it."

"Mr. Solberg tried to kill me again. Only the police shot him this time." Brandy tells Norman.

"I can arrange for counseling if you want." Norman answers. "Make sure you have the support you need."

"You can't build your life around me." Brandy shakes her head.

"The reality is I have. Even when you were in Africa, you were my reason for waking up in the morning. Realizing how selfish I was, trying to become a better person, buying this house, praying a dozen times a day that you would return, bargaining with God, it was all because I could not accept a life without you." Norman answers. "I will not put my church before you or bring someone home who will put you in harm's way."

Tears run down Brandy's cheeks. "I am not worth it."

"To me you are, you are worth every second of repentance and atonement God asked for, you are worth far more than I have paid. Now you are here I intend to cherish every moment we can spend together." Norman lifts her chin and kisses her lips. "I believe God understands my need to put you first after all these years. He went to great lengths to show his followers just how much he cared for them."

"No sermons." Brandy frowns.

. "No sermons, I promise. Just love, Brandy."

The phone rings. Norman picks it up. "Norman Kettering." He listens for a few seconds then hands the phone to Brandy.

"Brandy Hollander." Brandy answers.

"This is Jeffry Archer. I was the senior pastor when Ned Hollander worked in our little church." A voice tells her. "What did you want to know about your father?"

"Graham Solberg visited me today. He told me that the attack was my father's fault for interfering with his family and his wife would have never left him without my Dad's insistence."

"In my opinion, there is just enough truth in the statement for the devil to use his twisted logic to make your father sound bad." Jeffry Archer answers. "Mrs. Solberg was for lack of a more precise term was infatuated with Ned. She lied about her circumstances to desert a domineering husband. Only once she got free of her marriage, she refused to leave Ned alone. Ned thought that showing her that he had a wife and children might convince her that she had no future with him so he took her to your mother. Your mother was an insecure woman who did not trust God and her husband with the work he did. Mrs. Solberg played on your mother's fears and stressed your parents' marriage beyond its limits. Ned asked me a thousand times to pray for them."

"Did you tell him to send Mrs. Solberg away?" Brandy asks.

"I did, and he arranged a dozen times for her to leave but she used a thousand excuses not to go. I told your mother to force the woman out. I even used the example of Sarah and her maid as a scriptural example. Your mother thought that it would make her a bad Christian and her husband would be mortally offended by it."

"I take it that my parents did not communicate." Brandy answers.

"Your parents needed quiet time together and Mrs. Solberg did not allow for it." Jeffry Archer answers.

"I have one other question." Brandy pauses. "Why do I not remember going to church and Sunday School?"

"Your father's work with battered women left its mark on your father's life. He moved his family out of the city to a far suburb to protect your mother, your brother, and you from threats made against him and his family. He thought you were safer away from him."

"I would have thought then he would have found some nearby church to send us to Sunday school. No wonder my mother would have been insecure her husband sent her and her children away and did not even instruct them in his faith."

"Your father loved you."

"The truth is my father didn't bother with me. My mother was too anxious to be a good parent and they both dumped me on my brother who resented me. Then the church deserted me when I was in the hospital. It is not my memory that is faulty." Brandy puts the phone on it cradle and rolls her chair towards the kitchen.

Norman winces but allows Brandy to go. The phone rings again.

Norman picks it up. "Norman Kettering." "I am afraid that Brandy is not in the mood to speak to you." "I believe there is another scripture about the dangers exasperating children and yet another warning about turning them away from God." "Brandy has a right to her own feelings. The police had to shoot Solberg today because he attempted to stab Brandy. I would think shaming the victim for not agreeing that the best was done in the situation is petty and self-serving." Norman places the phone down before walking into the kitchen. "What do you need down, where you can reach it?"

Brandy looks at him. "With the helps David put in these cupboards, I should be able to reach it."

"With your back still being tender, a little help should not be unwelcome." Norman answers. "Now what do you need from up there?"

"Why did this happen to me, Norman? Why?" Brandy asks.

"Unfortunately why is a philosophical question, and the answer depends on what how you view life." Norman frowns. "You keep telling me not to preach to you and what ends in a dilemma when you ask me these kinds of questions."

"What would you tell one of your congregants?" Brandy asks.

"The correct question may not be why but what is God accomplishing in your soul with these events. Sometimes there is no question, God permits evil but does not condone it because people such as your father allow it into his life and by extension into the life of his family. Then Jesus does the most extraordinary thing, he puts his arms around us and weeps with us."

"And what good is that?"

"It tells us that we are right to weep, that the world has treated us poorly and the underlying power of the universe upholds our cause. Then he gives us the power to overcome our feelings of powerlessness and to stand up for others who evil has victimized."

"Like my father?"

"It sounds like your father's church placed too much of its identity in your father's works. That status brought pride rather than humility that comes from leading a godly life. Your father lost the Spirit's ability to judge between those women who needed him and the ones who merely wanted him."

Brandy frowns. "And you live a godly life?"

"I try Brandy but I don't always succeed. I once took it into my head to travel the world looking for you. My accountability group insisted I pray about it. God showed me in a dozen ways that I needed to be here to wait for you to return even though it brought me suffering to do so. Now I realize that even if I had found you, you were in no state of mind to listen to what I wanted to say."

"What would you say in this situation to a non-Christian?" Brandy asks.

"Brandy, you know the answer as well as I. There is no good or evil because everything in life happens strictly by chance."

"Can you not be an evolutionist and believe in the concept good and evil?"

"On what would, you base that belief?" Norman asks. "Good and evil lack the scientific basis. Whether something is good or evil is a value judgment we place upon acts that are not healthy or kind and are not an objective observation."

"You don't think that I've seen evil?"

"I believe in good and evil, Brandy. I know you have seen hatred and been hurt by it. Whether you are willing to label it evil that after being trained only to trust observable senses-"

"I sensed evil." Brandy answers. "I remembered the coldness at the heart of him more than I do what he looked like. He still carried it within him."

"I can't answer without knowing what his issue was." Norman tells her.

"So I have to live not knowing." Brandy sighs.

"It might be better not to know then his evil can't take root in your heart." Norman tells her.

Brandy pauses and thinks about it for a long time. "How do I get rid of fear without uncovering its cause?"

"This is one where the answer quickly becomes a sermon. I don't know what to do with fear except to place your trust in God." Norman answers. "That is all I will say on the subject."

Brandy nods and turns back to the cupboard.

"Now what did you want down?" Norman asks.

Brandy's eyes drop to the rest of what she has put on the counter. "I don't remember."

"Then how about I take you out to lunch?"

It only strikes Brandy that they might be walking into a trap when they pull up to the gated driveway of the Gilford's manor. Her hands begin to shake at the thought, Scott had gone over earlier to see Marianne and she had missed her opportunity to cancel.

"Do you know anything about the Gilfords besides they seem to be friends of Chastity's and your mother's?"

Brandy asks after the gate is opened in response to the buzzer.

"Mr. Gilford owns a group of businesses. I've never met the man." Norman asks. "Why?"

"I'm suddenly nervous." Brandy answers.

"I'm here and Scott will be there. You will be fine." Norman tells her.

Brandy nods but feels the tension building in her as they near the house. Scott comes out to meet them. "Thanks for coming."

Norman helps Brandy out of the car and into her chair. "Are there stairs?" Brandy asks.

"The house has an elevator. The dining room is on the ground floor." Scott answers. "Marianne is waiting inside."

Norman pushes the chair to the door of the house and Marianne is waiting to open the door. "Thank you for coming." She is dressed casually in a blouse and slacks.

"Thank you for inviting us." Brandy manages a tight smile. "How are you?"

"Nervous," Marianne answers. "My parents are starting to ask a whole lot of questions about what we want at the wedding and neither one of us have given it a whole lot of thought."

"Perhaps we should meet them and talk about the subject before we give any advice." Norman answers. "Find out what they have in mind."

Marianne nods and leads the way into a large living room. The Gilfords are seated on chairs facing each other across the room. Mr. Gilford is a medium sized man with just a touch of gray at the temples standing out from dark brown hair. He wears clothing appropriate for the golf course. His wife is a tiny woman with blonde hair piled high on her head dressed in a designer gown.

"Mother and Father, this is Scott's parents, his mother, Dr. Brandy Hollander and his father, Reverend Norman Kettering. These are my parents, Randall and Rachel Gilford." Marianne pauses and looks at her parents.

"We are pleased to meet you." Mrs. Gilford answers with a slight lift of her chin.

"What kind of doctor are you?"

"I am a university professor I hold two doctorates in the subjects I teach." Brandy answers. "Norman also holds a doctorate."

"Did I introduce him wrong?" Marianne turns red.

"I have made my living as a reverend for the past twenty years. I prefer Reverend to Doctor." Norman tells her.

Scott puts an arm around her shoulders. "You did fine."

Mr. Gilford gives Scott a slight nod. "We are pleased to welcome Scott into the family."

"We have offered our congratulations." Norman answers. "We understand that, at this time, they are busy finishing off their semester."

"Yes, but one must book somewhat ahead when one is planning a wedding. There are professional services required and many of them want lead time to prepare properly." Mrs. Gilford answers. "Churches are often booked months in advance if Scott and Marianne wish to-"

"If they wish a church wedding then I can arrange one," Norman answers, "With either myself or my associate officiating."

Mrs. Gilford blinks. "In eight weeks?"

"I believe I can manage that depending upon what

day of the week they wish to get married." Norman answers. "Do you want to get married in a church?" He turns to Scott and Marianne.

"Yes." Scott answers, Marianne starts nods before Scott speaks.

"I've heard many clergymen have rules about marriages and church membership," Mr. Gilford frowns, "And marriage counseling."

"I can give them the name of a marriage counselor, but neither me nor my associate would be able to supply marriage counseling," Norman answers, "as we are both relatives of Scott."

"Next we need a venue for the reception." Mrs. Gilford frowns.

"Do you know what I would really like, Mother?" Marianne speaks quickly. "To hold the reception on the lawn down by the pond using the gazebo, picture a tea with fancy sandwiches and old-fashioned baked goods and southern belle dresses. Wouldn't it be elegant?"

Her mother glances at her husband who nods and says. "I guarantee that it will not be booked."

"It would need to be a morning wedding if you wish a tea." Mrs. Gilford answers.

"That is easily arranged at the church." Norman answers. "Few people want to get married in the morning."

"What do the men wear to such an event?" Scott asks.

"A morning coat which is a form of a tuxedo," Mr. Gilford answers, "Or a civil war uniform."

Scott nods.

A bell sounds. "Time to go to dinner." Mrs. Gilford holds out her hand to her husband who then leads the way into the dining room where dinner awaits them.

Marianne hugs Scott's waist. "Thank you for not putting up a fuss."

He gives her a short hug in return. "Best we find our seats."

Brandy glances at Norman, who pushes her chair. He bends down and whispers. "A little fancy."

"Fancy enough to satisfy her mother." Brandy answers.

Norman pauses for a moment. "You might be right."

The formality of dinner at the Gilford's equals the formality of the court hearing the next morning. Norman sits at his lawyer's table with Brandy in the aisle behind him.

"All rise, this court is now in session, Judge Marvin Baker presiding."

Brandy rises to her feet then sits back down very slowly when the rest are seated.

"Norman Kettering versus Herman Golden." The clerk announces.

"The charge is the misuse of power relating to the divorce decree of Norman Kettering and Brandy Hollander." The clerk continues.

"Mr. Cameron, state your case."

Norman's lawyer rises to his feet. "Herman Golden filed the papers for, and then presided over a divorce between Norman Kettering and Brandy Hollander issuing a final decree when neither party even knew such steps had been taken. His object seemed to be to marry his daughter, Chastity, to Mr. Kettering. Chastity Golden had driven Brandy Hollander from town with harassing behavior and threats without Mr. Kettering's knowledge. Mr. Kettering wishes the court to rule on the legality of said divorce since neither he nor his wife signed the divorce papers." Mr. Cameron sits down.

"The defense can now make its case."

"The divorce papers were filed by Herman Golden on behalf of Mrs. Linda Kettering, Mr. Kettering's mother." The Goldens' attorney starts.

"Did Herman Golden know that Mr. Kettering had nothing to do with filing the divorce papers?" The judge asks.

"Judge Golden filed the papers on the behalf of Mrs. Kettering." The lawyer frowns at the question. "Not Norman Kettering, Mrs. Kettering assured the judge that is was in her son's best interests."

"Who filed them is irrelevant." Judge Baker answers. "Judge Golden knew that neither party to the marriage had wished to dissolve the marriage. That is the heart of this matter."

"Brandy Hollander left the country and did not return until a month ago. Had she wanted to save her marriage she could have objected when she was sent a copy of the decree. Mrs. Kettering was worried about her son's frame of mind. He turned away from his family and friends after Miss Hollander left the country. She thought that if he was free to start over then, he might return to normal." The Golden's attorney asserts.

"Brandy Hollander is present and ready to testify as to why she did not respond to the divorce decree, your honor." Mr. Cameron remains standing.

"Call Brandy Hollander." The judge instructs.

The court guard comes forward to assist Brandy and her wheelchair to a place between the lawyer's tables and the judge's bench. The clerk comes down to get her oath to tell the truth.

"So why did you not object to the divorce decree?" The judge asks.

Brandy takes out the letter and hands it to the clerk. "This is the letter Judge Herman Golden sent to me with a copy of the divorce papers." Brandy frowns. "In it, he clearly states that the decree was legal without my signature and then made it sound as if Norman Kettering's marriage to Chastity Golden was arranged and that legally I was a non-person as far as having any say in the divorce. It left me feeling as if my husband had never wanted to marry me. I didn't think I had any reason to return. It is only after I returned that facts have led me to believe that Herman Golden abused his position as judge and Chastity and Norman's mother abused my person to further their ends."

"And what did they do?"

"They arranged for a doctor to steal fertilized eggs from my body so that Chastity Golden could claim to be pregnant with Norman's child." Brandy answers. "Charges to that effect have been laid by the police."

"I have paperwork that outlines those charges." Mr. Cameron stands up and takes it to the clerk. The clerk hands them to the judge who skims them.

"Was there any other reasons that you did not respond to the letter?" The judge asks after taking a few minutes to read the letter.

"Yes, your honor. When I was eight years old, I was severely injured and my family killed by a man who was angry with my father. I had no part in their quarrel but I knew what extremes crazy people who threaten and harass are willing to go. Frankly, I was scared to return after the treatment I received at the hands of Chastity Golden."

"Objection, your honor, this has nothing to do with Herman Golden."

"Miss Hollander, can you refute Mr. Stapleman's

statement?"

"Getting her father to declare the divorce was another of Chastity Golden's harassment tactics. I might have contacted Norman to find out the truth and I had considered doing so until that letter came. Afterwards I had no hope of reconciling my marriage."

"Objection overruled." The judge answers. "May I ask why you are in that wheelchair?"

"In the attack, when I was eight years old, I was thrown out a second-floor window onto concrete, as a result, my spine was wired together. The years I spent in Africa, I did not eat a calcium rich diet so my previously damaged spine got more and more fragile. A young woman who was under Chastity's influence shoved me hard into a doorway and another section of my spine had to be fused about two weeks ago. I can stand and take a few steps but another sharp jarring is all it would take to take away what mobility I have."

"Has either Herman or Chastity Golden threatened or harassed you since you returned to town?"

"The first day I returned, Chastity came to my office and Herman phoned me, the security guards at the university were called to remove her." Brandy answers.

"We have records, your Honor." Mr. Cameron stands and brings them to the clerk.

"Do they still phone you?"

"Not since Norman started answering my cell phone late at night." Brandy answers.

"Are you and he living together?" Judge Baker asks.

"We have since I was released from the hospital after the incident that put me in the wheelchair," Brandy nods.

"Do you sleep in the same bed?" The judge asks.

"Yes." Brandy answers.

"Why do you believe Norman Kettering pursuing

this matter in court?" The judge asks.

"He wants to convince me that we are, and always were, legally married. He heard their phone calls and he wanted to stop the harassment." Brandy frowns. "He has spent the last twenty-five years trying to understand why I left because I didn't tell him what was happening at the time. Herman Golden was also arrested for kidnapping and drugging Norman after Norman had his lawyer file this suit." She pauses. "Oh, and he has a doctoral degree in ethics and the Goldens upset his sense of right and wrong."

Judge Baker nods. "I think I understand the situation. Mr. Adkins will help you back to your place in the gallery."

"I wish to cross-examine Dr. Hollander." Mr. Stapleman frowns.

Judge Baker answers. "Do you have cell phone records of the phone calls, Mr. Cameron?"

"I do your Honour." Mr. Cameron rises to his feet to deliver them.

The judge looks the papers over. "Phone calls from both the Goldens after midnight to a woman newly released from the hospital. Numerous mentions in the university security records, where Miss Golden was removed from the facilities. A physical attack at the university where the police were called and Dr. Hollander sent to the hospital. Legal papers that outline the kidnapping case against Herman Golden where he tried to discredit Reverend Kettering by getting him hooked on street drugs. No, Mr. Stapleman, you will not get to harass Dr. Hollander by cross-examining her in my court. You must build your case on facts and proof without doing so."

"Mrs. Kettering was acting in the best interests of

her son by arranging their divorce." Herman Golden jumps to his feet.

"Order! When a man holds an advanced degree in ethics, his mother no longer has authority over his life." Judge Baker answers. "Unless you can prove he was tricked into marrying Dr. Hollander."

Norman laughs.

The judge turns his way with a severe frown. "Do you have something to say, Mr. Kettering?"

"I was not tricked into marrying Brandy." Norman answers. "My mother is a wealthy woman who doesn't believe anyone should do anything without her approval and she used the Goldens to deliberately destroy my marriage. None of it was done for my benefit."

Judge Baker frowns. "Do you have proof of that?"

"She tried the same thing with her grandson Jared and his girlfriend. He and I have told her that we wish to be written out of her will." Norman answers. "Jared moved and refuses her calls."

"Is Jared in the courtroom?"

"No, he had class at the university this morning." Norman answers.

"I can speak to that." Marianne stands up at the back of the gallery.

"And you are?" Judge Baker frowns.

"Marianne Gilford, Anna Kettering told my father that she would bankrupt him if I did not marry her grandson, Jared Kettering." Marianne reddened. "Between my parents, Mrs. Kettering, and the Goldens I ended up in the psych ward until I realized that it was hopeless. Jared wanted nothing to do with me because of them and the tactics they suggested I use."

Judge Baker frowns. "Mr. Stapleman, do you have any other defense evidence?"

Herman Golden glares at his lawyer. Mr. Stapleman frowns. "No, your Honor."

"Then based on the preposterous of evidence I find that Herman Golden abused his judicial power and that the divorce between Norman Kettering and Brandy Hollander is not binding in this or any other court. I recommend to the state prosecutors' office that charges be laid against Herman Golden. Herman Golden shall be responsible for all court costs regarding this case." Judge Baker states and bangs the gavel.

Norman turns and smiles at Brandy. Brandy squeezes his hand but does not smile.

"What's wrong?"

"Your mother and Chastity will be looking for revenge." Brandy answers. "We've embarrassed them publicly."

"Right now, all I care about is you." Norman answers. "We are married and we are staying married no matter what Chastity and my mother do."

"But they can make our lives miserable." Brandy frowns.

"I know that I can't live in fear of them or they win." Norman answers. "Shall we go out to lunch to celebrate?"

Brandy pauses and looks up to see the young woman approach. "Marianne, I didn't expect you to come."

"Scott told me about the hearing. I feared that if I didn't show up, then they might get away with what they did." Marianne pauses. "I know my parents might get mad but I had to tell the truth to feel better about myself."

"Hopefully, your parents will understand," Norman says.

"Father may, mother…" She shrugs. "I have to get back to the university; I have a class later with a paper due." Marianne says as she glances around then gives them a small wave. "Bye."

Norman glances at one of the sheriff's deputies. The man follows Marianne out of the room.

"Time for us to go," Norman takes the handles of the wheelchair and pushes Brandy towards the door. Chastity Golden flings herself at them but a deputy sheriff intervenes.

Brandy waits until they are in the car. "When does throwing herself at us get old?"

"For me, the first time she did it." Norman answers. "For her, when it sinks in that it doesn't work."

"How long does that take?" Brandy sighs.

Norman laughs. "Longer than I am willing to wait." He takes her to an upscale restaurant for lunch. "Can I take you away on a honeymoon now?"

"Hardly, there are still other investigations and court cases." Brandy frowns. "Plus you want me to debate next week."

"The day after the debate then," Norman smiles.

The hostess shows them to a table and brings menus. "Your server will be with you shortly."

"You wanted to see Sweden." Brandy points out. "The conference isn't for another three weeks."

"That soon, we need to get airline tickets," Norman frowns.

"We have a wedding to attend. Jared and Leia are getting married." Brandy reminds him.

Norman frowns. "I wanted to take you to Sweden."

"There will be other conferences. We still haven't got Mary's wedding invitation but by the end of summer four of the five children will be living elsewhere with their spouses."

"You wanted to go to the conference."

"Conferences aren't holidays." Brandy answers. "You would be going crazy because I would be in sessions all day. I can see the papers and get the summaries of answers over the internet."

"But you don't get to ask your own questions?"

"I can e-mail my questions and get answers back." Brandy answers. "It wouldn't be the first year that I had to miss because I had experiments in progress that I couldn't leave. It's the face to face meetings and networking that I will lose."

Norman shakes his head. "How long is the conference?"

"A week but it's an intense week and it sitting that long in sessions would probably strain my back. I can handle the disappointment of not going, Norman."

"I don't know if I can." Norman answers.

Brandy laughs. "We can go later, Sweden will still be there. I should go visit the research stations in the next six months."

"Not once the semester starts." Norman frowns.

"The research stations are part of my work. As long as I am supervising students at the stations I can make the case for going." Brandy answers. "What you really want is a trip where I have time to concentrate on you instead of work."

"At the end of summer, you will be back to the university." Norman frowns.

"Let see how fast my back heals." Brandy frowns.

The waitress returns to take their orders. After they order Norman keeps her entertained with stories of what happened to their classmates after she left for Africa.

When they get back to the house, a woman in a car is waiting for them. She is an elderly woman who walks with a limp. "You look just like your mother." She tells

Brandy.

"How did you know my mother?" Brandy asks as she waits for Norman to bring her wheelchair from the trunk.

"My name is Mrs. Renfrew. Your father rescued me from a dangerous life. I know I don't look the part now but as a teenager, I was running with the wrong crowd and ended up in the hands of a pimp. It was a bad three years until I meet your mother volunteering in a soup kitchen. She got your father involved and he found me a place in a safe house in another town. I was his first rescue. I kept in touch with your mother until her death."

"Did you keep in touch with my father too?"

"It wasn't like that at least not with me." Mrs. Renfrew frowns. "I heard the rumours later and didn't believe them. Pastor Hollander was happy to help with lodging and transport but it was your mother who talked me into leaving that awful man."

"Brandy," Norman interrupts to lift her out of the car and into the wheelchair.

"It was my pimp who threatened your mother and caused Pastor Hollander to move her out of the city." Mrs. Renfrew admits. "Only the first plan was for him to change churches but his senior pastor talked him out of it. My rescue quickly led to another and another. Your mother thought he should stay where he was doing good works."

"Did that include Mrs. Solberg?" Brandy asks.

"I was out of town long before that happened." Mrs. Renfrew frowns. "Your mother was torn between doing good works and wanting her husband back. The more rescues he did and the greater his reputation grew, the less time he had for her. She wrote about her worry that the women were putting too much temptation in his way but she refused to talk to him about it because she didn't want to interfere with God's work."

"Did she ever concern herself with what she was doing to her children?" Brandy asks.

"She didn't mention you, your brother was mentioned a little more often but most of the letters concerned your father and his work." Mrs. Renfrew frowns. "I am afraid that I missed that fact at the time."

"I am afraid that my wife is tired and in need of a nap." Norman interrupts the woman. "She is not long out of the hospital and she's had a stressful morning."

"I came all the way from-"

"Which was your choice," Norman answers. "My wife is not obligated to you but she is under doctor's orders."

"How dare you?" Mrs. Renfrew states.

"We have seen pictures of my late mother-in-law and she looks nothing like her daughter." Norman answers. "Ned Hollander bio did not suggest that he rescued prostitutes just abused wives who came to his church from their husbands. Whoever you are you need to go home and leave Brandy alone."

The woman opens and closes her mouth many times as Norman wheels Brandy away from her and into the house.

"You don't think she knows anything useful," Brandy says.

"I don't think I want to get mixed up in whatever remains of your father's folly." Norman answers. "Now it's nap time."

"Is Scott here?" Brandy asks. Norman knocks on Scott's bedroom door but Brandy finds the note on the table. "He has gone to the library with Marianne. She is having trouble studying for a test."

"Either that or she is scared of Chastity." Norman frowns.

"It does not matter which he's spending the afternoon with her." Brandy answers. "If I have to be here alone I would prefer not to sleep."

"I am not leaving you here alone." Norman answers. "Let's get you into bed and I will write next week's sermon sitting right here."

"Don't you need your library of reference books?" Brandy frowns.

"I can look up references later," Norman tells her. "I have a fairly good memory for Biblical principles."

"This time, I am interfering with your work." Brandy shakes her head.

Norman pauses for a moment. "Brandy, are you scared to stay here alone?"

"Is she gone yet?" Brandy asks.

Norman goes and looks out the window. "No."

Brandy frowns. "What are the chances of her coming to the door if you leave?"

"Come on, you can come to the church with me. If Anne shows up maybe, you can go to coffee with her." Norman answers.

CHAPTER 19

Norman stops by a woman at a desk. "Cheryl, this is my wife, Brandy Hollander. Brandy, this is Cheryl James, the church secretary. We will be in my office. Is Hubert in?"

"No, Anne came and got him. She wanted his opinion on some furniture for their new house." Cheryl answers. "Shall I call him?"

"No, let them buy furniture." Norman answers. "Any messages I should answer?"

"Nothing this morning, everyone knew you were in court," Cheryl replies. "I am assuming prayers have been answered."

"My prayers have been," Norman tells her. He pushes Brandy into his office. She looks around. The adjacent walls behind the desk are lined with full bookshelves. On the wall on either side of the door hang pictures with inspiring sayings. On the fourth wall is a six-foot long, leather sofa with a cupboard at the end. "You can nap on it if you want. I can attest that it's comfortable."

"I think I would like a nap." Brandy nods.

Norman takes a blanket and pillow out of the cupboard and he drops the pillow onto one end and then helps her onto the couch finally he spreads the blanket over her.

Brandy opens her eyes and glances toward Norman. He has his shirt sleeves rolled up and is concentrating on what he is writing. Brandy watches him for a few minutes before moving enough to attract his attention.

"What time is it?"

"About three," Norman answers.

"I need to continue my research for the debate." Brandy frowns.

Norman takes a laptop from his desk and brings it to her. He helps her sit up and moves a fold up table to where it can hold the computer in the right position. "It's internet capable."

Brandy nods and goes to work while he goes back to his work. They sit and work without speaking for a long time. Finally, Cheryl breaks the silence when she says that she's going home for the night.

Norman glances up from what he is doing. "You want to go out to supper or should I get take out?"

"How far along is the sermon?"

"Not far but this is Monday. I have until Sunday morning to finish it." Norman answers. "How is the research going?"

"Slowly, I am trying to understand the logic behind the argument for Intelligent Design in genetics." Brandy frowns.

"Within Christianity, there are a few verses written for non-scientists the sum up the principles of DNA. The main one says that every kind of plant and animals mates with members of its own species and produces offspring after its own kind and it has been that way since creation."

"But plants and animals mutate over time, either through selective breeding or through isolation of populations which leads to limited breeding." Brandy frowns.

"Dogs don't become cats." Norman frowns.

"But they do compete in their species those with the best adaptations for their situation get stronger and out breed those who are less well adapted." Brandy answers. "So in an arid place like the desert, hairless dogs are more likely to survive whereas in colder climates dogs with thick, long hair are more likely to survive."

"Can you argue then that because animals adapt to their environments they will change from one species to another? Can a monkey become a man?" Norman asks.

"No, but did they once share a direct ancestor? Man being better able to adapt in to circumstance while monkeys adapted better in another." Brandy answers. "We have thousands of breeds of dogs, we have thousands of breeds of cats, why shouldn't humans have close relatives of common descent?"

"We have races. Wouldn't that be the equivalent?" Norman answers. "Not so far distant that interbreeding is impossible as it is with the great apes but humans adapted to different climates."

Brandy frowns at him. "Using human comparisons always leads to controversy, I would avoid it if at all possible."

"We are not in the court of public opinion. All I am saying is that in creationism man and monkey are two different created species and have no common ancestor." Norman answers. "Creationism also calls for a particular date when plants, animals and people were put on this planet so there are no billions of years for evolution to work the magic of turning one species into another."

"What about the fossil record?" Brandy frowns. "Is it to be thrown out without analysis?"

Norman sighs. "I don't want to have this conversation without food in my stomach. How about if we go to dinner and talk it out?"

"I don't think talk over dinner is going to settle the argument."

"Neither of us is going to change our minds over Chinese food. It will, however, help us understand the way the other person thinks." Norman answers. "Building our understanding of each other will strengthen our relationship. I meant it when I said I want to remain married to you."

A long sigh comes from Brandy. "I don't understand why. I left you without one word about where or why I was going. I blamed you for all the problems between us without looking at where my head was. I would have never returned without Manley manipulating me to undercut your lecture series. Jamison Forester wanted me to blackmail you into teaching. If it weren't for Jared and Scott we probably would never have started talking."

"And both I forgive them, each one of them, and thank them for their contributions to getting us back together." Norman answers. "There is a Biblical principle that when you find a great treasure you sell everything and buy it. I knew when I meet you that you were a treasure but wasn't smart enough to realize I couldn't have you and everything else. This time, I refuse to make the same mistake."

Brandy stares at him for a minute. "I doubt the treasure in the Bible is me."

"It is God and his kingdom but personally, I think of you in the same way." Norman answers.

Brandy shakes her head. "I am not certain I want to set myself up against God."

"You are not in competition. He's my God and you are my wife." Norman tells her. "I have him for eternity and as much as I would like you to join me there I want you for this lifetime if I can't get anything else." Norman frowns. "I am doing it again, pressuring you when I promised I wouldn't. Come we will go eat and then see if Mrs. Renfrew went home." Norman lifts her off the couch and into her chair.

Brandy allows him to take her to supper and then they return to the house. Mrs. Renfrew is gone and Scott is home. Norman uses the opportunity to go meet with his men's group. "Marianne is scared after court this morning. I am sticking close to her except when her father is home." He tells Brandy.

"Don't worry about hanging around here for my sake, I think I need your father's books, to get a firm grip on genetics from a creationist perspective. I may tag along with him this week."

The phone rings. Scott picks it up. "Kettering residence." "May I ask who is calling?" He puts his hand over the receiver. "Are you willing to speak to Jeffry Archer?"

Brandy frowns but holds out her hand. Scott gives her the phone and moves away.

"What is this I heard about you refusing to listen to Mrs. Renfrew?"

"Mrs. Renfrew showed up with no warning. The first thing out of her mouth was a lie.and then she wanted to interrupt our day to suit her whims." Brandy answers. "We are not ready to get into whatever tangle is leftover from my father's works."

"There shouldn't be any tangle-"

"The police shot Abraham Solberg in my backyard as he ran at me with a knife last week. Does it have to get more serious than that for you to understand that I do not wish to suffer anymore over my father's work?" Brandy answers.

"Just what are you saying?"

"In the last month doctors had to operate on my back because my spine is fragile from the original incident. Mr. Archer, I do not intend to allow these same people back into my life to relapse the mental and emotional anguish that losing my family and not having anyone willing to talk to me about them caused." Brandy answers. "All I wanted was to have my memories verified, not to allow every kook my parents associated with access to my family and me."

"Mrs. Renfrew did not get your name and address from me. A woman showed up at the church this last Sunday a Mrs. Kettering, who talked freely with everyone about you and your preacher husband."

"Not again." Brandy sighs softly. "You may tell Mrs. Renfrew and anyone else who knew my father and my mother that I do not wish to rehash old times."

"This Mrs. Kettering, who is she?"

"My mother-in-law who is estranged from her son, and I am told that she hates Christians, something to do with lack of acceptance of her lifestyle by a religious relative."

"What about her lifestyle?"

"According to her son, she is a controlling, manipulative social climber who thinks her money gives her the right to complicate the lives of everyone she knows." Brandy answers. "She believes that I am beneath her notice. I always hear about her latest stunt through a third party and by then the damage is done."

"You are saying she was here strictly to cause trouble." Jeffry Archer states.

"That is her usual method of operating." Brandy answers.

"I will speak to Mrs. Renfrew." Jeffry Archer pauses. "Good night."

"Good night." Brandy puts the phone down.

"Good news or bad news."

"Your grandmother is digging into my past." Brandy answers.

"Definitely bad news," Scott answers. "Marianne thinks Grandma will damage her father's businesses. Her mother was ranting at Marianne but her father took her mother aside and hushed her."

"You think Marianne is in danger?" Brandy frowns.

"I hope not." Scott frowns. "I have been texting with her all evening and she seems to think the storm is passed."

"Just keep in touch with her." Brandy tells him.

Scott nods.

Brandy waits up for Norman but he doesn't come in too late. "Archer phoned. He said a Mrs. Kettering showed up at their church this weekend and talked to the older people about us."

"What does she think that will get her?" Norman frowns.

"She was behind Mrs. Renfrew's visit and talked to other like-minded people."

"Anything else, you think she is meddling in?"

"Marianne is scared that your mother is putting pressure on Mrs. Gilford or that is what my guess from what Scott told me."

"Come and I will get you ready for bed then I have to make a visit to my mother." Norman frowns.

"And say what?" Brandy frowns. "Do you have anything to blackmail her with so she will leave us alone?"

"Blackmail is not a Christian activity." Norman answers. "I can't say I have any confidence that talking to her will change her ways but short of strangling her, what else can I do?"

"Ignore her. Just simply ignore her." Brandy answers. "We can call Lang and Turner tomorrow."

"And what can they do?"

"Arrest her for messing in an active police investigation." Brandy answers.

Norman hesitates for a few seconds. "That does sound like it might work." He smiles. "Come it's been a long day."

Detectives Lang and Turner arrive of their own accord just after Norman starts to make breakfast. "What is it?" Brandy asks.

"We have the lab reports on the birth control pills you were given and you were right they contained fertility drugs. We also have the files President Forester sent to us from the university about who was funding Dr. Conroy-Hamilton, and we have the final translation of Dr. Conroy-Hamilton's notes." Lang answers. "None of them point to your mother or the Goldens."

"Where do they point?" Brandy answers.

"Nathaniel Earl Kettering."

"My grandfather died when I was fifteen." Norman frowns. "All this happened ten years after his death."

"Who has control of his estate?" Lang asks.

"I don't know." Norman frowns. "No one ever

mentioned anything to me about an estate. He died in his sleep or, at least, that is what I remember."

"Do you know who his lawyer was?"

Norman shakes his head. "We had arranged to go fishing together and when I arrived at his place he was dead. I found him in bed."

"He lived alone?"

"Yes, but he had a housekeeper who came in once a week." Norman frowns. "I don't remember him being ill but at fifteen, I guess I thought he was old and old people die."

"At fifteen, we tend to see things that way. We would like to look into his affairs."

"Go ahead." Norman answers. "By the way, I understand my mother visited Ned Hollander's church to talk to the people who knew him."

"Where did you hear that?"

"I spoke to Jeffry Archer, the former senior pastor, on the phone last night after we got a visit from one of my parents' friends yesterday." Brandy answers. "We wondered if Mrs. Kettering was interfering with a police investigation. After all, Marianne accused her of threatening her father with bankruptcy."

"We heard about the court case and are going to visit Mr. Gilford to see if there is any truth in the accusation about the bankruptcy." Turner answers.

"Are you ready to charge any of them?" Brandy asks.

"Herman Golden is sitting in jail. He was arrested after the hearing yesterday. Chastity Golden is being held in the psych ward after her little display yesterday after court. Dr. Lansing-Conroy-Hamilton remains in jail. We have files for the lot of them in the hands of the prosecutors. It might take a few weeks to a few months to get them in front of the judge. I know it seems slow but we have to make certain the charges will stick."

Norman and Brandy both nod. Brandy goes to the church with Norman and spends time reading the Bible directly to try to understand the creationist side of the argument. She then goes back online to fit that with the basics of genetics.

At the end of the day Norman takes her out to supper, Jared and Leia find them in the restaurant. "We wanted to talk to you before the debate tonight." Jared pauses. "They arrested Grandmother for the murder of Nathaniel Earl Kettering. Who is he?"

"My grandfather." Norman answers. Brandy reaches out to take Norman's hand.

"Her housekeeper called me. She lives in and wants to know if she can stay until she can find another job." Jared pauses. "Apparently most of the money we thought was Grandmother's was actually willed to you by your grandfather. It seems she spent everything she inherited years ago."

"What kind of woman is the housekeeper?"

"She kept me from accepting everything Grandmother said as the truth." Jared sighs. "She also pointed out how crazy Chastity was."

"Tell her she can stay until the case is settled." Norman answers. "We wouldn't want the house to fall into disrepair and lose money in selling it."

"Thanks, Dad." Jared answers. "See you at the debates."

"Do you feel up to attending the debate?" Brandy asks after Jared and Leia leave.

"I am the moderator so I don't have much choice." Norman answers. "Why didn't I question his death? I knew what she was."

"You were fifteen." Brandy answers. "Unless your

grandfather told you about estates and trust funds, you wouldn't have looked for the money."

"He didn't." Norman sighs. "The most he would do is look at me and say that woman is crazy."

"Perhaps he thought you were too young."

"To understand?"

"To deal with the truth, I remember my first foster home where they stonewalled me for an hour at a time if I mentioned my parents. They had an elderly relative they called Aunt Gertrude. One day after they deliberately ignored my attempts to talk about my parents she pulled me aside and told me that they thought I was too young to know about the evils of the world."

"Did you point out that the evils of the world had already become known to you?"

"It wouldn't have done any good. They weren't comfortable talking about what happened to my family and not long after that I was moved somewhere else." Brandy shakes her head. "What's tonight's lecture topic?"

"The first week was physicists discussing the creation of the universe; the second week was geologists discussing the formation of land, sea and sky; this week is chemists talking about the chemistry necessary for life." Norman answers.

"Organic chemistry, a fun, light-hearted subject," Brandy shakes her head. "What is the creationist theory on the chemical soup that produced the first living organisms?"

"That organic matter has always been organic." Norman says.

"Hardly good debate material." Brandy frowns.

"Justin is tough, he knows his stuff." Norman answers. "Whether Professor West is as good is yet to be seen."

"Then let's eat up and go." Brandy answers.

"So what do you think?" Norman says as he helps her prepare for bed.

"If that's the quality of the speakers I am in trouble." Brandy answers. "Next week will be a disaster."

"You will be fine." Norman answers as he lifts her onto the bed. "I have faith in you."

Brandy frowns, but the phone rings cutting off anything she could say. Norman answers it. "Norman Kettering."

"No, I will not." Norman says to whoever is on the other end. "My mother killed my grandfather, a man, I respected and admired. I think she can spend some time in jail to realize that not everyone jumps to meet her every whim."

"I don't care what lies she told you about my grandfather, it changes my mind not at all." Norman answers. "She has made my life miserable for fifty years, she can be miserable now." Norman smiles, as the person on the other end, hangs up.

"Is that a Christian response?" Brandy asks.

"She hasn't asked for forgiveness just money." Norman says, "Unless you want to bail her out."

"Not me, I know she can't be stirring up more trouble if she is jail." Brandy answers. "And I don't trust her not to skip out if she has a chance to go. I judge people's characters before I put up bail money."

"I think you underestimate her ability to stir up trouble but she would skip if someone bailed her out." Norman strips off his own clothes and lies down beside her.

"Tell me about your grandfather. What did he like to do besides fish?"

Norman starts to talk and ends up crying. Brandy holds him while he does it and goes to sleep that way.

The rest of the week, Brandy studies genetics and the Bible and tries to reconcile what she knows with the creationist view. On Thursday, an extremely upset woman comes to visit Norman. He asks Brandy to leave his office so she goes out into the outer office with Cheryl. Hubert comes through and invites her into his office to discuss her subject.

Brandy rolls her chair into the smaller office and looks at his collection of reference books. "You don't have anything on creationism."

"The church I came from was much more interested in prophecy and the future than the past." Hubert shrugs. "Anne is over at your house cleaning today, I know you've been going out for meals but she would be upset if you didn't go home to eat what she cooked."

"She's a good cook. Now I know it will be there I can tell Norman. I don't think it will be a problem." Brandy answers. "Why don't you join us?"

"Anne wants to help you and you won't let her." Hubert frowns.

"I lost my family when I was eight and lived with ten different foster families until I was seventeen when I went to university. In my last year of a master of biology, I married Norman and we lived together less than a year before I went to Africa. Coming back to find Norman waiting and then learning I have five children and they have spouses is overwhelming when I allow myself to think about it. To have Anne and her sisters wanting to wait on me when I am so used to just doing things for myself is way too much. I would rather all my children were building their own lives and visiting once in a while."

"But the Bible says to honor your father and your mother."

"Then honor me by letting me have my way." Brandy answers. "I know Anne probably took over all the housework when her other mother died but I value education and independence for both my children and me."

Hubert frowns. "She did finish high school."

"And what will she do if something happens and you are not able to preach?" Brandy asks.

"God will look after us." Hubert frowns.

Brandy sits looking at him for a long time. "If that is true why did you go to seminary?"

Hubert opens his mouth then closes it without saying anything. "She would have to want to go back to school."

"You know she wouldn't go back without your approval. She wouldn't do anything that might upset you," Brandy tells him, "No matter what she really wants to do."

He frowns. "We are talking about starting a family."

After a brief knock, Norman enters the room. "How is it going?"

"Hubert needs to read a book or two on creationism." Brandy answers. "He apparently does not have an argument for creationism in regards to genetic evolution."

"God created everything. What more do I need to know?" Hubert frowns.

Norman smiles at Brandy. "Be fair, he has not been studying the subject for weeks."

"He tells me that Anne is at our house cleaning and cooking. I suggested he come home with us and they can stay for supper since she's making it." Brandy tells Norman.

"That would be pleasant. Why don't you call Anne and suggest she wait for us?" Norman addresses Hubert.

"I will do that." Hubert manages a half of a smile.

"What happened to your upset woman?" Brandy asks.

"Harry arrived and took over. He's much better than I at getting people to talk out their troubles." Norman answers. "Unfortunately, he has taken over my office until the crisis has past."

"Then I think I need some air." Brandy frowns. "I think I will go out and see what's in the planters." She wheels herself towards the door.

"Do you need company?" Norman asks.

"No, I think I need to identify some flowers." The sun was getting hot, as was the air coming from the asphalt parking lot. The flowers were bright against the light green foliage. Brandy sits there for a long time.

"The pansies are going to bloom soon."

Brandy glances up to note the short man with curly hair. "You're Harry, right, and Norman sent you to talk to me."

"He keeps telling me that you are brilliant." Harry acknowledges without directly answering her.

"I blew it." Brandy answers. "What more do I need to know?"

"How did you blow it?"

Brandy sighs rather than answering. "I put my thoughts and beliefs on someone else rather than remembering that my daughter is tough-minded and able to hold her own as I am."

"This is a church lots of that goes on here." Harry says with a smile.

"I didn't raise these children I can't expect them to think as I do." Brandy frowns.

"Most women take years of preparation to do a good job with their twenty-something kids. Norman tells me that you turned Scott around and Jared is much happier with you as his mother. Daughters take a special touch. Mother-daughter relationships are often complicated." Harry says.

"He's betting his future on God taking care of them." Brandy sighs. "I've read enough in the past week to know how much that is part of Christianity but-"

"Your experience is different."

"I've had to be self-reliant, I tried to lean on Norman once and it ended in disaster. Now I'm in this chair they all want to look after me."

"That's a hard leap to take." Harry answers. "It threatens your self-esteem and the meaning you have found in life."

"It threatens my security. I lived twenty-five years living in semi-isolation where the neighbors were opposed to what I was doing, with bad food, and disease-carrying mosquitoes without one incident and then come home to find all this family and within three weeks I am permanently in a wheelchair with people threatening my life over things that happened over forty years ago." Brandy frowns.

"And you are upset about saying the wrong thing to a son-in-law whose values are totally opposite to yours? Cut yourself some slack lady." Harry answers.

"Norman is going through the same things without the wheelchair." Brandy frowns.

"Norman has a support group. He has a whole congregation praying for him. The wheelchair has given him a way to get close to you when you wouldn't give him that chance if you were healthy." Harry frowns.

"I'm trying to figure out what I want that I can still do. Living in this chair in a research station would be nearly impossible. Moving to the university, I would have to change to analysis from pure research. If I do nothing, my daughters will make me their project."

"What about Norman?"

"We believe different things, our values are different, he doesn't think it should matter but I am afraid that I am going to destroy his life. There are so many things I am not, but he doesn't see it." Brandy frowns.

"There are other men in the world." Harry says.

"What?"

"Other men who you might like better," Harry answers.

Brandy shakes her head. "People are a gamble. Norman came into my life at the one time I was open to believing I could share my life with someone else. It ended badly and to open myself again even to Norman is difficult, someone else is unthinkable."

"Why unthinkable?"

"I've caused Norman too much pain now." Brandy shakes her head. "If there is one emotion I do understand it is pain."

"Pain isn't technically an emotion." Harry frowns.

"When you've lost your family to arson and you are tied to a hospital bed with a shattered back and no one wants you to talk about it, they treat you as if it never happened, then pain becomes more than a physical symptom." Brandy answers. "I know that cost, I can't knowingly do that to another human being."

"Norman is tougher than you think." Harry tells her.

"Norman waited twenty-five years for me to return and that is not the kind of man who is going to take no for a final answer." Brandy answers.

"Harry, Norman would like to talk to you about Mrs. Parker." Brandy looks up to see Hubert standing there with a glass of ice water in one hand.

The counselor frowns but goes back into the church. Hubert hands Brandy the drink.

"Sorry about interfering in your relationship with Anne. If she's as hard-headed as I was at that age then she would tell you if she wanted a career." Brandy takes the glass and then looks up.

"But she would give it up maybe without even discussing it if she thought her not working was important to me." Hubert answers. "Her father was strict with her and her mother when it came to things he didn't want them to do. She is trained to consider my wishes before her own. How do I get her to talk?"

"Ask her what she daydreamed about doing as a child." Brandy shrugs. "Only do it at a time when she doesn't suspect you of being serious so she can feel free to talk." She takes a sip of the water. "Thank you for the drink."

"It's hot out here." Hubert shrugs.

Norman comes out of the church. "What did Harry want?"

"To examine my state of mind," Brandy answers. "He calls violas, pansies."

"So does most of the rest of the English-speaking world." Norman answers. "You, on the other hand, use the proper botanical Latin names for plants. It's time to go home for supper."

"I will take the glass back in and make certain everything got locked up before coming over." Hubert takes the glass back.

Norman nods and starts to push Brandy's chair

towards the car.

"What did Harry tell you?"

"Harry said I was an idiot." Norman answers as he lifts her into the car. "Don't tell me he didn't try to steal you away."

"I don't think I gave him any encouragement if that was his intent." Brandy answers. Norman gives her a brief kiss on the forehead.

Anne has everything ready for them and frets a bit when Hubert is two minutes behind them. Brandy watches her daughter as she talks over supper. How she answers her husband's questions and her mannerisms. Hubert finds an excuse to take his wife home shortly after the dishes are done.

"You have a question," Norman tells her after their company leaves.

"Was I like that, glossing over all my problems and deferring to you if there were any points of contention between us?" Brandy asks.

"No, you tried to make me listen and when I refused you gave up trying and just dealt with problems how you thought best." Norman frowns.

"And I didn't get your attention because?" Brandy frowns.

"I needed to grow up." Norman answers. "I admit I was at fault. I know it now and I knew it then. I was shocked, hurt and disappointed but if I was angry, it was with myself when I realized that my immaturity drove you away."

"I didn't tell you what was happening." Brandy shakes her head.

"I knew you had trouble opening up to people, Brandy. If you knew what it took to get the coach to agree I needed tutoring in biology. Then I messed up so badly that I didn't dare even try to apologize. Perhaps you might understand why I was scared to try again for another year to get your attention. There was no excuse for treating you the way I did once I got the ring on your finger."

Brandy frowns and turns away. "It was all a long time ago."

"No Brandy, it is still here, right here, right now. That's why you can't let go of it. There is a place where time doesn't exist and those moments when we are touched by the sublime or the horrors of life exist there and until we can place them in their proper historical context they remain as raw and as immediate as if we were still living them."

"Is that a Christian tenet?"

"Not one I've read anywhere. It's a truth that's been with me since I first laid eyes on you. I relived the significant moments of our relationship every day of the twenty-five years we were apart. The first time I saw you, that first meeting, the second meeting, our first kiss, our vows, the first time we made love, the day I came home to an empty apartment. I would wake up with empty arms and I would cry because I knew I was to blame."

"And you want that put into its proper historical perspective?"

"No, I want to remember it all as if it was just a second ago so the lesson of how to treat my wife so she won't leave me again stays front of mind." Norman answers. "The horror of your injuries, mental and physical, plus the nastiness of my mother needs placing into perspective so you can release the pain and enjoy the rest of your life."

"The physical pain is not going away," Brandy

frowns, "not this time."

"No, but it would be easier to bear if the mental and emotional pain was gone." Norman answers.

"How do I attain a proper perspective on your mother?" Brandy asks.

"By smiling and waving as they haul her off to prison." Norman answers.

Brandy shakes her head. "Where in that is forgiveness that Christians are supposed to be showing?"

"Then she asks for forgiveness-"

"Somehow I doubt that you can manage it even then." Brandy frowns. "How am I supposed to know how to do this if you aren't going to give me a good example?"

"Scott-"

"That was to your personal advantage." Brandy frowns. "Not the same as your mother."

Norman frowns. "I am not paying for her attorney so she can get off. She's a danger to those around her."

"I am not suggesting paying for her lawyer or helping her get off, I am talking about letting go of the emotional pain that she caused. Just how is it done?" Brandy asks.

Norman sighs.

"You really don't know," Brandy tells him. "It's just platitudes."

"It's not, it's about letting God absorb the pain." Norman answers.

"Magical sounding but really not practical for me," Brandy answers. "I think I need to spend the evening on research."

Norman just nods.

CHAPTER 20

Friday Brandy spends the day continuing to research and learn everything she can about the Biblical version of creation. Saturday Norman asks her to attend the soccer pitch with him. She goes and sits back from the sidelines so she does not have to worry about being hit by the ball.

A man comes and stands beside her. "Jeffery Winters, I phoned you once about Chastity Golden."

"What do you want a statement on now?"

"You are starting to get a lot of bad press. This Abraham Russell thinks you are responsible for his father's death."

"His father attacked me when I was eight years old. He told that he believed my parents helped his wife escape him. The man did not attack my parents first, he attacked me and threw me through the glass of a second story window onto the pavement. Then he killed my parents and brother before setting the house on fire. The man had no reason to even know I existed unless his son or daughter told him, which also explains how he found us. I didn't like them, they took my toys. Their mother was trying to break up my parents according to my father's senior pastor, which was stressing my mother beyond what she could handle. Greg Solberg, which is his real name, is playing the blame the victim game to make himself feel better about his part in my family's deaths."

"You are still with Norman Kettering even after all the antics of the Goldens and his mother." The man says.

"Circumstance have brought us back together, whether it can hold us together has yet to be determined." Brandy answers. "I am taking the scientific theory side of the intelligent design debate Tuesday night. The outcome and its consequences are still in the future."

"What is the name of the senior pastor at your father's old church?"

"Jeffry Archer." Brandy answers.

"I wish you luck on the debate. It might be worth a column."

"It's open to the public." Brandy answers. "You don't need a ticket to get in."

"I will remember that." The reporter gives her a smile and leaves.

Brandy glances towards Norman, who is looking at her. She nods at him and goes back to watching the game. Norman comes over between games.

"Who was that?"

"A member of the press," Brandy answers.

"It might not be best to be giving interviews."

"It might get Tuesday's debate a little free publicity." Brandy answers.

Norman frowns. "The debate has all the advertising it needs."

"Advertising and publicity are not necessarily the same. Your team needs your attention." Brandy tells him.

"What are you not telling me?"

"We can't all be saints." Brandy answers.

"Brandy?"

"He wanted a statement. Abraham Russell is trashing me in the press over his father's mental state." Brandy answers. "So I gave a statement of what I believed happened."

"Did you lie?"

"No."

"Then why the evasion?" Norman asks.

"There was no forgiveness in what I said." Brandy answers, "Just plain deductions from the known facts."

"God has to give you the power to forgive; Brandy, it is not otherwise humanly possible." Norman kisses her before going back to his team.

Sunday morning Brandy goes to church with Norman but spends the service in his office with his library rather face his congregation. Norman pauses at the idea but Brandy says "I am not ready to meet your church family. Not with the debate so close, meeting everyone would be a distraction that would make the debate harder to handle."

He does insist that she go out to lunch with him. They are joined by one of the elders and his wife, Edmond and Lisa Gates. Edmond spends his time talking about Norman's sermon on the stewardship of man over the earth until Lisa pulls Brandy to the side. "I understand there is a marriage coming up in your new family."

"Three of them," Brandy answers, "Two sons and a daughter by the end of the summer if all goes according to plan."

"How are you going to handle it?" Lisa asks. "When our daughter got married I was harried enough."

"Right now none of them are asking for very much

help from me. Norman is more involved at the moment than I am."

"Have you brought your dresses yet?" Lisa asks.

"No." Brandy shakes her head.

"Thursday, by then you will have rested after the debate if you wish I will take you shopping." Lisa answers. "I know all the best places."

"I want to see how the debate turns out before I plan much beyond it." Brandy answers.

"I will phone you on Wednesday." Lisa tells her.

After lunch, Norman and Brandy return to the house to find Marianne there with Scott. Marianne turns away to wipe at her cheeks before greeting them. "Hi."

"I know you are probably going to object but can Marianne stay here with me until we leave town?" Scott asks Norman.

"I think I need to hear the whole story." Norman says.

"One of my father's companies took a big hit on the stock market. My mother said it was my fault for giving up on marrying Jared. She said that I should leave and not come back." Tears trickle down Marianne's face.

"It's time to figure out how to put a stop to my mother's schemes." Norman answers.

"Did you bring your things with you?" Brandy asks Marianne.

"Just a few things I could stuff quickly into a shopping bag. I don't remember her ever being this awful." Marianne tries to wipe her tears away.

"Let's see what you brought, I know a thing or two about starting with next to nothing." Brandy answers steering her chair between Marianne and Scott. "I left a lot of foster homes without much more than a bag of odds and ends."

Scott retreats leaving Brandy to deal with Marianne and goes to talk to Norman.

"Now what did you bring with you?"

"Not enough to start over." Marianne answers. "Now our wedding plans are ruined."

"You still have the plan you just need other help in putting it into place." Brandy answers. "I admit I don't have a gazebo but I do have a backyard."

Marianne sniffs. "But I can't pay for any of it."

"Don't worry about that today. The trick to getting through today is taking stock of what you do have and then figuring out what you need for tomorrow. Did you bring the computer that you were doing your papers on?"

"No, but I turned in the last of my papers last week, just exams are left."

"What do you need to study for your exams?" Brandy asks.

"My textbooks, which are in my car," Marianne answers. "They might make me return it."

"So long as you can get the textbooks out of it before they do." Brandy answers. "Do you have enough clothes for tomorrow or do we need to go shopping?"

"I think I have enough for tomorrow." Marianne answers. "I have an exam at nine o'clock tomorrow morning."

"So get your textbooks and try to concentrate on studying." Brandy answers. "Scott, Marianne needs some help studying."

Scott and Norman look at Brandy as she rolls towards them Scott bends down and says "What?"

"Keep things as normal as possible so she can understand that the world is going to keep turning and no drastic measures are necessary." Brandy answers. "We need her to handle only what she needs to do today."

Scott nods and goes to help Marianne get her textbooks out of the car. Brandy goes to her computer and looks up Marianne's father. She picks up her cell phone and calls the business number she finds.

"This is Brandy Hollander, please get Mr. Gilford to phone me." Brandy gives her number. "It concerns Marianne." She sets the phone down.

"Now what do we do?"

"We wait to see if he phones back but in the meantime as a backup plan, we find her somewhere to sleep tonight." Brandy answers, "Unless you are willing to let her stay here with Scott."

"Too much can happen in seven weeks." Norman frowns.

"Yes, we can plan and pull off a wedding." Brandy pauses. "Give me your phone."

"Why?"

"I need to know what Anne knows about weddings but I don't want to tie up my phone in case Marianne's father calls." Brandy answers. Norman hands her the phone.

Scott comes over. "I think I have it covered."

"What do you have covered?" Norman asks.

"I have a contact who occasionally needs people to work the night shift at his security company. I phoned him and offered to work tonight. I go to work, Marianne sleeps in my bed and I get home about the time she has to go to her exam so I can catch up on my sleep then."

Brandy looks at Norman. Norman nods. "I think I can manage to live with that."

"Thanks, besides I need the money for a wedding." Scott answers. "I got notice of my court date this morning, it's in three weeks."

"We will be there," Brandy tells Scott.

"Thanks." Scott kisses her cheek and goes back to Marianne.

Brandy stays home the next day. Marianne is up and dressed when Scott comes in and kisses her for luck and sends her off to her exam. Brandy is up when Marianne comes home. Marianne is upbeat about the exam results but worrying about the rest of it.

"You need to go shopping?" Brandy asks.

"I will wash the clothes I wore yesterday. I don't want to empty my bank account." Marianne frowns. "I don't get that many hours at the library and I refuse to use the credit card Dad gave me."

"Do you need a loan?" Brandy asks.

"I would rather not. I feel bad enough now about the wedding being dumped on you."

"I admit that the only wedding I organized was mine to Norman so you might have to lower your standards somewhat." Brandy frowns. "I didn't spend a lot of time or money on it."

"Did your father walk you down the aisle?" Marianne asks.

"No, my father died years before I married. Norman and I were married by a justice of the peace in the courthouse and there was no aisle." Brandy shakes her head. "When is your next exam?"

"Thursday," Marianne answers. "I will start studying for it tonight. Right now I need to relax after the last one."

"You can take a hot bubble bath. Scott's not likely to wake for a few hours."

"Sounds good, but I would like to talk over wedding plans." Marianne bites her lip.

"I am working on research for the debate but let's see what I can do." Brandy reaches for the phone. She pushes in some numbers and waits. "Anne, it's Brandy." "Yes, Scott's fiancé would like someone to help her plan her wedding. I am busy getting ready for the debate, can you help Marianne."

"Okay, I will tell her." Brandy gets off the phone. "Anne will be over in a few minutes."

Marianne frowns slightly. "But I don't know her, who is Anne?"

"Scott's sister, she's married to Hubert Mueller, who is the associate minister who works with Norman at the church. She will be a much bigger help with a wedding than I will." Brandy answers.

Anne arrives and talks Marianne into going shopping to look at wedding things so they have some idea of what Marianne wants. Brandy gets back to work and does not get interrupted until Scott wakes up.

"Where's Marianne?"

"Anne took her shopping to look at wedding stuff." Brandy answers. "She's starting to get frantic about the wedding."

"We can always elope." Scott answers.

"I don't think Marianne is the eloping type." Brandy answers.

"Probably not," Scott comes and looks over her shoulder. "There's something in one of Dr. B's latest papers about the likely rate of decay in human DNA as a species. I will find it for you."

Scott disappears back into his room and comes back with a printed paper opened to the appropriate page. Brandy takes it and reads it. "Interesting, how is the studying progressing?"

"I am hoping to be completely caught up by the trial date." Scott answers. "You have Anne's phone number. I should catch up with Marianne."

"Leave her to have a day with another woman who is not part of her current friends." Brandy answers. "Perhaps she will see a different set of values lived out."

"You think she is playing me?" Scott frowns.

"If her mother is this fearful about losing one of her father's many companies then Marianne probably has some deep rooted problems with being what she considers poor. Hubert and Anne are much more into letting God or providence look after them. She might learn that weddings and decent living don't require designer dresses for a supper at home." Brandy answers.

"You think she is as into money as her parents." Scott frowns. "I'm not going to be making that much."

"Give her a day or two with Anne and see what her reaction is." Brandy answers. "Consider it an experiment."

"Okay."

"Are you working again tonight?"

"I told Sam I would work another night. Then I am going to talk to Mr. Gilford and see if I should find another place to live where I can have Marianne with me." Scott answers. "I don't want to offend Norman but if his mother is feuding with her family, I don't want her out there alone. Not after the stories I've heard."

Brandy nods.

Anne brings supper with her when she returns with Marianne. Hubert arrives with Norman. Brandy breaks off studying to join everyone around the table. "How did the shopping go?" Brandy asks.

"I didn't know a bride had to make so many choices." Marianne frowns. "Mom always hires a shopper who winnows down the selections. I think I have to go back to studying until after my exam on Thursday or my brain will lose the last semester before I get serious about making that many decisions. Although I did see a gown, I really liked but it wasn't a hooped skirt so it might mean changing the ideas I had."

"If you can't find anything you like Ruth loves sewing projects," Anne tells her. "Not that it is much cheaper than buying once you buy all the material and trimmings."

"I will think about it Friday." Marianne answers. "We do need to figure out who to invite soon if we want to get the invitations out on time. Scott, can you start the list while I study?"

"My family, your family, and who else?" Scott frowns.

"Some of the people from school, I know you don't want alcohol there but not all of them drink at everything." Marianne answers. "We can talk about it later."

Hubert glances at Scott. "This is a dry wedding?"

"I would prefer it that way." Scott answers. "Is that a problem?"

"No, not at all," Norman answers, "Toasts can be made with sparkling juices of various flavors."

Scott asks. "Anything else?"

"I don't think there is anything will be harmed by waiting two days." Marianne shrugs before turning to Brandy. "How did the studying for the debate go?"

"It went well." Brandy answers. "One more day and it won't matter."

"I did look up a verse for you one that is not out of the Genesis creation story but applies." Hubert says. "Psalm 104 verse 30, it might help or it might hurt depending on how you use it."

Brandy looks at Norman, who shrugs. "I don't have

it memorized but I can lend you a Bible to look it up."

"I will, thank you for the verse." Brandy turns to Hubert.

"Ruth, David, Mary, Pat and some of the other members of our old congregation are coming out to see the debate." Anne tells everyone. "My father is coming."

Brandy glances at Norman. Norman smiles at her and winks, "You will do fine."

When Brandy opens up the Bible the next morning she sits and starts at Psalm 104 Verse 30 then she goes back to read the psalm in full before concentrating on the verse. Something deep in her mind relaxes and she feels more at peace that she has in many years. The rest of the day goes quietly but quickly. Scott and Marianne have gone to the university library to study and Norman is at church. Jared has come over to sit with her but he is studying for his last exam which is on Wednesday. Leia is writing an exam at the university, which she went to after dropping Jared off.

Brandy reads the Bible for the rest of the day leaving off worrying about the debate. It is nearly mid-afternoon when her phone rings.

"Brandy Hollander." She answers it.

"Randall Gilford here, where is my daughter?"

"At the university library studying for her exam on Thursday," Brandy answers.

"I mean where has she been living?"

"She's been living here. Scott didn't want her on her own when she could not run into trouble with Mrs. Kettering and her friends." Brandy answers.

"I have been out of town and I just got your message. My wife forgot to inform me that my daughter moved out of the house." Randall Gilford says.

"Should I get Marianne to phone you?" Brandy asks. "I don't know that I will see her before the debate at the church tonight."

"I will try her cell phone. Thank you for calling."

Brandy says good-bye but she senses that Mr. Gilford is not happy. She pauses but then decides to leave his problems to Mr. Gilford.

Jared and Leia take Brandy and Norman out for supper. Brandy just has a bowl of soup.

"Are you worried about the debate?" Leia asks.

"Not as much as I was." Brandy answers. "It's not confidence as much as acceptance. How are your wedding plans?"

"Mom has everything in hand. Now I am done exams I have to do my part. I know Saturday is coming fast." Leia pauses. "I am getting excited."

"What colors did you choose? I have to shop for a dress and I don't want to clash."

"Oh, I should have told you; a soft pink and a dark blue." Leia answers. "Do you need me to go shopping with you?"

"I have an offer to go shopping on Thursday with the wife of one of the church elders." Brandy answers. "You stay on track with whatever you need to do."

Norman takes Brandy to his study when they get to the church. "I forgot something until this morning, up until now the speakers have been standing I found three options. You stay in your chair, stand, or sit on a high stool so you are at the same height as your opponent. Which would you choose?"

Brandy frowns. "Height has its advantages."

"But also its dangers," Norman answers. "Should I

bring the stool in so you can try it before you make up your mind?"

"It might be helpful." Brandy answers.

Norman goes and gets the stool. He helps her to stand up and then to mount the stool.

"As long as I don't get too exuberant it should work." Brandy nods as he starts to lift her down then pauses.

"Something happened today." Norman comments.

"What happened?" Brandy asks.

"Something about you is different and don't say it's the suit because I've seen that suit before," Norman tells her.

"What sort of different?" Brandy asks.

"I am not sure but something is different," Norman tells her. He steps forward and kisses her. "For good luck."

"Do you kiss all your opponents?" Brandy asks.

"Only the ones I'm married to." Norman answers. "Shall I take the chair out then come back and get you?"

Brandy nods. There is a knock at the door and Norman goes to open it. "Edgar."

"Norman, Dr. Hollander, how nice to meet you again?" The trim mid-aged man greets her.

"Dr. Jefferson." Brandy answers. "I take it you are my opponent for tonight."

Norman glances at Edgar's smile. "Brandy, how do you know Edgar Jefferson?"

"We've worked together on research projects." Brandy answers, "Mostly over the internet or on conference calls. We have met at a conference or two."

"What's wrong, Norman?" Edgar frowns.

"He doesn't like other men smiling at his wife." Brandy answers. "Help me into my chair and tell me how you expect to get me up on the platform. I don't remember any ramps."

Norman pauses. "I will get Scott and Jared to help."

Hubert knocks. "The church is filling up."

Norman lifts Brandy off the stool and into her chair. He takes the stool out.

"A husband and a wheelchair, any more additions we didn't know about?" Edgar asks Brandy.

"Five children," Brandy answers. "Norman isn't a recent addition but a return to someone I left behind."

"Which explains why none of us could get your attention," Edgar shakes his head. "Are you up for another research project? I understand you had left the Chad station before it was destroyed."

"The cleric found out I had left a husband behind."

"So what are you doing now?"

"I'm on medical leave at the moment but living on a remote research station in a wheelchair would be awkward." Brandy shakes her head. "I may return to teaching at the university in the fall."

"You could do your part from here. The university would be an excellent site for what we have in mind, studying the impact of human settlement on the environment using the same measures we use at the remote stations we have operated. We would pay for the equipment and space. We can talk contract details after the debate."

"If anyone is still speaking to me," Brandy laughs.

"At the Stewards of the Earth we always knew your position and it was fair, tonight I expect you to do your best to put me in my place as you see it. It won't affect the offer of work because I know the work will be well done." Edgar Jefferson shakes his head. "You underestimate your charm, Brandy."

Norman returns, "Time to get you both out where the audience can see you."

Edgar gets out of the way by leaving the office.

"What did he offer you?" Norman leans down to where his head to hers.

"A research station at the university and the contract to operate it," Brandy answers, "Just like I had in Chad."

"What university?" Norman asks.

"The one I already teach in." Brandy answers.

Norman stops. "Here, where we can live together?"

"We need to get out there Norman before someone comes looking for us." Brandy answers.

Norman pushes the chair out to where Jared, Scott, Hubert, David and Pat are all waiting to help him lift it onto the platform. "Next week I will build you portable a ramp," David tells Norman after she is safely up. Then all the young men go down and sit next to their wives and girlfriends in the front pews.

Brandy looks over the audience to see people standing at the back of the church as the pews are full. She takes a deep breath and Norman sets her up to the stool. "Are you still good with this or does it feel too high?"

Randall Gilford comes through the church doors and walks up to the front. "Where is Marianne?"

"I'm here, Daddy." Marianne glances at Scott then stand to look back at her father. "We can go out and talk, the debate is about to start."

Randall Gilford holds out her cell phone. "You are to carry this so I can call you and I expect you back at the house tonight. Is that understood?"

"I will bring her home after the debate," Scott tells the man.

"Good." Randall Gilford walks out of the church.

Brandy takes a deep breath. Norman frowns. "What was that about?"

"Randall Gilford phoned this afternoon looking for Marianne. He said he had been out of town and had not heard about the problems between Marianne and her mother." Brandy answers as she stands slowly. "I will take the stool at least then I won't feel at a disadvantage."

Norman helps her sit on the stool. "Is that alright?"

Brandy nods. "You better stand back or someone might see this as special attention."

"I intend to give a full disclosure in the introduction," Norman tells her.

Hubert comes over. "Time to start or the crowd might get restless."

Brandy settles herself on the chair. Hubert goes down to sit with Anne. Edgar stands by the other microphone and Norman takes the pulpit between them.

"I am Norman Kettering of the Mount Vernon Presbyterian Church. Welcome to the fourth debate in our series about Intelligent Design. Tonight our question is What proof is there for Creationism in the sphere of genetic and environmental science? The pro-creationist side is represented by Dr. Edgar Jefferson of the Christian environmental group The Stewards of the Earth. Dr. Jefferson has a doctorate in Environmental Science. In opposition, we have Dr. Brandy Hollander of Lakeside University, who holds double doctorates in genetics and ecology. I will also tell you in the interests of full disclosure that Dr. Hollander is also my wife but is not a member of a Christian church. Dr. Jefferson I would like to give you the opportunity to bow out if you think that we have taken advantage of your good graces."

"It won't be necessary the Stewards of the Earth are well acquainted with Dr. Hollander and her work. In the interests of full disclosure, we have had her research stations under contract for years. She is the one of the best scientists in our field."

"Then we will begin with the affirmative side. You have ten minutes to make your opening remarks." Norman turns the attention of the audience to Dr. Jefferson. Brandy listens to the monologue wishing she had some way to write down the gist of his reasoning. Once his time is over, Brandy glances at the audience.

"In science, it deemed impossible to prove a theory absolutely which leaves me to find reason it can not be true. Creationism, therefore, cannot be proven it must be disproved. The flood story is a case in point. Could a boat of the size described hold two of every animal and seven of every clean animal on the earth at that time. I don't believe it could if you included all the animals found in the fossil record. So we need to ask could would two of all the creatures of the earth now fit in a boat of the same size. If they could not then we must deduce that animals, through interbreeding, have created many more species, a sign of evolution. This experiment would take some time to calculate and we cannot do it this evening.

The Bible says that God made man and the land creatures from the dust of the ground. Man is primarily made of water and while dust may contain microbes it hardly contains all the elements found in the human body. He made his creatures mate with their own kind and produce young in the same likeness. This has been proven with advances in genetics through DNA and RNA. Even people who were created male and female; note that the man is created first which speaks to the chicken and egg question but poses problems for scientists who assume that a new creature would start as a child. The problem with that is that it makes calculating the day of creation difficult. How old did he create them, were they teenagers, young adults or middle aged? He created them as adults without any childhood traumas to mislead them and they still turned on him." The audience laughs. "They also did not have any childhood traumas to teach them how the world works." Brandy draws a breath.

"The biblical recount of creation has some definite psychological truths about evil and its origin in the world. That it lacks is collaboration in the fossil record especially since the Garden of Eden is blocked by flaming swords to stop men from returning to eat of the tree of life. This makes it difficult to either prove or disprove the creation account.

The fossil record suggests that over time, and with mutations, people and animals are not static ideals but change slowly in small increments from generation to generation. Domestic animals have evolved with targeted breeding and wild animals from interbreeding caused by isolation. We know from studying plants that every niche in the spectrum of plant and animals are filled with some very odd variants including small animals that use chlorophyll to synthesize sunlight to plants which lack that ability. The argument for a creator making clearly distinct species defies the need for such assorted creatures." Brandy pauses.

"My worthy opponent has made much of the fact that fossils are only made in traumatic events where large amounts of earth shifted completely encasing animals and their tracks in an oxygen free environment. He states that this shows a world of dramatic changes such as the biblical flood but we see such landslides and volcanic eruptions every year. If this were the case, we should have few fossils of animals who lived on plains and more who lived on mountainsides that is simply not the case as most dinosaurs could not have handled steep hillsides easily. The truth is the earth changes as often as do plants or animals, this is not disputed by science."

"I admit I know little about Intelligent Design and its proponents, what I do see is Christians who are confused about their part in creation. As stewards are they like Dr. Jefferson to search out the answers to desertification to reverse it, or are they in domination to strip the world of all its riches because God will someday give us a new heaven and a new earth. As someone who believes we only have one earth I don't have that dilemma, I think we need to save that which we have. In his address which opened this series, Reverend Kettering said we need to look at that which works rather than bowing to our preconceived notions but using science to prove the biblical story he and his like-minded people are doing exactly that; taking an existing narrative and fitting the discoveries of science to it."

"My son-in-law gave me a Bible verse, Psalm 104 verse 30 which says that the spirit of God has the power to continue to create and God renews the earth as he pleases which may be the strongest argument for evolution. Dr. Jefferson tells me that he believes in God, the creator God, and his son Jesus. James, an elder in the early church, wrote to Jesus' followers that if anyone lacks wisdom he should ask God and it will be given him. Jesus also said if his followers have faith they can move mountains yet Dr. Jefferson has paid me for the last fifteen years to tell him how to reverse desertification and the other environmental damage caused by man. A commentator of Acts said it was the faith of the Apostles that causes the early church to grow and thrive yet I find just the opposite in the Christians I have worked with."

Brandy glances at Norman, who shakes his head.

"Dr. Jefferson, your rebuttal."

"I will deal with the strongest point first. My lack of faith does not negate the Biblical account of creation. Just as a mad man's insistence on his version of the facts does not negate the truth. I turned to science for my answers because I believe studying his creation leads me to know God better. God can with a thought stop the wind and waves but that does not make me stronger in character, and God is into character development for his followers. So far as plants that don't have chlorophyll and animals that do, God has a fascinating sense of humor once you get to know him."

Norman waits until it is clear Edgar is finished then he turns to Brandy. "Dr. Hollander."

"Are you accusing God of misleading us, Dr. Jefferson, as in God created man as adults, and therefore everything he created was fully formed and mature so the fossil record was simply part of what put into place at creation? Is this 'the sense of humor' you mentioned? I knew coming into this debate that this conversation was based on philosophy which is more my husband's field than mine. If education is not based on the knowledge and assumptions of those who come before us, we would have to start from scratch and we would never get beyond wandering the earth testing by trial and error which plants are edible. To argue creation by an intelligent being, we need to see in that creation itself, traces of God, his purpose, besides amusing himself, his character, and you have not pointed any of these out."

Norman pauses and looks at Dr. Jefferson, who nods.

"No, I am not accusing God of fraud, Dr. Hollander, just teasing. The answers are there but as Proverbs says it is the glory of God to hide knowledge and the glory of kings to search it out. I agree that we need to build on the knowledge of those who have come before us. As to seeing God's purpose and character in creation, we see the heavens and we put meaning into either by astrology, astronomy, or simply by being awe at their vastness. One is based on stories of Greek gods and the other by men with telescopes and both has its proponents. This is why as Christians we use science to prove the truths of the Bible so we can stand on the truth rather than another mythology. Even so we do not always agree what scripture means or what our response should be. That may be a bad argument but it is the truth whether my faith allows me to move mountains is up to God for ultimately He holds the power and decides where it is displayed."

Norman waits a few seconds and says. "Dr. Hollander."

"If God wants us to search out our answers then we need to be objective in our measurements and careful in our conclusions. Assuming that he is teasing and hiding information means that we must not take things at face value. This makes it impossible to disprove his existence. In his opening address at the beginning of this series, Reverend Kettering said we need to ask ourselves two questions about the theories people put forward. The first question is does it work. But this is a philosophical question about proof for creationism in genetics and environmental sciences, is creationism reflected in the genetic makeup of people and animals? Is the Biblical narrative equal to the test of factual data?

Genetic decay in people and animals exists. Every generation has new and somewhat different mutations that soon are seen as normal. Is God's creation fixed in stone, no, the Bible does not claim it and neither does the fossil record but is it fixed enough to say that on this date God created all animals or all people? Unfortunately neither science nor theology has all the data it would take to reach a definite conclusion.

Is the Biblical narrative equal to the test of factual data? The trouble with this question is that for an experiment to prove or disprove something data must be taken analyzed and extrapolated. I have spent the last few days attempting to do that with the creation story and I find that it lacks the detail and controls that I have become accustomed to having during such an exercise. Can I say that the facts are completely wrong? No. Can I say that they are complete? No. Have Dr. Jefferson's experiments over the years convinced me of his argument, no, and not just because of his lack of faith, but because their focus has been on what man can do and not the Biblical focus of what God can do if his people have faith. I can lecture for days on what humans could do if they believed their interests were served by restoring the earth rather than on living comfortable lives insulated from nature. But the Biblical focus is on what God did and can do. I must admit my personal history leads me to distrust rather than trust but the miracles recorded in the Bible are stumbling blocks and not proofs to me. If something intervenes in the ordinary course of events, does that mean God acted or does it mean that a random chance event disrupted people's expectation and the people at the event interpreted to mean that God acted. Without being there and taking measurements and observations is there a way to be confident of my interpretation?"

Dr. Jefferson frowns. "The experiments are based on what man can be simply because my fellows and I can control what we do and how we instruct others to act but we do not have the power of creation to return the earth to its pristine state."

"Have you tried an experiment to see if faithful Christians calling on God can turn back desertification?" Brandy asks.

"No."

"Why not, if you want to prove God exists and that he is creator would that not be a logical place to start?" Brandy asks. "The Bible says, without God, you can do nothing."

"You know what kind of experiments we fund." Dr. Jefferson frowns. "We hope to engage the world in dialogue about the consequence of sin on the earth and what it takes to atone for that sin."

"In other words, ecology is simply a side effect of your real goals which are to convict people of their sin." Brandy answers. "But that is not the role of Christian's in God's design. It is the work of the Holy Spirit to convict men of sin. It is the role of Christians to show God's love to their fellow men so that they can escape the consequences of sin."

"How long have you been studying theology?" Dr. Jefferson asks.

"A little over a week," Brandy answers, "I must admit that some verses read like nonsense but some tenets are reasonably clear. How was I to argue against creationism if I knew nothing about the Creator?"

"Shall we have closing comments?" Norman interrupts the back and forth between his debaters. "The negative side goes first leaving the affirmative side with the last word. Brandy."

"It is not just observations and data that make science but the interpretation we put on those facts.

Without a time machine to travel back and observe what happened and even then considering all the ways that creationists have claimed God could have worked creation there is no way to prove creationism. I am not an expert in fossils, I look for ways to create life in the arid places on earth or I did until recently. I do not often find new creatures although I did once witness a change in one of the world's smallest creatures. Am I willing to state categorically it was evolution? No. I am still searching for answers and that is as honest as I can be." Brandy finishes.

"My worthy opponent has not disproved creationism. She has admitted that she lacks the evidence to disprove God created the earth and everything in it. What she has done is agreed with God that people are unable to live out Christianity without God's power and that we often forget to align our attempts with his Spirit to do his work."

Norman nods. "I would open this to questions but our time is up. If you wish answers to specific questions e-mail them to me at the church and I will pass them on to our speakers. Thank you for coming and good evening."

Norman comes over to Brandy. "You look tired; time to take you home so you can rest."

"Are you still talking to me?" Brandy asks.

"It would take a million times worse than this for me to do anything but love you." Norman lifts her off the stool and sets her on her feet.

Dr. Jefferson comes over and shakes her hand. "Well done."

"I took you to task publicly." Brandy frowns.

"Perhaps God thought I needed it." Dr. Jefferson answers. "I hold no animosity towards you and the offer to fund another research station stands if you will direct it."

Norman brings the wheelchair over for Brandy to sit. She sits down. "It would have to be agreed to by the president of the university."

Norman leaves and returns with Dr. Forester. "Dr. Jefferson, this is Dr. Jamison Forester, president of Lakeview University. Dr. Jefferson has a proposal."

"Dr. Jefferson." Jamison answers.

"I want Dr. Hollander to set up a research station at the university and send us the same data from a temperate environment as a control on what we were doing in the Sahara, the desert in Australia, the Alps and the Arctic Circle."

"I would have to consult my staff and see if we have room." Dr. Forester starts.

"We will fund all the buildings and equipment that Dr. Hollander needs. We assume she will be as big a magnet here for the top graduate students as she was in Chad and the other research stations." Dr. Jefferson answers. "If you turn us down then I will simply have to poach and bring her to our head office in Geneva where she can plan out our experiments and analysis the data in comfort where her health will no longer be compromised." Dr. Jefferson answers.

"As I said, I must consult my staff and since Dr. Hollander is on medical leave until September, we will make our decisions when we have all the relevant data." Jamison Forester tells Dr. Jefferson. "It is too big a decision to make it off the cuff."

"I will send you the contracts and our requirements." Dr. Jefferson answers. "We will expect your reply over the summer."

Scott, Jared, Hubert, Pat and David arrive. "Sorry

about rushing things, Mom, but Marianne wants to get home to talk to her father." Scott grimaces.

"I understand." Brandy answers.

The men lifted her and her chair to the bottom of the stairs.

"Thank you." Brandy tells him.

"You used the verse well." Hubert tells her. "Don't feel sad about not finding proof against creation other scientists haven't been able to do in two thousand years."

Jared gives her the thumbs up and the girls including Marianne come over. "You did well."

"I want to make everyone a celebratory supper but you look tired so how about tomorrow night at my house." Anne announces.

"That would be fine." Brandy answers. Norman and Dr. Jefferson come off the platform.

"What would be fine?" Norman asks.

"Anne invited us to supper tomorrow night." Brandy answers.

"Tomorrow night is best." Norman says and introduces Dr. Jefferson to all their offspring and spouses.

"I have to take Marianne to see her father," Scott says. "I will see you at home later."

Brandy nods, and Norman glances at Marianne. He says, "We wish you well."

"Thanks." Marianne nods and they leave.

"Anne, get away from that woman." A white-haired man orders, "She publicly shamed her husband. I should never have allowed you to come."

Hubert draws Anne to his side. "As my wife, you no longer control what Anne does."

The man glares at Hubert and Norman steps between them. "I assume you are Nelson Riley."

"That woman is not a Christian!"

"None of us ever said she was." Norman answers. "She is a research scientist was excellent credentials just like all the other scientists we have had here debating topics around Intelligent Design. She is also Anne's biological mother as I am Anne's biological father. You have no right ordering an adult, married woman around and I, as senior pastor of this church, am asking you to take your emotional abuse and leave."

"How dare you?" The man rears back.

"You abused your late wife until she, innocently or not, felt compelled to work with the doctor who stole my children. You will not carry on with that sort of nonsense here." Norman answers.

"Hubert!"

"My wife is not going to be taken from her mother a second time. Brandy did a lot of studying opening her mind to the Bible so she could debate tonight and I respect her for it." Hubert answers. "Norman obviously does not feel shamed by the outcome."

"It is obviously time you came home, Anne."

"I am home. If a man should leave his parents and cling to his wife, a woman should leave her father and cling to her husband." Anne answers. "I am staying with Hubert."

"Now, it is time for you to leave," Norman tells Mr. Riley. "There is nothing here for you."

"I paid for that girl's raising."

"She worked as your housekeeper for years you have been more than paid back." Norman answers. "Now leave before the police are called."

"Why don't I walk you out?" Dr. Jefferson takes Mr. Riley's arm. "I will call you tomorrow, Norman, I have to stick around and negotiate with the university."

"Goodnight, Edgar."

"Goodnight Dr. Hollander."

"Goodnight." Brandy answers.

Dr. Jefferson walks a suddenly stoic Mr. Riley out the door.

"Isn't this against Biblical principles?" Patrick asks.

"God never instructs men to abuse their wives." Norman frowns. "Men are taught to love their wives and treat them kindly as co-heirs in Christ for to do otherwise means God will not listen to your prayers."

"Wives are to submit." David frowns.

"Wives are to respect their husbands but for them to do that, husbands must be worthy of respect. No abused wife, cowed as a man can make her, respects her husband. To force another to obey God usually means that you are not using that time to follow his edicts for yourself." Norman replies. "Believe me, when you walk into an empty house because you've driven your wife away, you understand that doing your part is more important than making sure she is doing hers."

Jared speaks first. "I am taking Leia home she has a busy couple of days before the wedding."

"Goodnight." Brandy says and both Jared and Leia give her a kiss on her cheek for before they leave. Everyone says goodbye to them.

Norman comes back to Brandy's wheelchair. She reaches up to squeeze his hand. Tears start streaming down her face. Norman crouches down by her chair. "I love you."

"If you want to take her home, I will make certain the church is locked up." Hubert offers.

"Thank you." Norman answers.

"Thank you for helping Anne." Hubert pats his

shoulder.

"It's one of those things fathers are supposed to do," Norman tells him, "Husbands too, when necessary."

Norman gets Brandy out of there as quickly as he can. They arrive at the house to find Scott already home.

"Marianne is staying with her father until the wedding. Her mother has gone to visit relatives." Scott tells them. "He is insisting on paying for the wedding and our moving expenses. He said that the drop in business had nothing to do with Mrs. Kettering."

"I'm glad that things worked out," Brandy says.

Scott kisses her on the cheek. "Goodnight, Mom, Dad." Scott disappears into his room.

Norman takes Brandy into the bedroom and gets her ready for bed. Once he has her in bed, he hesitates.

"Did I offend you with what I said in the debate?"

"No." Norman shakes his head and sits on the side of the bed. "I don't want to hurt you, Brandy."

"You asked earlier what had changed." Brandy reaches over and puts her hand on his arm. "The verse Hubert gave me Psalms 104 verse 30 it changed something inside of me. After I read it, for the first time since I truly understood the damage climate change is doing to the earth that I wasn't afraid."

"God looks after his creation Brandy." Norman lays his free hand on hers.

"I did that whole debate as if nothing had changed." Brandy frowns.

"But it has." The words are a declaration.

"Not completely, that didn't happen until you stood up to Nelson Riley." Brandy answers. "When I was attacked as a child I cried out in fear, I screamed in pain, but my father who could hear me didn't come. I went through foster home after foster home and no one took my side. I went through that hellish time with Chastity without support, and I faced the desert and the clerics alone." Brandy lifts her hand higher and places a finger on his lips to stop him from speaking. "You told me, this time, it would be different. That you would be there. You stood up to the Goldens even took them to court. You stood up against your mother and sent her away. You bent over the girls' arrival in our lives and befriended Scott even though it wasn't your first inclination." Brandy starts to cry silent tears. "The purpose of it all was so clearly to persuade me that you had changed."

Brandy covers a slight hic with her free hand. "Tonight was different. It may have even started because he attacked me but what's not what you reacted too. You acted because of his attempts to intimidate your daughter."

Norman removes her finger. "Our daughter, Brandy, she is our daughter even if she doesn't acknowledge me."

"I know, but something happened when you reacted like a father should instead of allowing Nelson Riley to take Anne away." Brandy answers. "It was like an acknowledgment that of what I knew to be true all along but never witnessed."

"You are overtired and overwrought. A good night's sleep and some time to think through what happened is what you need." Norman answers.

"You don't trust me?"

"I just couldn't handle a declaration made tonight if there is a chance to you will change your mind tomorrow. Just give yourself a day to think everything through." Norman answers. "I will see you in the morning."

Brandy lays there for about two minutes before she makes the first phone call and by the time she goes to sleep she has the next day arranged.

CHAPTER 21

Standing in front of the mirror in a long white dress, Brandy studies it. "There is a prettier one over here." Lisa Gates brings it over and holds it up for Brandy to see. "Or we could go off white."

"No, I want it white." Brandy answers, "Long and white."

"Then you should try this one on." Lisa takes the dress to the change room and waits to help her change clothes. In this dress, Brandy stands in front of the mirror. "I like this one."

"It looks lovely on you." Lisa answers, "Now hair and makeup to go."

Lisa delivers Brandy to the church where Anne, Mary and Ruth have decorated the sanctuary and everyone is wearing festive clothing. "Where is Norman?"

"Dr. Jefferson is keeping him busy for the day." Hubert says. "Do you want anything specific in the vows?"

"Traditional vows will be fine." Brandy answers. "Sorry the last time it was a justice of the peace and there was no choice."

"I can do traditional without any problems." Hubert tells her. "My traditional does have Christian overtones."

"That's perfectly all right." Brandy tells Hubert. "I think I have a better grasp on what they mean now."

"Come, Mom, we have a room at the back for you to wait in while the guests arrive." Anne comes and takes control of the wheelchair. "You still have to pick your bridesmaids."

"Bridesmaids!" Brandy frowns.

"How many bridesmaids do I need?"

"You need a maid of honor to sign the marriage registry. But you can have as many as you like?" Anne tells her.

"Then why not all five of you?" Brandy answers.

"That would be nice but Hubert is conducting the ceremony so I wouldn't have a partner and am a little busy arranging everything, how about four?"

"You need one of your sons to push you down the aisle." Marianne frowns.

"I am walking down the aisle." Brandy tells her. "One of you can go tell them what their part is."

"Are you certain?" Leia asks. "One of us can sit out."

" On Saturday, we will do things your way today we do things my way. I am able to get myself down the aisle." Brandy says. "Go talk to Jared."

Leia shakes her head but leaves only to return a short time later. "Jared is getting everyone together to help Norman get ready."

"How do we pick the order to go into the sanctuary?" Ruth asks.

"Whatever order your men choose to stand in."

Anne answers. "I will come and inform you the minute they come out and get in line. If you excuse me, I have a few more things to organize."

About ten minutes later there is a knock at the door and Edmond Gates enters. "I understand that you require an arm to lean on while you walk down the aisle. I came to offer mine."

Brandy blinks. "Thank you."

Anne sticks her head in the room. "Mary goes first, then Ruth, then Leia and Marianne gets to act as the maid of honor. I have to go take a seat. Come when the music starts." The door shuts.

Mary goes to the door and looks out as the music starts. Marianne puts a chair in the door so everyone can pass through without touchingit. Edmond pushes Brandy's chair to door to the sanctuary then stops and helps her to her feet. She rises and walks slowly down the aisle. The audience is standing so she does not see Norman until they almost reach the front. He immediately comes over and takes her arm from Edmond but instead of walking her before Hubert he lifts her off her feet and carries her the last ten feet.

Hubert glances at them individually before starting the wedding ceremony out of a book of sacraments. Brandy hears the words and responds. Scott hands Hubert two rings, the one Brandy had left in her boxes of personal belongs and a new one. Edmond Gates brings Brandy's wheelchair so Norman has enough hands free to place a ring on his wife's finger.

Brandy has no time after the ceremony to speak to her groom as Anne organizes a line with Norman and Brandy at the front and the groomsmen and bridesmaid in order and then her and Hubert at the end. Brandy feels as if she has meet Norman's entire congregation by the time the last person shuffles by and congratulates the pair of them.

"Do I have to remember all the names?" Brandy asks.

"I will try to help you with that later." Norman tells her.

"Dad and Mom, the ladies of the church put together a supper for us downstairs." Anne announces.

It is another three hours before Brandy and Norman shut the door of a hotel room the use of which for a night is a wedding present from their children.

"Brandy-" Norman puts his hand into the pocket of his jacket and pulls out half a dozen condoms. "Jared slipped something into my pocket as we were leaving the church."

"I guess he doesn't want another sibling." Brandy jokes. "It could have been worse it might have been Viagra."

"Brandy-" Norman flushes.

"Help me take this dress off Norman," Brandy stands. "So I can show my husband how much I love him."

"I don't want to hurt you."

"Then don't treat me like I'm broken." Brandy answers.

Norman comes and stands in front of her and Brandy thinks he's going to argue when he puts his arms around her and unzips the dress. He kisses her on the lips but as soon as the dress slips down her shoulder his lips follow the material until it reaches the top edge of the strapless bra then he loosens his hold enough to drop the dress to the floor. "Not broken, Brandy, beautiful."

ABOUT THE AUTHOR

Rosalyn Marie Francis lives in Naramata, B.C. She is a wife and
the mother of three children, also the grandmother of one.
She likes writing, reading, and gardening.
Rosalyn is also the author of the book Math Troubles.

www.ingramcontent.com/pod-product-compliance
Lightning Source LLC
Chambersburg PA
CBHW060538180626
46817CB00002B/625